A FOREIGN AFFAIR

'Kate realized that her interest in Rudi was increasing rapidly. She wondered if she'd been too ready to fend him off. After all, he *was* a Crown Prince, and the most handsome boy she'd ever met . . .'

However, it takes more than a brush-off to dampen Rudi's interest in Kate – especially as he's very keen to meet her influential father. And in the end an invitation to his tiny country, Essenheim, proves irresistible.

But things don't turn out quite as expected. For a start, Rudi appears to have lots of girlfriends and Kate feels hampered by the presence of George Ormerod, a talented young reporter her father has sent with her to investigate the political situation and to act as chaperon. Kate's irritation with this state of affairs is startlingly dispelled when she and George are caught up in a *coup d'état*. As the plot thickens and Rudi appears in an amazing variety of roles, Kate and George find that they too have a vital part to play in the future of Essenheim.

John Rowe Townsend

A Foreign Affair

PUFFIN BOOKS

Puffin Books, Penguin Books Ltd, Harmondsworth, Middlesex, England
Viking Penguin Inc., 40 West 23rd Street, New York, New York 10010, U.S.A.
Penguin Books Australia Ltd, Ringwood, Victoria, Australia
Penguin Books Canada Ltd, 2801 John Street, Markham, Ontario, Canada L3R 1B4
Penguin Books (N.Z.) Ltd, 182–190 Wairau Road, Auckland 10, New Zealand

—

First published by Kestrel Books 1982
Published in Puffin Books 1984
Reprinted 1985

—

Copyright © John Rowe Townsend, 1982
All rights reserved

—

Made and printed in Great Britain by
Richard Clay (The Chaucer Press) Ltd,
Bungay, Suffolk
Set in 10/11½ Ehrhardt

For RICHARD BECK

with memories
of
Mecklenburg
Brandenburg
Wurttemberg
Alsace-Lorraine
Lausitz-Altenberg
and
Thurn-Taxis.

Author's Note

This story has no message
and no hidden meanings that I am aware of.
Don't take it seriously. It is for fun.

J. R. T.

I

Kate Milbank wouldn't have gone to Essenheim if she hadn't met Rudi. She wouldn't have met Rudi if she hadn't gone to Susan Baker's party. She wouldn't have gone to Susan Baker's party if she hadn't had a row with her father. She wouldn't have had a row with her father if he hadn't left the kitchen in a mess when he went to work in mid-afternoon the previous Monday. He wouldn't have set off for work in mid-afternoon if he hadn't been a newspaperman. And if he hadn't been a newspaperman, he and Kate and George Ormerod wouldn't have got involved with Essenheim anyway. That's how chancy it all was.

Kate and her father quarrelled about once a month on average. It was usually over something trivial. They loved each other dearly and often found each other irritating.

Edward Milbank sometimes described his daughter as bright and bossy. Kate admitted she was bright but denied that she was bossy. Actually Edward was right: Kate *was* bossy. It was mostly because she had considered herself to be in charge of the household since she was twelve, which was nearly five years previously.

Let's begin with Edward. He was tall and thin, with wavy silver-grey hair. He looked distinguished. When people met him for the first time, they often thought they'd seen him before, or at any rate heard of him; and so they had. This wasn't because of his job as Foreign Editor of a London newspaper.

9

It was because he appeared briefly on television from time to time, to be consulted about the significance of events in some country that had come into the news. Not that Essenheim ever came into the news. Nothing happened in Essenheim to interest the rest of the world until Kate went there.

Kate's quarrel with Edward had been going on all week. Until the day of Susan's party it was conducted by correspondence. This was because, five days a week, Edward and Kate didn't see each other. Kate got up at half-past seven and left for school soon after eight. Edward got up at noon, made himself some lunch, listened to the radio news, read a pile of daily newspapers, and went to work at three. Kate came home from school at four, did her homework, read, watched television, and went to bed about eleven. Edward came home at half-past one, wound down with a novel and a couple of small whiskies, and went to bed at three. Kate got up at half-past seven and the cycle continued.

This may sound an odd way of life, but it's not unusual in households with a newspaperman in them. In fact it was really why Edward's marriage had broken down. Anne Milbank had complained bitterly about staying at home five nights a week with only a child for company. In the end she'd met someone who worked less unsocial hours and gone off with him, leaving Kate and her father together.

After that happened, Edward had got himself on to day work for a year or two, but he was back on nights now. And during the week, when he and Kate had things to say to each other, they left notes. Edward's job on the *Morning Intelligence* involved a lot of decision-making on questions such as whether to spend large amounts of the paper's money sending reporters on overseas assignments, or whether to print reports that might lead to diplomatic crises. When he got home the last thing he wanted to do was make decisions. So Kate had gradually taken over the management of the house. She did the shopping and organized the repairs and replacements. If a room needed decorating, Kate decorated it, and Edward didn't even notice it had been done.

Anyway, on Monday night that week Kate left a note for Edward. It asked, coldly, '*Must* you leave dirty saucepans around and crumbs on the carpet?' On Tuesday morning she found a reply scrawled at the foot of her note saying, 'In yesterday's circumstances, yes.' On Tuesday night Kate inquired, '*What* circumstances?' On Wednesday morning the note was still there, with no further comment from Edward. Actually he hadn't seen it.

On Wednesday afternoon Kate had a tiresome interview at school about the subjects she was to do next year; then she had to go and buy some cleaning materials for the house. She was hot and cross and just in the mood to be irritated all over again. So underneath the words '*What* circumstances?' which she'd written the previous night, she added a row of five question marks, each bigger than the last, followed by an enormous exclamation mark; and she put the note where Edward couldn't fail to find it, under the coffee-pot.

On Thursday morning she found that Edward had added the one word 'Crisis'. On Thursday night she wrote crossly beneath this, '*What* crisis?' On Friday morning the note still lay on the kitchen table, with the further message, 'Can't remember now. Too much water under bridge.' On Friday night Kate filled the remaining space on the scrap of paper, which by now was a bit grubby and smeared with marmalade, with the words 'Oh, you are *hopeless*!' And on Saturday afternoon, when at last they were at home together, they had a row.

Like all such rows, this one generated more heat than light. Old grievances were brought out and old accusations thrown around. It was all made worse by the fact that Kate and Edward were so involved with each other emotionally. Otherwise they wouldn't have been so nasty over something so unimportant. Kate claimed that she worked her fingers to the bone for an unhelpful and unappreciative father. Edward claimed that he risked heart failure or nervous breakdown in a gruelling job to support a nagging and bad-tempered child. And so on. In the end, Kate declared that she was longing for the day when she could leave home, and Edward proclaimed that it couldn't come too soon for him. Both statements were untrue, but that didn't prevent them from hurting.

At about tea-time the battle ended, both sides having run out of ammunition. But neither of them was ready yet to make peace. Kate having said she would never speak to her father again, and Edward having indicated that this would be no hardship, a long and heavy silence fell between them. And in mid-evening Kate announced that she would go to Susan Baker's party after all.

Edward said, 'Who's Susan Baker?'

This question refuelled Kate's annoyance. 'At a modest estimate,' she said, 'I have mentioned Susan Baker one hundred and seventy-seven times this year so far. It just shows how much you listen to me. Susan Baker is an awful girl in my form at school.' She added bitterly, 'I expect it will be an awful party.'

'If she's an awful girl and you expect it to be an awful party,' Edward said, 'why go?'

There are some conversations that can be likened to tennis matches, in that the aim of each participant is to score points off the other. Applying this comparison, it could be said that Edward had now lobbed up a weak return and given Kate the opening for a forehand smash. She took it.

'*Anything*,' she declared, 'would be better than spending the evening in this God-forsaken house with you!' And she flounced out with an air of having won game, set and match.

It was a hollow victory. To begin with, it had started to rain, and Kate had to battle her way for half a mile on foot to Susan Baker's house. And the party was every bit as bad as she'd feared. Susan's parents, instead of considerately going out for the evening, were lurking in the background, worrying over the possibility of broken glasses and stains on the carpet. The drink was sweet fizzy cider, which Kate particularly disliked. She didn't think much of Susan's music, either. There wasn't room to dance, but people were trying to do so and treading on everybody's feet. After half an hour Kate had had enough and was also beginning to feel remorseful about the things she'd said to Edward. She was on the point of slipping quietly away home.

It was Cecily Higgins who prevented that from happening. Cecily buttonholed Kate on her way to the bathroom and asked her to come and meet Rudi. Cecily was one of the more OK girls at the independent school in West London which Kate attended. Her father was a knight. He didn't wear shining armour or ride a battle-charger; he was a senior civil servant in the Foreign Office who sometimes entertained important people from abroad. It appeared that Rudi was one of these, and that as he was nearer to Cecily's age-group than to her father's she'd brought him to Susan Baker's party. She took Kate across to meet him.

He was sitting in a corner of the room, surrounded by girls. He wore a well-cut and obviously expensive lounge suit. He was dark and very handsome. And his first words to Kate were among the most surprising she'd heard in her life.

He said, 'Hello, beautiful!'

2

Kate didn't have any exaggerated idea of her own attractions. The truth is that she was dumpy. She was a little below average height and a little above average width. It wasn't her fault. She didn't nibble between meals or eat a lot of candy. It was all in her genes. What's more, it was in her genes from her mother's side. Edward ate twice as much as she did and was as thin as a rail. As she often pointed out, it was grossly unfair.

Kate's face was as round as the rest of her. Her hair was a mousy brown. True, she had nice, dark eyes and a good complexion. But beautiful? Oh, no. She was under no illusions about that. And she didn't expect such compliments from good-looking young men.

There was no doubt that Rudi was good-looking. Spectacularly so. He was probably in his early twenties, and had a thin oval face, dark hair with a slight crisp wave in it, and dark straight brows. His eyes were as brown as a moorland pool, his skin olive but not swarthy. He spoke perfect English with the faintest of foreign accents.

Kate couldn't quite believe she'd heard him correctly. 'Do you mean me?' she asked.

Rudi flashed a stunning smile at her. 'Of course,' he said. 'Who else?'

'Well . . .' Kate, still a little bemused, indicated those around her. Rudi dismissed them with a shrug of the shoulders.

'I have been watching you for twenty minutes,' he told her. 'And I said to myself, "There goes the girl I want to meet."'

A girl called Deirdre Thomas who had been sitting next to Rudi rose to her feet.

'Seems to me you two should be getting together,' she said sourly, and took herself off. Rudi patted the vacant space and Kate sat down beside him.

'Do you have a boyfriend?' he asked her.

'As a matter of fact,' said Kate, 'I haven't. Not just now. I have had before and I dare say I will have again. At the moment the post is vacant. But I don't know why that should interest you.'

'I am astonished,' said Rudi. 'I should have thought you would have a dozen at least.'

'I think you're taking the mickey,' said Kate.

'To take the mickey,' Rudi said thoughtfully. 'I assume that has the same meaning as to pull the leg. You have nice legs.'

'Good-bye,' said Kate.

'Oh, don't go, Kate.'

Kate didn't go.

'How did you know my name?' she asked.

'I inquired, of course. I have a tongue in my head, as they say in this country. I asked Cecily.'

Kate was flattered. A wild hope sprang up in a corner of her mind that perhaps after all she *was* the kind of girl that young men like Rudi inquired about. But she beat it down instantly.

'Listen,' she said. 'I'm quite intelligent. I get As in most subjects. But you couldn't know that from looking at me across a room. In appearance I only get B minus. Or maybe C. Some would say F. So what are you on about?'

Rudi flashed the smile.

'The English,' he said, 'have a strange taste in women. They like them tall and skinny. Latins like them fat. But in my country we like them ...' (he looked her up and down appreciatively) '... just right.'

Kate said coldly, 'Do you have to treat us as sex objects?

How would you like it if I said that, according to my taste in men, you were "just right"?'

'I should like it very much,' said Rudi. He smiled for the third time. It did have a curiously melting effect. Against her will Kate found herself half smiling in return.

'Don't trust him, Kate,' said Deirdre Thomas, coming back.

'Anyway,' Kate demanded of Rudi, 'who's "we"? Which *is* your country?'

'A country you've never heard of,' said Rudi.

'Tell me,' said Kate. 'And I bet I *have* heard of it.'

A new tape started up. It was particularly noisy, and drowned Rudi's reply. Then somebody at the other side drew him into conversation. Kate was left momentarily to her own thoughts. Her attention was caught by a man, several years older than the other guests, who was standing on his own beside the window. He was blond with close-cropped hair and a pale, expressionless face. His shoulders were broad and he looked decidedly tough.

Deirdre Thomas had followed Kate's eyes.

'That's Rudi's interpreter,' she remarked. 'The funny thing is, he doesn't seem to know much English.'

'Whereas Rudi knows plenty,' said Kate. 'Odd.'

'Very odd.'

'Well,' said Kate a minute later, 'I was asked to meet him, and I've met him. I think I'll go now.'

She started to get up. Rudi hadn't been looking at her, but his hand went out and took hers. He stopped talking to the other person and turned to Kate.

'Stay where you are, darling,' he said.

'I'm not your darling,' said Kate.

'That's a pity,' said Rudi.

Cecily Higgins came up. 'You wouldn't have heard the doorbell,' she said to Rudi, 'but my father arrived just now. He's come to fetch you. He wants to take you to the Courtenays'. You remember?'

'I remember,' Rudi said. 'A tragedy. The party has just become interesting. Now, where is my hostess?'

'Susan?' said Cecily. 'Oh, she's around, somewhere. I wouldn't bother in all this crush. I'll say good-bye for you, Rudi. I'll tell her you had a lovely time, OK?'

'OK,' said Rudi. He rolled the syllables round his tongue. 'OK. You are very tactful, Cecily. Good-bye, Kate. I shall see you again, shall I not?'

'I doubt it,' said Kate.

'What is your telephone number?'

Kate didn't answer.

'Oh well, I expect it is in the book,' Rudi said. He allowed himself to be led away. The tough-looking blond man detached himself from the wall and followed him, a few feet behind. Kate stayed where she was, meditating. She had just decided to go home when Cecily Higgins reappeared.

'Well, he got to know you,' she said. 'I think that's what he came for, really.'

Kate was startled. 'You mean, he wanted to know me before he'd even seen me?'

'Yes.'

'But why? Why should he want to know *me*? How did he know I even exist?'

'I think my dad mentioned your dad, and I said I knew you.'

'Did you say I was a goer or something?'

'Frankly, Kate, no. But he does rather seem to fancy you, doesn't he?'

'How long is he here for? And where *does* he come from, anyway?'

'He's only here for a week or two, on a visit. He comes from Essenheim.'

'Where's Essenheim? In Germany?'

'No. It's an independent country.'

'He said I wouldn't have heard of it,' Kate said. 'And he was right. I haven't.'

'Neither had I until a few days ago. It's a tiny place in the middle of Europe. That's all I know about it. If you want to know any more, you'll have to ask Rudi.'

'You seem to think I'm going to see him again.'

'I'm sure you are,' said Cecily.

'I still don't understand,' said Kate. And then, after a pause, 'So Rudi comes from Essenheim. What does he *do* there?'

'He's the Crown Prince,' said Cecily.

3

When Kate got home, there was a great big reconciliation scene between her and Edward. This was usual. Actually, the reason why they could throw all inhibitions overboard and have enormous rows about practically nothing was that they knew perfectly well there'd be a lovely hug-and-make-up afterwards.

Edward explained that the crisis which had led to the unwashed saucepans was a sudden recall to his office over an international incident which had now blown over. He apologized for the mess and for pretending to forget the reason. Kate apologized for putting saucepans ahead of international affairs. Both of them blamed themselves with all the energy they had previously devoted to blaming each other. Then they fell into each other's arms, swore undying affection, and sat down at the kitchen table to drink coffee and swap the week's gossip of school and office. After a while Kate said to Edward, 'What do you know about Essenheim?'

Edward said, 'As much as anybody does. Which isn't much.'

Kate said, 'Why isn't it much?'

Edward said, 'Nobody goes there and nothing happens. I can't remember when we last had a story from Essenheim. There isn't even an agency reporter there. It's just a backwater.'

Kate said, 'That can't be *all* you know. Tell me more. To begin with, where exactly *is* Essenheim?'

Edward said, 'You know where Switzerland is. And beyond

Switzerland is Serenia, right? Serenia's like another Switzerland, but more so. Rich and comfortable. No inflation, no crime, no unemployment. No drunkenness, no immorality. No fun. Well, Essenheim's at the far side of Serenia. It's a bit of the old Austrian Empire that got forgotten in the peace treaty after World War I. Just a few thousand people, mostly peasant farmers, but they make good wine there, or so I'm told.'

'I like the sound of it,' said Kate. 'Could we go there on a package tour?'

Edward said, 'You're joking. There aren't any package tours to Essenheim. It's ruled by an old fellow they call the Prince Laureate, who doesn't like anything as modern as tourism. His family were princes of Essenheim under the overlordship of the Austrian Emperor. There isn't an Emperor any more, but Essenheim still trundles on as if World War I had never happened. Now, why the sudden interest?'

'I've just met somebody from there,' said Kate.

Edward sat up straight. A newspaperman always pricks up his ears when he hears something that sounds as if it might lead to a story. In a moment, Edward was transmuted from Kate's dad, chatting in the kitchen, to the Foreign Editor of the *Morning Intelligence*.

'Who is he?' he asked. 'What's he doing in London?'

'You don't know that it's a he,' said Kate. 'It might be a she. Why is it always assumed that a person of unstated sex is masculine?'

'Oh, don't be women's-libby about it,' said Edward. 'I know it's a he. I can tell by the look in your eye.'

'All right, it is a he,' Kate admitted. 'And what he is, is the Crown Prince.'

Edward pondered this for a moment. Then he asked, 'Who says?'

'Cecily Higgins says. He's staying at their house. And her father came to collect him from Susan's party.'

'Hmmm,' said Edward. 'It sounds as if he's the genuine article. James Higgins wouldn't be entertaining a phoney.

20

Now, let's see if my memory can supply me with your man's name. Prince Rudolf, is that it?'

'That's right,' said Kate. 'Rudi. And by the way, he said he wanted to see me again.'

'Does he know your address or telephone number?'

'I didn't give him them. I wasn't sure I liked him. But he can easily find out.'

'Why weren't you sure you liked him?' Edward asked.

'He was trying to pick me up. Calling me "darling" and "beautiful".'

'That sounds interesting.'

'It sounds ridiculous,' Kate said. 'I mean, you only have to look at me to see how ridiculous it is. The Crown Prince of Wherever-it-is making advances to the plump, plain daughter of a London journalist!'

'You're not plain at all,' said Edward loyally. 'Or plump either, really. Just pleasantly rounded.'

'Come off it,' said Kate. 'You may deceive yourself but you can't deceive *me*. It's Rudi who's beautiful. I'm not.'

'As to that,' Edward said, 'we'd better agree to differ. But anyway, if he does show up, I'd be quite glad to meet him. Why not ask him here for a meal? Unless of course you really don't want to see him again.'

'Oh, I expect I could stand it,' said Kate.

Actually she realized as she spoke that her interest in Rudi was increasing rapidly. She wondered if she'd been too ready to fend him off. After all, he *was* a Crown Prince, and the most handsome boy she'd ever met, and the only one who'd said such things to her . . .

She lay awake that night thinking about him.

The next morning, Sunday, she was still thinking about him. And by now she knew she hoped very much that he'd meant it when he spoke of seeing her again. She was on tenterhooks all day. The doorbell rang twice and the telephone four times, and each time her heart pounded, but each time it turned out not to be Rudi. There was no sign of life from him on any of the next three days, either. On the fourth day, Thursday, she brought herself to telephone Cecily Higgins and inquire. But Rudi had only been with the Higginses for the weekend. Cecily knew nothing about his later movements.

On Friday Kate was in a sensible mood and told herself that the incident was of no importance, nothing was going to come of it, and she might as well put Rudi out of her mind and get on with her life. Then on Saturday he telephoned.

Kate was out shopping, and Edward answered the phone. It was his day off. By the time Kate came back, Edward had invited Rudi to come round as soon as he could, and had asked him to lunch.

Kate found her heart was bumping again. But all she said was, 'What are we going to give him?'

'Oh, you can go out and get some Chinese or Indian food,' Edward said.

'That doesn't sound very princely.'

'He's only a *minor* prince,' said Edward. 'And anyway, a princely stomach is much the same as any other.'

'He might not *like* Chinese or Indian.'

'He does. I asked him.'

'You always know the right question to ask, don't you?' said Kate.

She just happened to be looking out of the sitting-room window half an hour later when Rudi arrived. In fact she'd have just happened to be looking out of the sitting-room window whatever time he'd arrived. He was in a big old-fashioned Bentley, which drew up impressively in the Milbanks' drive.

Rudi wasn't alone: there was a man in a peaked cap sitting beside him, looking like a displaced chauffeur, which presumably he was, because Rudi was at the wheel. And there was another man sitting in the back, half-lost amongst the upholstery and giving the impression of trying to look as if he wasn't there at all. She couldn't be sure, but he looked rather like the man who'd been with Rudi at Susan Baker's party.

Kate answered the doorbell with Edward standing just behind

her. Rudi was on the doorstep. In contrast to the expensive suit he'd been wearing at Susan's party, he was in jeans and a T-shirt and looked rather like a student of a few years earlier. Inappropriately, though, he was carrying a large and showy bunch of flowers. The other two men stayed in the car.

Rudi thrust the flowers into Kate's arms; then, having freed his own hands while hers were occupied, kissed her emphatically on both cheeks. And while she was still dazed, he pressed forward so that she had to step back, and in a moment they were both inside the house.

Once the door was closed behind him, Rudi seemed to relax, and said in a cheerful, friendly tone, 'Hello, Kate. Thank you for letting me come.'

'It wasn't me, really,' Kate pointed out. 'It was my father. Here he is. Dad, this is ...' She paused, then appealed to Rudi, 'How do I describe you?'

'Just Rudi.' And, turning to Edward and putting out his hand, 'How do you do, sir?'

'Come in, come in,' Edward said. 'Nice to meet you.'

'Thank you, Mr Milbank.'

'You know who I am, then.'

'Of course, Mr Milbank. I know quite a lot about you.'

'Somehow I thought you probably did,' said Edward.

4

The next twenty minutes seemed slightly unreal to Kate. In the sitting-room of the Milbanks' Victorian semi-detached house, Rudi sat at ease and chatted to her father, while she was very conscious that outside in the driveway two men sat in the car waiting for him. After the display of flowers and kisses on the doorstep, he hadn't paid any special attention to Kate. He and Edward made small-talk about weather and Essenheim wines and their respective European travels. It was mildly interesting but by no means riveting. Kate had the impression that they were circling round each other, not yet ready to come to grips.

Rudi hadn't mentioned the two men outside. When, after a few minutes, Kate offered to make coffee, she asked Rudi if she should take some to his companions.

'Oh, *those*!' said Rudi. 'No, Kate, you need do nothing for them. It is by no wish of mine that they are here. I would have come by myself and greatly preferred it. It was the Essenheim Consul in London who provided me with a chauffeur and an interpreter. I have no need for either, but I've had the doubtful pleasure of their company all week. They are, as you say in English, keeping an eye on me.'

'Oh,' said Kate. She went to the kitchen and loaded the coffee-making machine. When she returned to the sitting-room with a tray, the talk between Edward and Rudi had taken a more interesting turn.

'You see,' Rudi was saying, 'nothing can happen in Essenheim

24

while my uncle – he is actually my great-uncle – remains Prince Laureate. He will retain Dr Stockhausen as Prime Minister; he can't imagine doing anything else. Dr Stockhausen has been in charge for thirty years. He is very rigid in his views. And while this state of affairs lasts, we shall continue in isolation, with no democracy, no new science or technology, no tourism, no industry, and no increased production or exports of our excellent wine. We shall vegetate.'

'There are some in other countries who would envy you for that,' Edward remarked mildly.

'It doesn't seem enviable to *me*!' Rudi said with vigour. 'And the wealth and power stay in the same hands for ever. There's an aristocracy, which is the princely family, and there's a professional class, which is mostly connected with the Stockhausens. The rest are shopkeepers and peasants.'

'Presumably you're part of the aristocracy yourself,' Edward observed.

'Yes, indeed. But that is no great privilege. It's a very small aristocracy and very – what's your word? – stuffy.'

'You're pretty frank about it,' Edward said. 'After all, you only met me half an hour ago. Does the Prince Laureate know how you feel?'

'Oh, yes, Uncle Ferdy knows, but he's not too worried yet. He still thinks I'll grow out of it. He's not a bad old boy in his way.'

'Yet he has you watched?'

'Dr Stockhausen has me watched. He and Uncle Ferdy put their heads together and decided to send me on a kind of Grand Tour, visiting friends and relations. Descendants of deposed monarchs, most of them. The Prince hopes I'll return to Essenheim reconciled to my lot. Well, I'm almost at the end of the tour. I go home next month.'

'And are you reconciled?' Edward asked.

'No.'

'What do you want, Rudi?' Kate inquired.

'I want a free, modern Essenheim.'

'It's easy to say you want your country free and modern,' Edward pointed out. 'Everybody says that everywhere. What do you plan to *do* about it?'

'Well ...' Rudi began. He hesitated, then went on, 'I will, if I may, speak to you off the record. I am, as you know, the Crown Prince. But that gives me very little influence while my uncle retains the throne and Dr Stockhausen retains my uncle's confidence. Moreover, Dr Stockhausen would like to replace me as heir by my cousin Friedrich, who has a weak personality and would do as he was told. Now if *I* were Prince Laureate, things would be different.'

'Can't people vote for a new government?' Kate asked.

'We don't have elections in Essenheim. My uncle is an absolute ruler. He thinks elections have been the ruin of Europe. If it hadn't been for elections, he says, the old kings and emperors would still be on their thrones and the world would be a better place.'

'Doubtful,' Edward remarked. 'However, in circumstances such as you describe, an army coup is what usually happens.'

'That is true. In Essenheim the army, which is very small, is led by a certain Colonel Schweiner, who was a sergeant until my uncle promoted him. He has a dominating personality but no intelligence. He is far too stupid to lead a revolution. Fortunately there are some who think that I myself am qualified to head a movement to bring Essenheim into the twentieth century.'

'You mean *you* want to lead a coup?' asked Edward.

'Not unless all else fails. If I could persuade my uncle it was time for him to step down in my favour, the way would be open for peaceful change.'

'And what are you asking *me* to do?'

'I suggest you should print an article on the unrest in Essenheim and dissatisfaction with the reactionary old régime.'

'Maybe I will,' said Edward, 'when I'm convinced of it.'

'I can give you a great deal more information,' Rudi said. 'But you must agree that it will not be attributed to me. And

I must ask you not to print it for a few weeks. If it appeared now, my uncle and Dr Stockhausen might well guess that I was the source.'

'How will a story in the *Morning Intelligence* help your cause?' Edward asked. 'People overestimate the effect of newspaper articles. I don't suppose for a moment it would demoralize the old régime or bring you to power.'

'No. But it would win the support of your liberal-minded readership. Soon after it appeared, you would receive a letter from an exiled Essenheimer in London, Dr Falkstadt, appealing for support for a "Free Essenheim" campaign. I trust you would print it. And, the generosity and liberal principles of your readers being well known ...'

'You think they'd stump up,' said Edward. He thought for a moment. 'Well, they might. *Morning Intelligence* readers yearn for worthy causes to support, and the more distant the better. We haven't had a suitable one for quite a while. Yes, Rudi, you've interested me. And now let's have some detail to back up your general assertions.'

Kate said crossly, 'You won't be needing me. I'll go out for that Chinese food. Then Rudi can regale you with further fascinating information over the sweet-and-sour. I'll have mine in the kitchen and get on with some homework.'

She could have wept with humiliation and disappointment. It seemed clear that Rudi was interested in the *Morning Intelligence*, not in her. He'd only wanted to get to know her so he could talk to Edward. Now she'd played her part she was of no further interest, or so it appeared. Beautiful, indeed! Darling, indeed! As for the flowers, she'd a good mind to pitch them into the bin.

But now Rudi surprised her. 'Perhaps you'll let me come with you, Kate,' he said. 'I should love to go for a short walk. No doubt your father can be preparing the further questions he will wish to ask me.'

Kate looked inquiringly at Edward.

'No doubt I can,' he agreed drily. 'Try not to be too long.'

The big old Bentley was still in the drive. The chauffeur had moved to the driver's seat. He was now reading a popular newspaper, folded back to display the picture of a nearly naked pin-up girl, but he pushed it down on the seat beside him when Rudi appeared.

'He's a Brit,' Rudi said to Kate. 'He hasn't two ideas to rub together. It's the other one who counts.'

The other man was standing in the driveway ahead of them. Seen at close range, his pale face was rubbery and thick-lipped, and his nose slightly squashed. He looked the sort of man you wouldn't care to pick a quarrel with. And he spoke to Rudi in a language unknown to Kate, full of plosives and gutturals.

'Speak English, not Essenheimisch, please,' Rudi told him, and went on, 'This is Miss Milbank. She is a very special young lady. I am taking her for a walk.'

The man's face cracked into a kind of grin, which sat on him like lipstick on a gorilla.

'Good-day, gracious young lady,' he said, and stood aside.

'Karl is an Essenheimer,' Rudi told her. 'In Essenheim, all ladies are young and gracious, and all gentlemen are gallant. It's our standard form of address.'

He put an arm round her waist as they turned out of the drive.

'No, don't push it away,' he whispered. 'I'll explain to you in a minute.'

'I think you'd better,' Kate said when they were out in the street. 'You make passes at me in public, and then in private you don't show any interest. Just what are you up to?'

'Kate,' said Rudi, 'please forgive me. My life is rather complicated at present. Let me explain that Karl, though described as an interpreter, is really my bodyguard, escort, warder and, you might say, resident spy. I don't doubt he reports on me to Essenheim every day.'

'And you have to give him something to report?'

'That's not far off the truth,' Rudi said. 'You see, the Prince and the Prime Minister will not care in the least if I show interest in a girl. To their minds, that is harmless. It is what they expect of a young man of my age. But talking to the Foreign Editor of the *Morning Intelligence* is quite another matter. That would make them instantly suspicious.'

'That's all very well,' Kate said as they turned into the local park, 'but it's not very nice for me, is it? You said all those silly things at Susan's party, and you've got your arm round me now, and I'm nothing to you really but a way of getting to know my dad.'

Rudi looked contrite. 'I'm sorry, Kate,' he said. 'And you are wrong. I like you very much. I liked you when I first saw you. I liked the way you talked to me. You are independent We don't have girls like you in Essenheim.'

Kate felt herself relenting. She realized she was dangerously ready to be mollified. She'd been meaning to push Rudi's arm away, but she didn't. Then he said, smiling, 'But I ought to tell you I am engaged to be married.'

Kate broke away from him at once. It was absurd to feel shattered, as she did. It wasn't surprising, was it, that he should be engaged? No, not at all. Yet somehow it made his advances to her all the more insulting.

'I saw my prospective bride in Florence, three weeks ago. The wedding day, however, is still distant. She is just ten years old.'

'She's *what*?'

'Ten years old. She's heiress to a once-royal family and fortune. The match was made by my uncle. Under Essenheim law, such engagements are legal and binding.'

'And what does *she* think about it?' Kate demanded.

'She doesn't understand at all. The wedding cannot take place until she is sixteen. In the meantime, nobody talks to her about it. So far as those around her are concerned, it is none of her business. But now, dear Kate, I hope you see one reason why I hope for change in Essenheim. I should like to marry to please myself.'

'I should think so!' Kate declared. Then, 'They can't *make* you marry, can they?'

'If I am to succeed to the princedom, yes. I should forfeit my claim if I broke the engagement. My cousin Friedrich would step into my shoes, which would delight Dr Stockhausen.'

Then, out of the corner of her eye, Kate saw the big old Bentley. It was crawling along the road that bounded the park, keeping them in view all the way.

'They're still watching you,' she said. 'Is it like that in Essenheim, too?'

'Not quite as bad. But bad enough.'

'Seems to me it's a dog's life,' said Kate.

'It *is* a dog's life. And I don't look forward to being back in Essenheim. In a way, I would prefer to give it up, and find a nice girl of my own choice. Like you.'

'I wonder if you really *would* like to give it up,' Kate said. 'I don't quite know what to believe.'

'You can believe me about liking you.' Rudi gave her a slightly shamefaced grin. Kate preferred it to the stunning smile.

'All right,' she said. 'I will, for now. You can put your arm round me again, if it'll make Karl happy.'

After lunch, Kate left Edward and Rudi alone for a couple of hours, during which time she sat at her desk in her own room and did an exceedingly small amount of homework. She wondered whether there would be a further public display of affection when Rudi left. But in fact he looked slightly downcast, and the leave-taking was cool and formal.

Kate stood beside Edward on the doorstep to watch the Bentley pull away. This time the chauffeur was driving and the interpreter sitting beside him. Rudi waved from the back window.

'Well, what do you think of him?' she asked her father as they went indoors.

'I haven't made up my mind. He's ambitious, rather devious, ready to take risks but not quite so confident as he seems. Incidentally, he told me a bit more about what's brewing in

Essenheim. It does seem as though things might start happening there.'

'Are you going to do as he asked and publish a report, so that this exile he talked about can launch his "Free Essenheim" fund?'

'I might. But if so, it would be purely on news value, not because he *asked* me.'

'And will you take his word for what's going on?'

'Ah, well, that's another question. I don't like relying too much on what interested parties claim, however much they're acting in good faith. I shall put a reporter on to it.'

'How will *he* get his information?' Kate asked.

'He'll go to Essenheim, of course.'

'I thought you told me they don't like visitors.'

'No more they do. But if a keen young *Intelligence* reporter can't get in, nobody can. I have just the right young man in mind. George Ormerod, who joined us last year from the North. And, talking of right young men, what do *you* think of Rudi now?'

'I don't really know,' Kate admitted. 'First I didn't like him, then I thought perhaps I did like him, then I thought again I didn't. And now I think perhaps I do. But I'm not sure.'

'You'll see him again quite soon, all being well,' said Edward. 'I've asked him to come here next Wednesday and meet George.' He paused meditatively. 'I must say, Rudi didn't seem exactly delighted. I'm sure he thought we could have done without George. Whether he saw George as a threat to his monopoly of news from Essenheim, or a threat to his monopoly of *you*, I wouldn't care to guess.'

5

Kate couldn't stop thinking about Rudi during the next few days after he'd been at her house. She thought about him at all hours of the day, and once or twice she woke up in the night and thought about him some more.

Next Wednesday, the day he was due to come to the house again, she woke early with butterflies in her stomach. She went through the school day as if sleepwalking, then hurried home. There was a small car in the drive, but no Bentley. Letting herself into the house, she heard male voices in the sitting-room, and pushed the door open.

Edward was there, but it wasn't Rudi with him. It was a stocky, serious-faced young man with reddish hair and freckles who got up from the sofa as she entered.

'Kate,' Edward said, 'this is my colleague George Ormerod. George, my daughter Kate.'

Kate's mind had been so full of Rudi that she'd forgotten she was going to meet George.

'Hello, Kate,' George said. He extended a hand, rather awkwardly. Yes, she thought, he *would* be called George. He seemed pleasant enough and not bad-looking, but a bit shy and, compared with a prince, decidedly ordinary.

Kate wasn't always tactful. She looked at George and said, 'I wouldn't have guessed you were on the *Morning Intelligence*.'

'Oh?' said George. 'Why?'

'Well, I've met *Intelligence* reporters before. They're usually

32

ever so bright – you can hardly look at them for the shine in their eyes – and rather classy. You can tell at a glance they went to Oxford or Cambridge . . .'

Then she realized she was saying the wrong things and added lamely, 'Of course, I expect *you're* madly brilliant, too.'

'I'm not madly brilliant,' said George, 'and I didn't go to Oxford or Cambridge. But I *am* a reporter. I trained on a local paper in Yorkshire.' He added, not without pride, 'I've covered weddings and funerals and agricultural shows and all the local paper stuff there ever was.'

'In short,' said Edward to Kate, 'he's a professional. We could do with more of them on the paper.'

'Thank you, Edward,' said George gravely.

'That's why I'm putting him on the Essenheim story. I don't want clever witty essays by a bright young man from Oxford or Cambridge. I just want to find out what's happening. Speaking of which, I hope Rudi will turn up before too long.'

But half an hour went by and Rudi didn't come. George and Edward exchanged newspaper gossip. Kate felt increasingly let down, and finally couldn't bear to sit waiting any longer. She decided she could excuse herself once again on the grounds that she had homework to do, but Edward inconveniently forestalled her by remembering he had to make an urgent telephone call and disappearing for twenty minutes. Kate, now rather cross, made small-talk with George, discovering that his father was a steelworker, now redundant, and that he had two older sisters, both married. It was heavy going, as George tended to answer her questions briefly and wait for others.

Meanwhile, Rudi still didn't come.

Edward reappeared from his telephone call and took up the conversational running. Earlier in the week he'd looked up Essenheim in the reference books. He could now tell Kate and George that the total population was just under ten thousand, that the capital and only town was itself called Essenheim, and there were also three or four small villages. The present ruler, Prince Ferdinand, had succeeded his father in 1952. He lived

33

in the princely palace, a massive late nineteenth-century structure, from the battlements of which there were magnificent views
over the town of Essenheim and the Esel valley towards the
Serenian frontier.

All very well, thought Kate, but *where's Rudi*?

After an hour, they gave up. Edward sighed, and said it was
clear that Rudi wasn't keeping the appointment.

Kate said, 'Does this mean you'll drop Essenheim?'

Edward said, 'Certainly not. Far from it.'

George said, 'It means a bit more work for me, that's all.'

Kate didn't know whether to be worried or indignant. If Rudi
could have come and hadn't, she felt indignation was appropriate
and she wanted to know why not. But suppose he'd been prevented? What had happened to him?

'Tomorrow, Kate,' said Edward, 'why don't you ring the
Essenheim Consulate and see what you can find out?'

'That's my job, really,' said George.

'No, it's not,' Edward told him. 'This is a case for discretion.
Rudi took a risk by getting in touch with me. It might not help
him at all to have inquiries made by the *Morning Intelligence*.'

Then he poured drinks for himself and George, and after ten
more minutes, during which there was still no sign of Rudi, they
went off to the office in George's five-year-old Mini.

Kate was quite willing to ring the Essenheim Consulate. But
it turned out not to be as simple as it sounded. She tried for half
an hour at lunch-time next day, and for an hour after school,
and there was never any answer. The following day she tried at
the same times with the same result. The day after that was
Friday, the beginning of a long mid-term weekend, and Kate
didn't have to go to school. Half a dozen calls still brought no
reply. When Edward got up at midday, Kate was almost weeping
with frustration.

'Why not go along there yourself?' Edward suggested. 'What's
the address?'

Kate read it out: 'Seventeen, Forster Street.'

'Oh, yes, I know that street. It's not far from South Kensing-
ton station. You could go in on the tube. It wouldn't take long.'

'If he doesn't want to see me,' Kate said, 'it might seem as if I was chasing him.'

'I don't think it will. He probably won't be there anyway. But if you do see him you can tell him I still want to talk to him.'

Kate found Forster Street easily enough. It wasn't quite so easy to find the Essenheim Consulate. She had imagined a building the size of the American Embassy. But there was no such building in Forster Street. No. 17 was a florist's shop. Kate thought at first she'd made a mistake over the number. Then she saw, beyond the florist's window, a side door with three or four modest nameplates beside it.

GREEN & CORNFORD
Architects
First floor

said one of them.

SAFETY-FIRST INSURANCE BROKERS
Second floor

said the next.

HAROLD BROWN
Novelty imports
Third floor [front]

said the third. And finally:

CONSULATE OF THE PRINCIPALITY
OF ESSENHEIM
Third floor [back]

There was one more nameplate, which was actually a piece of grubby card. Written on this, in straggly capitals, was the name:

J. THOMPSON
Fourth floor

There was no lift. Kate slogged up three flights of stairs. The business of Green & Cornford, on the first floor, appeared to be rather a small one, and that of Safety-First Insurance Brokers even smaller. On the third floor [front] the tiny office of Harold Brown, Novelty Imports, stood open, and a gentleman with ginger hair and moustache, who was presumably Mr Harold Brown himself, was talking loudly and volubly on the telephone in a jargon composed largely of mysterious initials.

Across the landing was a door with ESS NHE M C NSULA E on it in somewhat eroded gold letters. This, too, stood open. Inside it was a counter, beyond which was an office just large enough to hold a table and a pair of plain wooden chairs. On the table were a telephone and a pile of unopened letters, and behind it was a large filing cabinet. On the wall hung a calendar for the year before last.

On the counter was a bell. It seemed somewhat pointless, as nobody could have entered the room unobserved by its occupants, had there been anyone there. Kate rang the bell all the same and, after a minute or so, rang it again. It didn't produce any sign of life. To pass the time she scrutinized the calendar more closely.

There were only three pages left on it, covering the months of October to December. On the October page was a picture of a marvellously complicated Gothic castle, sprouting from a hilltop like some monstrous plant and throwing out towers and battlements as it went. November showed a scene of cobbled streets, overhanging houses and little old-fashioned shops. December offered a distant prospect of a small town clinging to a hillside, seen across the valley of a sizeable river. The captions however were uninformative. Each consisted of the one word 'Essenheim'.

Kate turned her attention back to her present mission and rang the bell again. A moment later the gingery gentleman came across the landing from the office opposite.

'You got the wrong door, dear?' he asked. 'If it's the architects or the insurance people, you'll have to go back downstairs. If it's Harold Brown you're after, that's me.'

'It's the Essenheim Consulate I want,' said Kate.

'Do they know you're coming?'

36

'No,' said Kate.

'You'll be lucky, then,' said Mr Brown. He added, 'Mind you, if you had an appointment you'd *still* be lucky to find anyone there. A law unto themselves, they are.'

He picked up the handbell, went out on to the landing, and rang it vigorously. Kate now saw a tiny staircase winding still farther up towards the roof. After a minute, during which Mr Brown showed no sign of tiring, a head appeared at the top of this staircase.

'Who's making all that row?' a female voice demanded.

'It's me,' Mr Brown called back.

'You? Harold? What you on about?'

'There's a young lady here for the Consulate.'

'Oh.' The owner of the voice came down the tiny staircase and took a good look at Kate. She was a full-blown blonde in early middle age.

'What you want the Essenheim Consulate for?' she asked.

'I have business with them.'

'What sort of business?'

'If you don't mind,' Kate said politely, 'I'd rather tell someone from the Consulate.'

'Listen, duck, the Consulate means the Stockhausens. Old Mr Stockhausen and young Mr Stockhausen. Relatives of the Prime Minister, I believe. But young Mr S is away at present, and the old man doesn't come in all that often. There, there, don't look so disappointed.' Her tone was casual but not unfriendly. 'I have a phone number for him. I can get in touch if it's important enough. What have I to tell him?'

'You won't get anywhere if you don't tell Jenny what it's about,' said Mr Brown. 'Anyway, I've done my best for you. I'm not curious. 'Bye, my dear. 'Bye, Jenny.'

Kate said reluctantly, 'I want to find out what's happened to Rudi. To Crown Prince Rudi, I mean.'

'Oh. His young Nibs. Well, I'll ring Mr Stockhausen and find out if he'll see you. Probably get an earful myself in the process. Here, let me get at that telephone.'

Jenny dialled a number. It was answered, and Kate heard half the conversation: 'A young lady wants to see you. A young lady. Yes. Kate Milligan. Milligan. No, sorry, she says Milbank. It's about Prince Rudi. She wants to know what's happened to him. No, I don't know what it has to do with her. All right, I'll ask her.'

She put a hand over the mouthpiece, grimaced, and called to Kate, 'What's it to do with you, duck?'

'I'm a friend of his,' said Kate.

Jenny uncovered the mouthpiece. 'Says she's a friend of his.'

There followed a period in which Jenny listened, pulling faces from time to time. Kate could faintly hear a distorted voice, but couldn't hear what it was saying. Jenny, still holding the receiver, made circling motions with her free hand, as if to indicate that somebody was going on and on. Finally she said, 'All right' and put the receiver down.

'Well?' asked Kate. 'What did he say?'

'He said Prince Thingummy's left for Essenheim, and didn't leave any messages for anyone. And whatever it is you want, Mr Stockhausen can't do anything about it.'

'And he won't see me?'

'No, duck, he won't.'

'Can you give me that telephone number?'

'No. Confidential. There, now, it's no good getting upset. I hope His Nibs didn't get up to any little tricks, that's all.'

She looked hopefully at Kate, but Kate maintained a dignified silence.

'Well, there you are, then. On your way. No good hanging about.'

Disconsolate, Kate picked up her handbag from the counter.

'I might as well lock up,' Jenny remarked. 'He won't be back today.' And then, 'He don't pay me for this, you know. And gets rude with me into the bargain. I don't know why I do it. Too kind-hearted, that's my problem. This Consulate don't even bring me any business.'

'What *is* your business?' asked Kate.

'You mind your own.'

Kate trudged down the three flights of stairs. She told herself that her time hadn't been wasted. At least she'd learned what had happened. Rudi had gone, and had left no word for her. But there wasn't any comfort in that.

Edward was just leaving for work when she got home. She told him the results of her journey, and he pulled a face.

'That seems to finish Rudi as a source of preliminary information,' he said. 'George will have to find out what he can, where he can.'

'Is that all you have to say?' Kate asked plaintively.

'Don't look so forlorn,' Edward said. He took his daughter's hand. 'You hardly know Rudi. A couple of weeks ago, you weren't aware that he existed.'

'But what will become of him?' Kate said. 'He may be in trouble. And I don't like the sound of that Dr Stockhausen at all.'

'I shouldn't worry too much. He *is* a prince, and Essenheim's not a dictatorship. And I formed a very strong impression that that young man can look after himself.'

'I hope you're right,' Kate said; and then, wistfully, 'I wonder if I'll ever see him again.'

'Frankly,' said Edward, 'if I were you, my dear, I wouldn't count on it.'

When Edward had gone to work, Kate sat and stared at the wall for a while and then came to a decision.

Perhaps it was an odd decision to come to. She didn't know at the time that she'd ever go to Essenheim. It may have been an unconscious effect of seeing those three pictures on the calendar: the castle, the cobbled streets and overhanging houses, and the little town clinging to the hill. Or it may have been just because she needed to do *something*.

Anyway, she decided to learn Essenheimisch.

6

It turned out that taking up Essenheimisch wasn't all that easy.
There wasn't a teach-yourself book about it, and the local library
didn't have an Essenheimisch grammar. Kate decided to consult
her languages teacher at school. Most of the staff at her school
were young marrieds, but Miss Bond was a traditional teacher
of an earlier generation: a kindly but severe-looking lady in her
late fifties. And she was surprised.

'Essenheimisch?' she said. '*Essenheimisch?* Wonders never
cease. In thirty-odd years of teaching languages, I've only ever
met one person who learned Essenheimisch. It's quite an interesting language, I believe. Basically a peasant tongue that
evolved on its own, cut off by all those mountains. But they've
had to import a good deal: bits of French, bits of Italian, bits
of the Slavonic languages, lots of German ...'

She looked at Kate speculatively.

'I don't suppose it's all that difficult,' she went on. 'A girl as
good at languages as you are would probably pick it up quite
quickly. But when you've learned it, what have you got? There's
no literature in Essenheimisch, no trade between Essenheim and
the outside world. Essenheim doesn't have anything that anybody wants. Maybe that's why it's stayed independent ... Tell
me more, Kate. Why are you interested?'

'I met somebody from there,' Kate admitted.

'Well, you can't learn Essenheimisch in this school, that's for
sure. *I* can't teach you, because I don't know it myself. And I'm

not going to encourage you. You've enough on your plate already if you're going to pass your exams for college next year.'

'Do you know where I *could* learn it?' Kate asked.

'I don't. There might be a class somewhere in London, though I doubt it. Leave it with me, Kate. I'll inquire in the usual places, and let you know if I have any success.'

Kate left it with her. It stayed with her for three weeks. Then she called Kate over at the end of a lesson.

'There's not one official class in Essenheimisch in the whole of London.'

Kate's face fell.

'But don't despair. I've heard of someone who might teach you. He's a certain Dr Falkstadt.'

'I think I've heard that name,' Kate said.

'He's an exile, apparently. Didn't get on with the powers-that-be in Essenheim. He's living in London rather precariously, and teaching a couple of pupils to make ends meet. I gather he wouldn't in the least mind having one more.'

'I've found a teacher of Essenheimisch,' Kate told Edward next day.

'Interesting,' Edward said. 'We were told there wasn't any-body. But George has found one as well. He was telling me about it only today. The man George has found lives in Highgate. His name is Dr Falkstadt.'

'Snap!' said Kate.

Dr Theodor Falkstadt took George and Kate up several flights of stairs to the tiny apartment he rented at the top of a narrow house in Highgate Village. He was a small, elderly man, com-pletely bald, with a gentle voice and expression, and he was neatly dressed in clothes which had reached a state of terminal shabbiness.

'Gracious young lady and gallant gentleman,' he said, 'I shall be delighted to teach you what I can of the language of my unfortunate country. But let me impress on you that I am not by profession a language teacher. I do a little teaching because, to be frank, the money is welcome. As a foreigner I do not qualify for your retirement pension.'

'I understand you're an exile,' George said.

'Not an exile, exactly. I had to leave Essenheim because I could make no living when I lost my royal appointment.'

'What appointment was that?' Kate asked.

'I am a musician. I led the Palace Ensemble. We performed, from time to time, in the music-room of Essenheim Castle. But one evening, when we were giving a concert for the Prime Minister and a party of his guests, I had to reprove them for talking all through the performance of an immortal work by our national composer, Kammerjungfer. Dr Stockhausen thereupon led his party from the room; and the following month my appointment was not renewed. What can a musician do in Essenheim without a royal appointment? I came to London to earn my daily bread.'

'And have you worked as a musician here?' Kate asked.

'Alas, no. I cannot find a job. But I have a little part-time work as an assistant in an antique shop near here. And now, I hear the doorbell. In a minute you will meet my other two pupils.'

The other two pupils were a plump, round-faced, cheerful young man in a dark red velvet jacket and a tall girl with a very pale face, a severe expression, and long straight black hair parted in the middle. Dr Falkstadt introduced them as Aleksi and Sonia.

'They are both Essenheimers,' he explained, 'and they come to me to improve their English. You two are English and you come to me to learn Essenheimisch. So we form a good group, do we not? I shall insist that Aleksi and Sonia speak only English, and when you two have learned a little Essenheimisch I shall insist that you speak only that.'

'And what do you do, Aleksi?' George asked.

'I am poet,' Aleksi said. 'Essenheim has as yet no national poet. I shall be he.'

'But you don't need English to be an Essenheim poet, do you?'

'I study works of great English poets. From them is much to be learned, even by me. When I have studied enough, I shall write great poetry in Essenheimisch. I shall be Essenhcim's Shakespeare, Milton, Wordsworth, all three.'

'That sounds quite a programme,' George said, impressed.

'And what about you, Sonia?' asked Kate.

'I am a revolutionary.'

There was a moment's surprised silence. Then George said, 'That's not usually a way of making a living.'

'Sonia teaches in the University of Essenheim,' said Dr Falkstadt.

'That is true,' said Sonia. 'I have taught in the university. But it is a tool of princely reaction. Since last year I leave it. I shake the feet of it off my dust.'

'The dust of it off my feet,' Dr Falkstadt corrected her. 'But Sonia, you haven't actually left, have you? I thought you were on a year's paid leave.'

'That is so,' Sonia admitted. 'I go back soon. But I return only because revolution is coming to Essenheim. And when it comes, the dust shall be back on my feet with a vengeance! The Prince shall be overthrown and the university shall serve the people!'

Kate could see that George's professional interest was mounting.

'Who,' he inquired, 'will lead the revolution?'

'As to that,' said Sonia with contempt, 'I tell you nothing. I have heard about you. You are a lackey of the capitalist Press. I trust you like I trust a steak.'

'Snake,' said Dr Falkstadt.

'I've heard,' said George cautiously, 'that the army, or perhaps someone else, might be planning a coup.'

'The army!' echoed Sonia. 'That is another tool of oppression. Army rule would be no revolution. I spit on the army like I spit on the Prince, the university, the fascist Press. I spit on them all!' She pursed her lips as if about to demonstrate.

'To me,' said Aleksi, 'hope lies with the young prince.'

'I spit on him too,' said Sonia with an air of impartiality.

'I hear,' said Aleksi, 'that young prince is friend of Colonel Schweiner of army, and Klaus Klappdorf of university, and Herr

43

Finkel of much money, and that it is because he have too many friends that young prince is sent abroad.'

Dr Falkstadt intervened, looking anxious.

'I think that's enough of that subject,' he said. 'We are not here to gossip. You all pay me for this lesson, and I must earn my money. Now, George and Kate, let me give you books.'

He handed each of them a battered copy of a young children's story-book, printed in heavy old-fashioned Gothic type.

'It is not ideal,' he said. 'It has many misprints. There is only one printing house in Essenheim, and it is not very good. That will not matter greatly, as I teach by the direct method. But first of all I wish you to see Essenheimisch in print. Let me now read you the story, and you will follow the action from the pictures. After that, as their next practice, Aleksi and Sonia will tell you it in English. Thus we shall kill two birds with one stone.'

The story was easy enough to understand. It was about a small black sheep that strayed from the flock and was found and revived by a kindly shepherd. Having gravely read it aloud, Dr Falkstadt turned to Sonia.

'Now,' he said, 'you tell us the story in English.'

'I refuse,' said Sonia. 'It is bourgeois sexist racist ageist élitist fascist propaganda. I spit on it.'

7

Weeks went by during which Kate heard nothing from or about Rudi. Curiously, however, as her expectation of seeing him diminished, her interest in Essenheim itself increased. She wanted more and more to see it for herself, and had an occasional daydream in which she was wandering in the grounds of Essenheim Castle when suddenly Rudi appeared round a corner. He was as handsome as ever and had been writing to her every day, but his mail had been intercepted by the obnoxious Dr Stockhausen. 'Kate,' he said in the daydream, 'dear Kate, there has never been a moment when you were not in my thoughts . . .'

Meanwhile, in real life, the days lengthened, the summer term at school began, and Kate had her seventeenth birthday. Learning Essenheimisch became part of a routine. Every Wednesday George picked her up in the Mini and drove her to Highgate, where they sat in Dr Falkstadt's apartment and conversed, first in English and later in halting Essenheimisch, with the other two pupils. Aleksi was amiable and lived in a haze of anticipated future greatness, though at the moment he appeared to be decidedly hard up. Sonia remained intense and fierce, especially if the conversation went anywhere near Essenheim politics. Then Dr Falkstadt would look unhappy and stop the discussion.

George didn't pick up the language as easily as Kate, but he worked at it much harder than she did, so their progress was roughly equal. After the class at Dr Falkstadt's, he would take Kate to a near-by coffee bar and they would discuss their lives and philosophies. George was always serious; Kate was inclined to be flippant. George found this attractive. In fact George seemed to find Kate attractive altogether. This wasn't very welcome to Kate, because the proximity of George did absolutely nothing for her.

George also got into the habit of coming to her house on Saturdays and days off. He always talked earnestly to Edward, addressing him by his first name but with a tone of deference which made it sound like 'sir'. Edward, who had a low boredom threshold, became weary of George's visits but hadn't the heart to choke him off.

'All the same,' he confided to Kate when George went home rather late after a long evening of solemn discussion, 'I shan't be sorry when we've packed him off to Essenheim. I've told him to take as long as he likes on the story but make it a good one.'

'When will he be going there?' Kate asked.

'Oh, in about a month, I should think. Some of the other reporters are jealous. A country in the middle of Europe as little visited as Tibet: they'd all like to go there.'

'I think I'm jealous, too,' said Kate. '*I'd* like to go there.'

Edward made no comment. Neither of them guessed that Kate would be in Essenheim before that month was up.

On the morning of the day her school term ended, Kate came into the kitchen to find that a bleary-eyed and dressing-gowned Edward was there before her. He was drinking coffee and leafing through the pile of newspapers which had descended as usual on the Milbanks' mat.

'Hello!' she said. 'What's up?'

'I am,' said Edward.

'I can see that. But it's only half-past seven. I can't remember when you were last around before double figures.'

'Kate,' said Edward, 'there's a funny twist to the Essenheim story. You won't like it, I'm afraid.'

Kate sat down opposite him, feeling apprehensive.

'You remember,' Edward said, 'that when you went to the Essenheim Consulate you were told Rudi had flown back there?'

'Yes, of course. How could I forget?'

'Well, now, the *Morning Intelligence* has a correspondent in Serenia, the next-door country to Essenheim, and the correspondent himself, like all correspondents, has various sources of information. One of these happens to be near the Essenheim frontier. And our man – or rather, our man's man – has been picking up some curious stuff on Essenheim radio.'

'That's the first I've heard of Essenheim radio,' said Kate.

'Oh, they have a radio station. It's a one-horse affair that's always breaking down, and when it *is* working it can only be heard a few miles beyond the frontier. And most of the time it just plays last year's pop. But anyway, the person I'm telling you about is within its range. And what he's picked up is that Prince Rudi has not returned to Essenheim.'

'What?' Kate was aghast.

'He hasn't got back to base. Or so their radio says.'

'What's happened to him, then?'

'I don't know. I wish I did.'

'And what are the Essenheim authorities doing about it?'

'Nothing, apparently. It's being presented as a desertion. The old Prince, it's said, sent Rudi on this Grand Tour, and Rudi repaid his kindness by deserting him for wine, women and song.'

'Do you believe that's what's happened?' asked Kate.

'How would I know? I'm merely reporting what Essenheim radio says. And I haven't told you it all yet. This non-return of Rudi's was quite a while ago.'

'Twelve weeks,' said Kate, who remembered exactly.

'Right. It was some time before our source in Serenia happened to pick this up. He doesn't spend his days with his ear glued to Essenheim radio. And by the time he latched on to it, the story had developed further. It seems that the old Prince has decided, or been persuaded, that this means removing Rudi from the succession. The new Crown Prince will be his cousin

Friedrich. Friedrich will be proclaimed heir to the throne as soon as he's eighteen, in a few weeks' time.'

'Oho,' said Kate. 'What if Rudi turns up?'

'I have no idea. But there has to be a Crown Prince to secure the throne; otherwise if anything happens to the old boy there's a strong chance that the country will fall into anarchy. And the Prince rates the continuance of the Monarchy above all else. Hence the proclamation of Friedrich.'

'I suppose,' Kate said reluctantly, 'they must be right and Rudi just didn't want to go home. We heard him say he wasn't keen on the "prince" business. But why did he have to get *us* involved?'

Edward said, 'Why indeed? That's a serious question, Kate. Why should Rudi involve you, me and the paper, and then disappear into thin air? There's a curious smell about this affair. I think *somebody* is up to something peculiar.'

'What are you suggesting?' Kate asked.

'I'm not exactly suggesting anything, just wondering. Didn't Rudi say the interpreter was there to keep an eye on him?'

'Bodyguard, escort, warder and resident spy,' said Kate, remembering. 'Rudi also told me Dr Stockhausen would be delighted if Friedrich stepped into his shoes.'

'Well, then, what if Stockhausen wanted to get Rudi out of the way? And succeeded?'

'If *I* said that,' said Kate, 'you'd accuse me of being melodramatic.'

'All right,' said Edward. 'Point taken. However, I was interested enough to get on to James Higgins about Rudi's departure. Getting information from him is like getting blood out of a stone. However, so far as the Foreign Office is concerned, Rudi left London Airport all those weeks ago on a scheduled flight to Serenia, intending to change there for Essenheim. What he may have done since then is nobody's business. Least of all, James gave me to understand, that of the *Morning Intelligence*.'

'Did anyone actually see him go?'

'Apparently not. James's department would have seen him

off, but the offer was declined because Rudi's visit was a private one. He was travelling under his family name of Rudolf Hohenberg.'

'Could he still be in this country, then?'

'Unlikely. His name was on the passenger-list. Though as a matter of fact we've had another report which I'd better tell you about, although I'm sceptical of it myself. One of our reporters – not George – thinks he saw Rudi in a Mayfair night-club with a lady whom this reporter knows very well by sight. A rich young lady. A *very* rich young lady. The daughter of an oil millionaire.'

'Oh, *no*!' cried Kate before she could stop herself.

'He was probably mistaken, Kate. He'd never seen Rudi except in photographs. Most likely it was someone quite different.'

Kate hoped it was.

'Then again,' said Edward thoughtfully, 'he could duly have gone back to Essenheim, in spite of what the radio says, and been spirited away out of sight. He could be languishing in the dungeons of Essenheim Castle.'

'He couldn't. Oh, he *couldn't*! Could he?'

'Don't be upset. I don't really think so. But there's no end to the possibilities.'

'Then what is the *Morning Intelligence* going to *do*?'

'We talked about it a good deal in the office last night. We could, of course, run a story on the strength of what we have already: a "Mystery of the Missing Prince" affair. But that would blow the whole thing and get the popular Press on to it. At the moment nobody but us seems to know. I think instead we shall try to do a proper job on this. We've brought George's departure forward; he's off to Essenheim later this week.'

'How's he going to get in?' Kate asked.

'I don't know, but he'll manage it somehow. In the meantime, we're getting in touch with everyone Rudi is known to have seen during his tour. It may still turn out that he's simply got tired of the whole scene, thrown in his hand and gone to stay with some minor royalty on a country estate somewhere in Europe. If so, we'll trace him. If not ... well, it may be quite a story we're on to.'

'It's more than a newspaper story to me,' said Kate dismally.

'I know it is, my dear,' said Edward. He rubbed a sympathetic though unshaven cheek against hers. 'That's why I wanted you to know what's happened as soon as possible. And now, you'd better get ready or you'll be late for school.'

'It doesn't matter today,' said Kate. 'It's the last day of term.'

'Oh well. Take your time then, but forgive me if I totter back to bed. I wasn't home until nearly four, and I'm not as good as I used to be at managing on three and a half hours' sleep.'

'Thank you for getting up,' said Kate, touched.

Edward crawled from the kitchen and went to his own room. He was asleep in five minutes. He didn't know it would be weeks before he saw Kate again.

8

Kate walked part of the way home from school with Susan Baker that afternoon. It was the end of term and also of the school year; she didn't have to go back until mid-September, which was eight weeks away. She'd just parted company with Susan when there was a squeal of brakes and a car drew up precipitately a few yards ahead of her. The door on the passenger side flew open, and a bearded man called from the driver's seat, urgently, 'Kate!'

Kate, startled, went up to the car.

'Jump in!' the driver told her.

It took her a second or two to recognize him. The driver was Rudi, a bearded Rudi.

Kate didn't stop to think. She got into the car, which was a newish Triumph. Rudi leaned over to kiss her with extreme brevity, then steered instantly into the traffic. The whole incident had taken less than a minute.

'Where are we going?' Kate asked when she'd caught up with herself. 'And why the beard?'

Rudi was driving rather fast in the busy streets, nipping in and out between other vehicles.

'Never mind the beard just for now,' he said. 'You ask where we are going. We are going to your house. I shall talk very rapidly with your father. Meanwhile you will pack a bag. You will do it very quickly, in five minutes, no more. I hope you have a passport.'

'Yes, I've a passport. But why do I need it? Where am I going?'

'You are going to Essenheim Castle.'

'Thank you for telling me,' said Kate. 'But how do you know I want to go there? And what's my father going to say? And what would I do for money? And what . . .?'

'Be calm,' Rudi said. 'All shall be arranged. I shall speak to your father. He will not refuse a request from me.'

Kate thought her father capable of refusing a request from anybody except perhaps herself. But what she said to Rudi was, 'He won't be at home. He goes to work before this time. He'll be at the *Morning Intelligence* office by now.'

Rudi was momentarily taken aback, then retorted, 'Has the *Morning Intelligence* no telephones?'

'Of course it has. But are you going to spring a thing like that on him over the phone? Anyway, as I said before, how do you know I want to go to Essenheim?' In spite of the daydream, she found the prospect rather alarming.

'Kate,' said Rudi, 'it is very urgent, very important, and there is no time to lose. When I've explained to you, you will understand that you *must* come to Essenheim. In any case, how could you refuse? You are invited. My sister, Princess Anni, invites you. I convey the invitation to you now on her behalf. It is not usual to reject a royal invitation. In my country it would be considered unbecoming conduct on the part of a subject.'

'I thought you didn't believe in the royalty stuff,' Kate said. 'And anyway, I'm not a subject of yours. Or of Princess Anni. I'd never heard of her until this moment.'

'It's true you're not a subject.' Rudi turned his face aside for long enough to give her a smile which was halfway between his stunning special and his shamefaced grin. It melted her to the core. 'But you will come as a friend. You must. Kate, I am in deep trouble and cannot get out of it without you. I will tell you when we are on the way.'

'How long do you want me to go for? And what about money? I've just seven pounds and sixty pence in the bank.'

'There will be no expense. You will stay as a guest at the castle for at least a week. That will be necessary. Then it will be for you to decide whether you wish to stay any longer. I am not abducting you, Kate.'

He gave her the melting smile again.

'Look, we have arrived at your house. I have remembered well the way, haven't I? Jump out. You have your key? Open the door, quickly. Good ... Now, where is the telephone and what is the number?'

Kate told him the number and stood by as he dialled.

'Don't wait here!' he instructed her. 'Get your passport and pack your bag. Go on. Go, go, go!'

Kate, who was inclined to be bossy herself, found that for once she was being successfully bossed. She hurried upstairs to her room. With part of her mind she stood outside herself, watching herself throw things into a suitcase, wondering why she was doing it, and not really believing in the situation at all. She had just finished packing and taken her passport from a drawer when Rudi's voice came commandingly up the stairs: 'Kate! Kate! Speak to your father!'

Rudi wasn't looking too pleased. Kate wondered if Edward had objected to the trip. But soon it was clear that he hadn't.

'This is a mad caper, isn't it?' he said cheerfully on the phone. He didn't sound as if he thought it impossibly mad, though. And if Kate had had the time or the presence of mind to think, she'd have realized that Edward was about the least likely parent in the Western world to object to a sudden journey overseas. As a foreign editor he lived in a world in which people were forever going off abroad at a moment's notice. To him it was a normal way of life. He went on, calmly, 'You do really want to go, Kate, do you?'

'Yes,' said Kate, although until she heard herself say it she hadn't been quite sure.

'And I suppose you know what you're doing?'

'Yes,' said Kate again, more confidently than she felt.

'Well, Rudi says Essenheim's as peaceful as ever and it will

53

just be a holiday for you. In those circumstances I won't try to stop you. In fact, strictly speaking I *can't* stop you. You're over the age of consent.'

'Hey, half a minute. I haven't consented to anything,' Kate said. 'What's more, if you mean what I think you mean, I'm not going to.'

'Well, that's wise of you. I hope you'll stick to it,' said Edward. 'And anyway, you're going to have a chaperon of a sort.'

'A *chaperon*?' Kate echoed, startled.

'Well, not that exactly. But George is going with you. I got Rudi to say he could.'

Rudi was standing close by Kate, looking cross and anxious and glancing pointedly at his watch.

'I thought George wasn't going till later in the week,' Kate said.

'He wasn't. We hadn't worked out a way of getting him into Essenheim. But we mustn't miss this opportunity. Rudi can get him in.'

'Oh,' said Kate. The thought of George as a member of the party was something of a dampener.

'And don't lose contact with George, will you? If you have any problems, he'll get through to us.'

'Oh,' said Kate again.

'And have a good time. And I hope you're not too long away. I shall miss your cooking.'

Kate knew that was his way of saying he'd miss *her*. 'I'll be thinking of you,' she told him. 'And don't worry, I'll be back before too long, as good as new.'

'All right. I'll see you when I see you,' Edward said. 'Good-bye, my dear.'

Kate might have said something more, but Rudi had picked up her bag and was jingling his car keys impatiently.

'Good-bye then,' she said, and put the receiver down. And next minute she was being tugged out by Rudi to the car.

'That's not the way to the airport,' she told him two or three minutes later.

'We're not going to the airport.'

Kate said, 'Listen, Rudi, will you *please* put me in the picture. Here am I, dashing off to regions unknown with nothing but a toothbrush – well, *practically* nothing but a toothbrush – and you've hardly told me the first thing about it. Where *are* we going? Why are we in such a hurry? Where have you been these last three months? What about George? What ... ?'

'One question at a time, please,' Rudi said.

'All right. Just where are we going?'

'I've told you. We're going to Essenheim Castle. Which happens to be my home.'

'Then *how* are we going, if we're not on our way to the airport?'

'We are going mainly by road. We shall cross the Channel from Dover to Calais and drive through France and Switzerland to Serenia. There we shall catch a plane to Essenheim. It's all quite straightforward.'

'How long will it take?'

'Three days, all being well.'

'But I thought we were in a tearing hurry. So why aren't we going by air all the way?'

'The hurry was not a hurry to arrive in Essenheim,' Rudi said. 'We are in a hurry because it is possible that we are being pursued. And we are not going by air because I see the airport as a danger point for us. It will be safer by sea, I hope.'

Kate's heart bumped.

'Pursued!' she echoed. 'Who by?'

'By Karl and Josef. You may remember Karl. He accompanied me to your house on my previous visit.'

'I do remember,' Kate said. She shuddered at the thought of the pale, thick-lipped man. She had not liked the look of Karl.

'Josef I think you have not met,' said Rudi. 'I hope you never will. Josef makes Karl look like a Victorian maiden aunt.'

'But why?' demanded Kate. 'Why, why, why?'

'Let me return to your earlier question,' Rudi said. 'You asked where I had been these past few weeks. The answer is that I have been in a farmhouse in a remote part of Somerset. Imprisoned. That is why I have the beard.'

'Imprisoned!' Kate's heart bumped again. 'You mean you were kidnapped?'

'Precisely. On the way to the airport. It was very simple. Young Stockhausen – the son of the Essenheim Consul here and nephew of our Prime Minister – was to drive me there in his own car, which is the one we are in now. Soon after picking me up, he drove into an enclosed yard, where Karl and Josef had already parked another car. They came over to us and, when I asked what was happening, Josef said, "This", and hit me on the head. I gather that Albrecht Stockhausen went on to the airport in the other car, with my passport and ticket, and flew to Serenia in my name. Karl drove me to Somerset in this one, and Josef took the other car from the airport.'

Kate said, 'I can't believe it! Kidnapped! In England!' And then, 'How did they treat you?'

'They treated me well, but I was very bored. Karl was bored, too, and probably told me more than he should have done.'

'What were they aiming to achieve?'

'They'd have held me until Dr Stockhausen's protégé, my cousin Friedrich, was installed as Crown Prince, and their future power assured. Then I expect they'd have let me go. If I'd gone home and told the tale after that, it would have been my word against everybody else's, and no one would have believed me. I have, I'm afraid, some reputation for irresponsibility. Anyway, I've escaped just in time, and all being well I shall put matters right.'

'How *did* you escape, Rudi?'

'That was quite simple, too, when the opportunity came. Through the window of the room where I was confined, I saw Josef set off in the other car, I suppose to do the shopping. When Karl came to my room I hit *him* on the head. With a leg screwed off the bed, as a matter of fact. It gave me great satisfaction. Then I took his keys and young Stockhausen's car, and here we are!'

'Well!' said Kate. 'When you put it like that it *does* sound simple.'

Rudi said, 'I don't know how much start I had. Probably it wasn't long before Josef returned. Then they'd be after me. However, there are only the two of them; so far as I know they have no organization. Don't worry, dear Kate. Prepare to enjoy your holiday.'

'Did you tell my father you'd been kidnapped?' Kate asked.

'No. There was not time.'

'I think it was a bit sneaky not to tell him. Even *he* might not have been keen to let me come if he'd known about that. It's a wonder I'm not scared out of my wits.'

'I had no wish to worry your father. And I did desire his consent, or rather his goodwill. That's why I agreed to take George.' Rudi frowned at the recollection. 'I hope that will not spoil the party, so to speak. I have not met this George. What is he like?'

'Oh, George is all right. He's not the most exciting person in the world.'

'Good. I'm glad of that. I must try to fill the role myself.'

'Well, you have a head start,' said Kate. 'It's not everyone who can involve a girl in a nice exciting pursuit by a couple of thugs.'

'I don't think they're pursuing us now,' Rudi said.

'Anyway,' Kate went on, 'where are we picking up George?'

'At the home of a friend and compatriot of mine, in Highgate.'

'Dr Falkstadt!'

'Yes, indeed. Dr Falkstadt. Obviously you know him?'

Kate realized that Rudi was unaware she had been taking language lessons. She told him so, in Essenheimisch. He looked at her with surprise, then commented, 'Not bad. Not bad at all. You have a good accent. They will like that in Essenheim.'

'I'm glad to hear it,' said Kate. 'But when are you going to tell me what all this is about?'

'Later, dear Kate, later. You must allow me to give you a little surprise.'

'You've given me a big surprise already. I don't think I need a little one as well.'

Rudi made no comment. A minute later he said, 'I shall park the car here.'

'Dr Falkstadt's is two or three streets away,' Kate told him.

'Actually I'm aware of that. But this is Albrecht Stockhausen's car, and we are abandoning it. We shall change to the car of another friend of mine, Aleksi Wandervogel.'

'I know Aleksi, too,' said Kate.

Arriving at Dr Falkstadt's, Rudi rang the bell three or four times, insistently, in rapid succession. Dr Falkstadt himself opened the door. He embraced Rudi warmly.

'My dear Rudi!' he said. 'My dear Prince! At last!' So briefly that Kate was hardly sure she'd seen it, he dropped to a knee, then straightened up. 'Come!' he said. 'There are friends to meet you!'

In Dr Falkstadt's sitting-room were Aleksi and Sonia. Dr Falkstadt introduced Sonia to Rudi. She looked at him with disfavour.

'I do not care for princes,' she told him.

'Prince Rudi is not on the side of the old régime,' Dr Falkstadt told her. 'He is the hope of many of us for reform.'

'Reform, pah! I spit on reform. It is worse than no change at all. It causes only confusion. I am for the revolution, Prince!'

'That is your privilege,' said Rudi civilly.

'Privilege! I hate privilege!'

Sonia's eyes had the glazed look which always came over them in political discussion. Kate noticed a somewhat similar look in Rudi's eyes, and guessed he'd taken an instant dislike to Sonia. But he said no more. He bowed slightly and turned to Aleksi with a totally different expression.

'My dear old genius!' he said. 'I can't tell you how glad I am to see you. When shall we be able to talk together?'

'Soon, I hope,' Aleksi said. 'For I learn that you are on your way back to Essenheim. And I beg that you will allow me to come with you. My time in England is nearly up, and my money exhausted. It is right that I should return to Essenheim and place my gifts at the disposal of my own nation. Yet I have not the cost of the fare. I am, as you might say, hitching a lift.'

Rudi looked momentarily taken aback. Then he said, 'You are not hitching a lift, Aleksi. I propose to borrow your car for the journey. A man cannot be said to hitch a lift in his own vehicle. I'm glad you are coming.'

'But alas,' Aleksi said, 'I no longer have the car. I sold it last week, to pay the rent I owed.'

Rudi swore in Essenheimisch.

'We rent a car?' Aleksi suggested.

'Yes, I suppose we can. But it will take a little time. And I do not wish to stay here. I wish to be on the road, and at once.'

'I can help you, Prince,' said Sonia coldly. 'At a price.'

'Oh? How? And at what price?'

'I have a car. You may borrow it. The condition of doing so is that I am to come with you, and you will help me to enter the country.'

There was a brief silence.

'And do not deceive yourself, Prince,' Sonia added. 'I re-enter the country to further the revolution.'

'Whether your services will be a help to any cause is doubtful,' said Rudi. 'In the circumstances, I'm prepared to accept your suggestion.'

'That'll make five of us when George arrives,' said Kate, awed.

'It will not be comfortable,' Sonia said. 'Mine is a small car, a car of the people, not a drawing-room-on-wheels. But needs must, when the Devil drives it.'

'And can you get us all into the country, Rudi?'

'As to that,' said Rudi, 'there is no problem. You will not be required to present yourselves at any immigration post.' He looked around him dubiously. 'I had not however expected a party of this size. I am sorry, dear Kate. I had thought that you and I would set out for Essenheim in comfort.'

'You will not dislike your company any more than I shall dislike mine,' said Sonia sternly. 'There is no friendship involved.'

'You spit on friendship, I suppose,' said Rudi.

'If you do not wish me to change my mind,' Sonia said, 'I suggest that you begin the journey.'

'It can't be too soon for me,' said Rudi. 'I must make a couple of telephone calls to arrange our further movements. I hope that by the time I have done so George will be here.'

Five minutes later a hot and slightly flustered George arrived by taxi. Five minutes after that, everyone trooped down to the street, where farewells were said to Dr Falkstadt. Sonia indicated a small blue Fiat.

'This is it,' she said. 'I shall drive. You, Prince, will pay for the petrol and the passage. You will not sit beside me. I shall have ...' Her eye roved around the party. 'I shall have Kate to sit beside me. You male chauvinists can all sit behind.'

'I'm not a male chauvinist,' said Aleksi plaintively.

'You are not *anything*, Aleksi!' said Sonia with scorn.

'You spit on him?' suggested Rudi.

'Be quiet, Prince, and know your place!' commanded Sonia.

'There still doesn't seem to be anyone chasing us,' Kate remarked as they drove away.

The journey from London to Dover was slightly fraught. Kate by now was feeling overwhelmed by the events of the day. Rudi, crammed into the back of the little car with George and Aleksi, seemed diminished, silent and a little sulky. George clearly regarded himself as being on professional duty; he listened intently to such conversation as there was, making unobtrusive notes on the back of an envelope. Sonia drove emphatically, with a fixed scowl on her face and a total disdain both for her passengers and for other road users. Kate was silent but gripped the edges of her seat.

Aleksi alone was in excellent spirits. 'I have served my apprenticeship,' he informed them all. 'I have learned all that the literature of England can teach me. Now I return to become our national poet.'

'What will your poetry do for the revolution?' demanded Sonia. 'Poet and prince are equally useless. You are not the real people. But one day the real people of Essenheim will speak. They will speak through us. Then you will have to listen.'

'Yesterday,' said Aleksi, 'I compose poem in Essenheimisch. It is excellent poem.'

'Do read it out to us,' said Kate.

'Willingly.' Aleksi drew a piece of paper from his pocket and read out his poem. It was not very long. The subject-matter sounded familiar. Kate and George looked at each other with a wild surmise. Then George said, 'Read it again, please, Aleksi.'

Aleksi read it again. Kate translated to herself as he went along. 'I moved at random in isolation similar to that of a mass of fog drifting at a considerable altitude across mountains and valleys when without warning I observed an assemblage, an army, of yellow flowers on long green stalks ...'

'Why,' she said, 'it's Wordsworth's "Daffodils"!'

Aleksi inclined his head. 'I acknowledge an influence,' he said with dignity. 'It is better in Essenheimisch than in English, is it not?'

'It is rubbish,' said Sonia. 'It is totally irrelevant to the class struggle.'

It was raining when they reached Dover. There was some delay over the formalities, and a wait in line to drive on to the ferry. Rudi looked several times at his watch, and made anxious-sounding remarks to Kate under his breath about Karl and Josef. Only when they were on board the ferry and the crossing had begun did he seem entirely relaxed. Then he said quietly to Kate, 'We are on our way. In three days we shall be in Essenheim. You will like it.'

Kate hoped they would and she would. But she couldn't quite believe it. For the moment the whole trip seemed to have taken on an air of the higher unreality.

9

So Kate was on her way to Essenheim.

Conversation on the journey across France and Switzerland was sometimes in English, sometimes in Essenheimisch, which Kate and George spoke fairly well by now and wanted to practise. Rudi appeared on the second morning without his beard and looking more handsome than ever. Nothing was seen of Karl or Josef, and there were no mishaps along the way, though there might well have been.

Sonia drove the little Fiat well but fiercely; then, after some hours, complained of having to do all the work, conveniently forgetting that she herself had insisted on driving. She was succeeded in turn by Rudi, who relied on his quick reactions and drove alarmingly fast; George, who was so careful that the rest of them could have screamed and eventually did; and Aleksi, who wandered absent-mindedly all over the road, perpetually forgetting whether he was supposed to be driving on the left or the right. Kate didn't drive; she'd only just reached her seventeenth birthday and didn't yet have a licence.

On the third morning, in brilliant sunshine, they drove out of Switzerland into Serenia, along a straight smooth highway with superbly clean service areas, smart and tasteful restaurants which served rich pastries and hot chocolate, and vantage points at frequent intervals for viewing the spectacular mountain scenery. In early afternoon they left the highway and took to smaller, winding lanes, passing through villages of bright wooden houses carved like musical boxes. They began to descend, leaving the snow-capped peaks behind them; the landscape became grassy and wooded, hilly rather than mountainous.

And at last they came to a road sign, of elegant design and typography, pointing to SOUTH-EAST SERENIAN AIRPORT 3 KILOMETRES.

The airport in fact was tiny, but had neat, immaculate terminal buildings. There was a parking lot with room for a thousand cars and holding perhaps half a dozen. Kate and Sonia went in search of the ladies' room. Inside the automatic doors, the concourse gleamed with black tiles and pinewood walls and plate glass. But the airport wasn't doing a lot of business at the moment. A single flight of Air Serenia was listed on the destination board, and the plane itself sat in lone splendour on the tarmac. There was no sign of Essenheim Airways.

'This is the civilized end of the field,' Rudi said when they returned to the car. 'They've left *our* terminal at the other end, where it was before all this progress.' He put the car in gear and drove for some distance round the perimeter. At the farthest corner of the field was a wooden shack, in front of which stood a small two-propeller aircraft of a type which Kate, who didn't know about such things, could not identify. Over the door of the shack and on the side of the plane was printed, in Gothic lettering, 𝕰𝖘𝖘𝖊𝖓𝖍𝖊𝖎𝖒 𝕬𝖎𝖗𝖜𝖆𝖞𝖘 and beside this inscription, a bunch of grapes. Neither shack nor craft looked as if it had been painted lately.

'Look well on this,' said Rudi. 'This is our one and only plane, all ready – I hope – to fly on its one and only route, between here and Essenheim. It's just a hundred miles. With a bit of luck, I dare say we shall make it.'

Half a dozen men sat facing each other on a couple of baggage trolleys. They were eating out of paper packages and passing a bottle around among them. Three wore dirty overalls; the other three wore equally dirty purplish uniforms with wings on the chest and rings around the sleeves. All six got up. One of the uniformed men, a spider-like figure with a short torso but unusually long arms and legs, stepped forward and extended a hand.

'Hello, Highness,' he said cheerfully. 'We got your message and held the flight for you. We'd been told you were never coming back, but I knew you'd be along, one of these days.'

'Hello, Fritzi,' Rudi said. 'Good to see you.'

'You've quite a party with you, haven't you?' said Fritzi. 'Any of them *supposed* to be here? Or are we smuggling 'em in?'

'Don't use words like that, Fritzi,' said Rudi. 'We don't smuggle things into Essenheim, or people either, do we?' The two winked at each other, and the other men chuckled.

'Anyway, this young lady is an official guest,' Rudi said, indicating Kate, who was somewhat relieved by the description. 'The others are not here, so to speak. They are optical illusions.'

He introduced them, none the less. The six men turned out to be two thirds of the entire staff of Essenheim Airways. Fritzi was the Chief Pilot; there was also the Deputy Chief (and only other) Pilot, the Flight Engineer, two mechanics, and an Airline Director, whose broom was leaning against a side of the shack. It appeared that in Essenheim itself were two more mechanics and another Airline Director.

'Excuse us while we finish our snack, Highness,' said Fritzi, 'and then we'll be on our way.' He dug the Airline Director in the ribs. 'Pass us that bottle!'

Kate whispered to Rudi, 'I don't think he's quite sober.'

'Of course he's not!' said Rudi, and added, without bothering to drop his voice, 'He's as drunk as a lord.'

'Drunk as a prince, we say in Essenheim,' remarked Fritzi.

'Watch it, Fritzi!' Rudi warned him. 'If I were Prince Laureate, that'd be high treason. You'd finish up in the bargain basement.'

All six men burst out laughing.

'What's the bargain basement?' asked Kate. There was more laughter.

65

'It's our name for the dungeons of Essenheim Castle,' said Rudi.

'You must allow us a little drink, Highness,' said Fritzi. 'Especially as this is the whisky run.'

'And what's the whisky run?' Kate inquired, amid more laughter.

'It takes place every week,' Rudi explained. 'It is not only whisky. A number of delicacies are flown in. Not for my uncle, whose tastes are simple, but for the Prime Minister and his friends. And Herr Finkel.'

Kate would have liked to ask, 'Who's Herr Finkel?', but felt that her questions were giving enough opportunity for mirth already. However, Fritzi gave her the answer.

'That's Herr Moneybags, gracious young lady. The richest man in Essenheim. He owns the Spitzhof Restaurant, and lives pretty well himself.'

'How are all these things paid for?' asked George. Kate recognized the tones of the inquiring reporter.

'There's a good market for our finest wines,' Rudi said. 'And Herr Finkel controls their production. The same plane flies them out. It is well organized.'

'Time we were drinking up, lads,' said Fritzi, putting the bottle of red wine to his own lips and taking a deep swig. 'What time's the flight supposed to leave?'

'Midday,' said the Airline Director, dusting crumbs off his overall.

'Five hours late. That's not very good, is it?'

'I've known flights later than that at Heathrow or Kennedy,' said the co-pilot. 'And it's on account of his Highness, remember. If we'd left earlier, he'd have had to wait for a week.'

'I take it we have the goodies on board?' Fritzi said.

'Yes, she's loaded up. All except the passengers.'

'Come on then, people,' said Rudi. 'Prepare for the last lap.'

He manoeuvred the seating so that he sat beside Kate in the pair of seats just behind Fritzi and the co-pilot. Kate was relieved to see that the co-pilot, who appeared to be sober and competent, was in the pilot's seat. There was some cross-talk with ground control on the radio, and the plane taxied out to the runway and took off. The ground reared up sharply, first on one side then on the other. Kate felt apprehensive; she'd flown only once before, and it hadn't been quite like this.

'It's all right,' Rudi said as the plane levelled out and headed down the valley. 'We got the co-pilot and the mechanics from an American airline. They know what they're doing. Fritzi is called Chief Pilot, but he isn't really in charge, thank God.'

At a point where two rivers flowed together, the plane took a sharp turn left and headed up a different valley towards high ground.

'We're in the Esel valley now,' Rudi told Kate. 'We just follow it up into the hills and we come to Essenheim.'

Kate looked down with interest, first at broad meadows and lush farming country, then at increasingly steep riverside slopes covered with vines. High mountain-tops could once again be glimpsed in the distance. At one point was a series of dams and small lakes.

'That's the Serenian hydro-electric scheme,' Rudi said. And, a few minutes later, 'See the village down there? That's on the frontier. We're passing into Essenheim airspace now.'

The radio crackled. Fritzi turned to speak to Rudi. 'It's working today, Highness,' he said. 'Are we to tell them you're coming?'

'No, Fritzi. The news would get to officialdom before it got to the Prince. In fact it might not get to the Prince at all. What if I was arrested?'

'All right, Highness,' Fritzi said. 'We'll just land quietly and leave you to it. All they're expecting us to have on board is the whisky and the pâté and smoked salmon and so on. So long as that's delivered, nobody cares.'

In another ten minutes they were above the town of Essenheim. You could see even from above that it was a steep little place, divided by chasms where swift mountain rivers ran into each other, and criss-crossed by bridges. Pink-roofed houses clung to the slopes. Near the centre, soaring skyward from a crag, was the dynamic shape of the high Victorian-Gothic castle, which Kate recognized at once from the calendar.

'Am I actually staying *there?*' she asked incredulously.

'You are. As my guest. Or rather, as the guest of my sister Anni. She will like you. You will like her.'

'What about George?'

Rudi frowned. 'Oh, yes, George. That's all rather tiresome. I could have given your father's paper all the information it needed. However, George is fortunate. He doesn't know it yet, but he is on his way to the biggest story of his life. What do you call it? – a scoop?'

'What will it be?'

'You must be patient, Kate. I don't want to spoil it.'

'You're very secretive, Rudi. I never know what you're up to. I don't know even now whether you really like me.'

'As to that,' said Rudi, 'you need be in no doubt.' He kissed her lightly. 'Out of courtesy to your father I would ask George to be a guest at the castle too, but it wouldn't be the best vantage point for him. The authorities don't like journalists. But if George will be patient for a few days and keep his eyes open, the story will come to him. I suggest he stays at our Ritz-Albany Hotel, where he will be tolerably comfortable. It used to be Frau Schmidt's boarding-house. Indeed, it still is.'

'I must keep in touch with George,' said Kate. 'My father insisted on it.'

'You think of George as your lifeline, for use if I leave you struggling in the deep blue sea, so to speak?' Rudi smiled. 'Well, admittedly my position is not secure. However, you will have little difficulty in maintaining contact with George. The telephone service works most of the time, and if it fails there are messengers. Fritzi will fly you out in case of emergency. There is another way out of Essenheim: by boat down the river into Serenia. I assure you, Kate, you are in perfect safety.'

At that moment, Kate was concerned with a more immediate

question of safety. The airstrip at Essenheim was in sight below, and was a small field located disconcertingly between a deep chasm and a cemetery. But the little aircraft dived straight in to make a safe, smooth landing. Fritzi, beside the pilot, turned round and gestured with clasped hands over his head, like a footballer who'd just scored a goal.

'I hope a safe landing is not too unusual an achievement,' observed Aleksi. 'However, we are here. Home, sweet home. Home is the sailor, home from sea. Be it never so humble, there's no place like home.'

Across the chasm, the Gothic castle dominated the townscape. It didn't look all that humble or, for that matter, homely.

'Did you say it's less than a hundred years old, Rudi?' Kate asked. 'It looks kind of *battered*. Was it attacked in the war?'

'Indeed, no. Essenheim was neutral until the final weeks, when it came in on the winning side. The battered appearance of the castle was built in, at great expense. The Prince's grandfather insisted on it. He wanted it to be medieval and partly ruined, yet at the same time modern and splendid. It made him bankrupt. And in spite of the expense, it is, I'm afraid, rather draughty and inconvenient.'

'You can disembark now, Highness and gracious young lady,' said Fritzi.

The Essenheim airport was somewhat grander than the Essenheim Airways establishment in Serenia: there were two shacks instead of one. Over the first shack was the legend 𝕽𝖔𝖞𝖆𝖑 𝕰𝖘𝖘𝖊𝖓𝖍𝖊𝖎𝖒 𝕮𝖚𝖘𝖙𝖔𝖒𝖘 𝖆𝖓𝖉 𝖎𝖒𝖒𝖎𝖌𝖗𝖆𝖙𝖎𝖔𝖓 and against a doorpost leaned a somewhat shaggy official in coarse purple uniform. On one shoulder-tab were the words ROYAL ESSENHEIM CUSTOMS and on the other ROYAL ESSENHEIM IMMIGRATION. He advanced, grinning.

'Well, Fritzi, who've you brought us?' And then, 'Why, Highness, it's you! Welcome back to Essenheim!'

'One Prince,' said Fritzi. 'Four other passengers. Plus the usual. Twelve cases of whisky, six of brandy, three each of gin and the usual liqueurs, fifteen kilos of smoked salmon, twelve of pâté, one of caviare ... and it's all on ministerial authority, so don't try charging me duty.'

'And what are you smuggling, Fritzi?'

'Nothing.'

'Don't give me that garbage. Twenty per cent on what you tell me about, fifty per cent on what I find myself, that's my terms, Fritzi.'

'Bloodsucker!' said Fritzi amiably. 'I'll talk to you about it later. Don't keep his Highness waiting!'

'There'll be Unofficial Arrival Money, Highness, I'm afraid for the other people,' the official said. 'I'm not supposed to le anyone in without orders from the Prime Minister's office. And I haven't had any orders today. So, strictly speaking, they can come in.'

'They are all my guests,' said Rudi loftily.

'That's right, Highness,' said Fritzi. 'Don't let him get away with it. He's only trying it on. Anything he can collect goes into his own pocket.'

'If it wasn't his Highness,' said the immigration officer, 'I'm telling you, they'd have to pay up or be turned back. And it's dearer than it used to be, with the inflation.' He sounded wistful at the loss of revenue.

'That'll do,' said Fritzi. 'Good-bye, Highness. See you again one of these days.'

The other shack, the Airline Director's office, was empty.

'He'll be out at one of the wine-cellars,' said Rudi. 'If we did see him tonight, he wouldn't be sober. But we can use his telephone, that's the main thing. If it's working, of course.'

The telephone was an old-fashioned upright type with separate earpiece. Kate watched as Rudi unhooked it.

'Hello! Exchange!' he said; and then, at intervals, 'Hello! ... Hello! ... Hello! ... Adela, dear, I'm glad it's you on duty. This is Prince Rudi ... I said it's Prince Rudi ... No, I'm not a joker, don't you know my voice? ... Remember that evening down by the river-bank when we were both eighteen? Well, doesn't that convince you? ... Yes, I've come back and I'm staying ... Yes, I know they'll be surprised, they'll be knocked sideways ... Listen, Adela, I haven't time to chat, I want you to put me through to the castle. I want the Prince Laureate's private number. You know which it is; they call them hot lines these days ... No, I don't want his secretary ... No, I don't want his aide-de-camp ... No, I don't want *anybody* else ... No, you won't get into any trouble ... No, no, no, NO ... That's right, Adela dear, just put me through to the Prince!'

There was a brief silence. Rudi looked up and winked. Then, 'Hello, Uncle, it's me. Rudi. Yes, I'm here in Essenheim. At the airport. Yes, I've just arrived ... You can't believe it? You'll believe it in a minute ... Yes, I know about Friedrich ... He's not been installed yet, has he? You can send him packing, then ... Yes, I'm coming back as Crown Prince ... Yes, I know your conditions and I've met them ... Yes, she's perfectly suitable. She's ideal. You'll love her ... Oh, never mind what Dr Stockhausen says. You're the ruler, aren't you? Well then, rule! ... Yes, I'm overjoyed, too. Yes, please have a guest room prepared ... Yes, my love to Anni ... Yes, send the car round right away ... Good-bye, Uncle, see you in a few minutes.'

Rudi hung up, grinning. 'There!' he said. 'All fixed up!'

'Is the guest room for me?' inquired Kate.

'Yes.'

'And what am I perfectly suitable for?'

'You'll learn before long, dear Kate.'

'What about the rest of us?' asked Aleksi.

Rudi looked round the remaining faces. 'Well, first there's George,' he said. 'When the car comes, George, I will tell the chauffeur to drop you at the Ritz-Albany. We don't have anything you could call a real hotel in Essenheim, but Frau Schmidt is a motherly soul and you'll be quite comfortable. Now, Aleksi ... ?'

'I shall be all right,' said Aleksi. 'I shall walk to the university. It is proper that a poet and poor scholar should walk. It will be remembered when the cultural history of Essenheim comes to be written. Today will go down as the day when I returned to my country and walked from the airport with my pack on my back. Little, it will be said, did anyone guess that Aleksi Wandervogel ...'

'Quite so,' said Rudi. 'And you, Sonia?'

'For the moment, I shall go to my father's house.'

'Who is your father?' Rudi asked. 'Do I know him?'

'He is Count Zackendorf.'

'O-ho!' Rudi whistled. 'Next to Herr Finkel, he's the richest man in Essenheim, is he not?'

'That may be so. It is nothing to do with me. I did not ask to be begotten by a reactionary plutocrat. I spit on his wealth. But he is my father, he will have to find me a room.'

'It seems to me,' said Rudi, 'that you can probably afford to take a taxi.'

❦ 10 ❦

The day seemed to have been going on for ever, and it wasn't by any means over yet. In the Airline Director's shack, Kate sat in an awkward threesome with Rudi and George. A decrepit taxicab had appeared and been engaged by Sonia; Aleksi had decided that his intention to walk from the airport need not be interpreted too literally and had accepted a lift from her. From the customs shack near by came the sounds of a prolonged but amiable haggle between Fritzi and the Essenheim official.

Then there was a crunch of wheels on gravel. Kate and George followed Rudi outside. A stately but elderly Rolls-Royce drew up, with a stately but elderly chauffeur at the wheel and a coat of arms on the side. From the back jumped a teenage girl, a year or two younger than Kate, wearing T-shirt and jeans. She flung her arms round Rudi, covered his face with kisses, then turned to Kate and repeated the performance.

'It's great to meet you!' she declared. 'Boy, do I *need* you? It's been desperate here!'

She peered through a long blonde fringe at George. 'Who's he, Rudi?' she asked.

'He's an English journalist,' Rudi said. 'He knows everybody.'

'*Everybody?*' the girl said. 'You mean he knows *famous* people? Like ... like *DJ*s?'

'I'm afraid that's not my line,' George said. 'Political and diplomatic journalism, that's what I do, mostly.'

73

'Oh.'

'I should have introduced you,' Rudi said. 'Kate and George, this is my sister Anni. My *little* sister.'

'Get stuffed, Rudi!' said Anni. And then, 'Sit beside me in the car, Kate. I want to talk to you. Oh, it'll be so *good*, talking to someone from London again!'

'Again?' Kate asked.

'Yeah. My best friend is from London. Was. That's Betsy. She's the British Consul's daughter. Well, her dad *was* the British Consul. He got axed in an economy cut. They don't have any consul in Essenheim now. Nobody does. I guess we aren't in the world anymore.' She sighed deeply.

The Rolls left the airstrip and crossed a bridge over a steep narrow valley. Houses straggled up and down the slopes and a river flowed far below.

Anni was chattering into Kate's ear about the delights of London. Kate half listened as the car moved off the bridge, drove along a tree-lined avenue, across another bridge and through a gateway, and began a winding ascent to the castle, which loomed gloomily above.

'How'd you like to live in *that* load of architectural crap?' asked Anni.

From the car, Kate could see only that the castle was built from huge blocks of rough stone and that there was a great deal of it. The Rolls drove past a massively forbidding front entrance, with great studded wooden doors firmly closed, and then for some distance round the side of the castle. Near the back was a modest doorway with a light over it, and beside it a sentry-box with a single guard who stood upright but might well have been asleep with his eyes open.

'Well, here we are!' said Rudi to Kate. 'George, I've told the chauffeur to take you on to the Ritz-Albany.'

George seemed uneasy at leaving Kate. 'Do take care of yourself,' he urged her. 'Remember me if you're in any trouble. Will she be on the telephone, Rudi?'

'Of course,' said Rudi smoothly.

'Then I'll ring you tomorrow,' George said. 'Good-bye, Kate. Good-bye, Rudi. Good-bye, Princess.'

'*Princess!*' echoed Anni in disgust. 'What do you know, he said *Princess*! How old is he, Kate? He looks twenty-two, but he sounds about a hundred and three!'

Inside the entrance was a stone-flagged passageway, and from it Kate could see, through an open door, a vast echoing kitchen with enormous ranges, a great fireplace with a spit that looked big enough to roast a whole ox, and huge copper pans hanging from the walls. It was obviously disused. Farther on, the passageway ended at another door; and at the far side of that, looking remarkably modern by contrast, was a fully-lit carpeted hallway of modest size. In this was a desk with a bell on it, which Rudi rang.

'My uncle had part of the servants' quarters made into a private apartment,' Rudi said to Kate. 'The castle was totally unliveable-in.'

'Still is,' said Anni.

A dark-suited functionary appeared, bowed to Rudi, and said to Kate: 'The Prince Laureate sends his apologies for not coming down to greet you in person. He doesn't get around very easily these days. I'll have somebody show you to your room, and then perhaps you'll be kind enough to go and see him before dinner.'

Kate was still amazed by the attention being paid to her. Rudi said, 'I must have a word with my uncle right away, and then I'll come for you. You'll have plenty of time to change.'

'I haven't much to change into,' said Kate.

'You have a dress, I suppose? Just a pretty dress is what my uncle likes. In spite of all this modernity, he's very old-fashioned. And, Kate ...'

'Yes?'

'Don't react to anything he says, however much it surprises you. I'll give you the explanations afterwards.'

*

A very young, round-faced maid showed Kate into a bedroom which might well have been in a London apartment block if it hadn't been for the extremely high ceiling and the narrow, pointed, deeply-recessed window. Kate went over to this and looked out. Light was beginning to fade, and lamps were coming on to mark the many layers of the hilly little town below. She unpacked her suitcase, put out one of the two dresses she'd brought — a floral patterned cotton — and went into the tiny bathroom which opened out of her room. When she came out, freshly showered, Anni was sprawling on the bed.

'Hi, Kate,' she said. 'I just came visiting.' Seeing Kate's eyes on the new butcher-blue jeans she was wearing, Anni added, 'Rudi brought me these. And some records.' She looked Kate up and down as Kate put on the dress.

'So you're his new girlfriend,' she said.

'Oh, am I?' said Kate. 'I didn't know that.'

'Come off it, Kate. You wouldn't be here if you weren't.' She added thoughtfully, 'I must say, he could have chosen worse. Of course, you're special, aren't you? Uncle Ferdy has to like you, or Rudi stays out in the cold.'

'I don't know what you're talking about,' Kate said. 'I don't even know Rudi very well.'

'Then why have you come to Essenheim?'

'I thought I was invited by *you*.'

It was Anni's turn to look startled. She said, 'Rudi told you that?'

'Yes.'

Anni laughed. 'OK, let's make it true. Kate, I invite you to Essenheim. Stay for ages. But don't rely on what Rudi says.'

'He's very persuasive,' Kate remarked ruefully.

'Oh, sure, he's persuasive. Rudi can make anybody do any-thing. But if I was in London, you couldn't pay me to come to Essenheim.'

'Why not?'

'There's nothing to do here. No dances, no concerts, no discos. Just one boy in all Essenheim that I like, and I can't

76

have anything to do with him because he's only an apprentice. Apart from him, there's nothing but peasants and my cousin Friedrich. And Friedrich is the wettest thing since Noah's flood. You know something, Kate? I'm still a virgin.'

'Oh,' said Kate.

'I am, truly. Isn't it *disgusting*?'

'How old are you, Anni?'

'Nearly sixteen.'

'I wouldn't say it's actually a disgrace to be a virgin at that age,' Kate said. 'In fact ...' She had a sudden inspiration and went on, 'In fact it's quite fashionable in London. Lots of people think it's *sexy* to be a virgin.'

'Oh!' said Anni. The thought was obviously a new one to her. She was silent for a minute or two, considering it. Then there was a tap at the door and Rudi came in.

'Kate!' he exclaimed. 'What a pretty dress! My uncle will be enchanted. He would like to see us both now.'

The door of the Prince of Essenheim's private apartment was a commonplace modern flush door, such as Kate had seen in hundreds. Rudi tapped at it and they went in. The room inside had obviously been cut out of a very much larger one. Apart from a high triple-arched window and an elaborate turreted clock the size of a telephone booth, the room was furnished in mid twentieth-century style. The furniture was in limed oak with curved edges and chromium trim; there were rugs with geometric patterns and light fittings in the guise of coy young ladies. An electric fire occupied a fireplace of multicoloured tile. Beside it flickered a television set. Prince Ferdinand Franz Josef III, who had been watching it, rose with some effort to his feet.

'Enchanté, Mademoiselle,' he said.

He was old and decidedly bulky; his eyes were a watery blue and his cheeks heavy. He had sidewhiskers and a large drooping moustache. He wore a plum-coloured army uniform, much wider in the waist than in the chest, with high collar and epaulettes.

Kate made a somewhat awkward curtsey.

'Vous parlez français?' the Prince inquired.

'Un petit peu,' said Kate modestly.

'But of course, you are English,' the Prince said. 'I fear my English is not what it was. Neither, indeed, is my French, though it was the language spoken by those around me in my youth, now, alas, so long ago ...'

He studied Kate as openly as Anni had done.

'So you are the young lady in Rudi's life,' he observed. He seemed to be favourably impressed. 'I must congratulate him on his choice. You are quite charming.'

Kate tried to think of some way of disclaiming the role assigned to her, but remembered Rudi's request that she should not react to anything the Prince said. Fortunately Prince Ferdinand didn't seem to expect any comment.

'You are of course a commoner?' he said. 'That is quite acceptable. We live in a democratic age, do we not? What does your father do, my dear? He has an occupation, I suppose?'

'He's a journalist,' Kate said.

'A journalist!' The Prince seemed startled, as if that were rather extreme, even in a democratic age.

'An editor,' Rudi added hastily.

'Ah. The editor, perhaps, of *The Times* newspaper?'

'Well, not exactly,' said Kate.

'It is not a distinguished calling,' the Prince observed. 'Still, no doubt some of those who follow it are not wholly ignoble. I myself am but a simple soldier.'

The clock in the corner suddenly went into action. A procession of elaborately costumed figures made a circuit of its turreted summit, while a wooden figure of a black lady played a tune on a built-in dulcimer; the words FLOREAT ESSENHEIM appeared in wildly ornate lettering at a window; and a pair of heraldic birds emerged from hatches, turning their heads from side to side, opening and closing their beaks and flapping their wings. The activity ceased, the window and hatches slammed shut, and with an air of anticlimax the clock struck eight.

'I'm sorry if that startled you,' the Prince said to Kate. 'I've been meaning to get rid of it for thirty years. It is out of place here, is it not? It was made for my great-grandfather by an excessively loyal craftsman. I don't notice it myself, I'm so used to it. However, it is a reminder. Eight o'clock already. Dr Stockhausen and his lady will arrive any minute. They are invariably prompt.'

He sighed and cast a wistful glance towards the television.

'It's Monday,' he said. 'At eight o'clock on Monday evenings we get "Dallas", relayed by Serenian TV. Ah well, one must sacrifice occasionally for duties of state. And, thanks to Rudi's arrival, this is a more important occasion than the ordinary dinner which I originally arranged with the Stockhausens. Let me not neglect to say, my dear, that I am delighted to meet you and that you will be a welcome ornament to my dinner-table.'

A minute later Dr and Mrs Stockhausen were announced. The Prime Minister was an erect, precise-mannered gentleman whose thin hair was strained to the limit to cover his scalp, and whose sharp eyes behind rimless spectacles gave the impression of an accountant who has spent a lifetime detecting irregularities in the books. His wife was a very large lady in a low-cut dress displaying impressive expanses of bosom and back.

Dr Stockhausen bowed stiffly to the Prince but didn't seem at all pleased to see Rudi.

'I only heard five minutes ago from the chamberlain that you were here,' he said. 'No one had the courtesy to inform me. Am I to understand, Prince Rudi, that you have not deserted us after all, and that it is still your wish to be considered your uncle's heir?'

'If my uncle pleases,' Rudi said respectfully. He switched on the smile at its maximum stunning power. It had a devastating effect on Kate and also, she guessed, on Mrs Stockhausen; but the Prime Minister had clearly developed a resistance.

'Under our Constitution it is indeed a question of whether your uncle the Prince pleases,' he said drily.

At that moment there was a tap at the door and a small, pale, slightly pop-eyed young man sidled into the room. He blinked on seeing Rudi.

'Hello, Friedrich,' said Rudi affably.

'H-h-hello, Rudi. I didn't expect to see *you*.'

'I have to inform you, Prince Friedrich,' said the Prime Minister, 'that your cousin has arrived with the intention of supplanting you.'

'Oh,' said Friedrich, 'has he? I see.' And then, in a bemused tone, 'No, I don't see. I thought *I* was supposed to be supplanting *him*.'

'Somebody will explain to you later,' said Rudi kindly.

'I will explain *now*,' said Dr Stockhausen. 'Prince Rudi has no automatic right to succeed. The Constitution provides that a ruling Prince who has no direct male descendant may nominate his heir ...'

'I don't want to go into all that *yet*,' said the Prince Laureate in a tone of some irritation. 'Have a drink, and we'll talk about something else, such as this charming young lady my nephew has brought home.'

Kate was introduced to the Stockhausens and to Prince Friedrich. The Prime Minister inspected her with an auditor's eye, and appeared to find her in order.

'I am delighted, gracious young lady,' he said. 'Welcome to Essenheim.'

'I'm only here on a visit,' Kate said.

'Then may your stay be a long one.'

'That's right,' said Friedrich, beaming with successful comprehension. 'A long stay. Stay a long time.'

Kate was about to say it wouldn't be more than a few days, but Rudi slipped neatly into the conversation ahead of her.

'Kate has just arrived,' he said. 'There is a great deal to show her. How do you think we should begin?' And there was a discussion, into which Mrs Stockhausen entered enthusiastically, on the merits and priorities of the various delights of

Essenheim. Dr Stockhausen, obviously busy with his own thoughts, took no part. It lasted until dinner was announced.

The Prince gravely offered his arm to Kate, Rudi likewise to Mrs Stockhausen, and the Prime Minister to a reluctant Anni. Prince Friedrich tailed along behind, on his own. The dining-room was another modest chamber in the converted corner of the castle, and the meal was not what Kate would have thought of as princely. A thick, appetite-blunting soup was followed by a casserole of beef and then by a cheesecake; a heavy red wine by a cloying white one. The Prince ate steadily, as if conscientiously performing a duty; Mrs Stockhausen munched in a stately manner that combined thoroughness with speed and efficiency. The Prime Minister ate little and, towards the end of the meal, in spite of the Prince's earlier irritation, returned to the subject of the succession.

'Though I am sorry to raise it in the presence of the two princes,' he said, 'I think it only right that the matter should be discussed in front of them rather than behind their backs.'

'I don't want to discuss it either in front of them *or* behind their backs,' said the Prince Laureate.

'We have already made it known,' Dr Stockhausen said, ignoring this comment, 'that Prince Friedrich would be proclaimed Crown Prince in Prince Rudi's place. We should not lightly reverse that decision.'

'Cheese?' said the Prince Laureate.

'No, thank you. Now Prince Rudi will not deny that his behaviour has not always been responsible. It would not be tactful at the moment to remind you of some of his actions, but, to take only the most recent example, after being fortunate enough to enjoy a Grand Tour at the expense of the Principality, he absented himself without explanation for almost three months.'

'He was kidnapped,' said Kate.

'He was *what?*' There was no mistaking the astonishment of both the Prince and Dr Stockhausen.

Kate became aware from Rudi's frown that she had spoken

out of turn. Suddenly, with all eyes on her, she felt out of her depth.

'You didn't tell me not to tell them,' she pointed out, speaking to Rudi.

'Come now, what's all this about?' the Prince demanded.

Rudi smiled, apparently quite at ease.

'I'm afraid I was teasing you, Kate,' he said. 'I was not really kidnapped. My uncle and Anni will tell you that I have always had a weakness for story-telling and self-dramatization.'

'*That's* true enough,' remarked Anni. 'I never know when to believe what Rudi says.'

Kate sat dumbfounded. The Prime Minister said coldly, 'Since it seems you were not kidnapped, Prince Rudi, perhaps you would care to tell us what you have actually been doing in these past few weeks.'

'Oh, just visiting friends,' Rudi said.

'You see, sir,' said Dr Stockhausen, addressing the Prince Laureate, 'it is impossible to know what he will do next. He grows more rather than less irresponsible. We cannot rely on him to behave in a manner suitable for a Crown Prince. And we must of course be prepared for a certain eventuality which is, we hope, still far distant ...'

'You mean I might die,' said the Prince Laureate. 'Then say so. It's obvious, isn't it. I'm only mortal. Fruit?'

'If Prince Rudi were to succeed to the throne, he might bring it down in ruins. The tide of republicanism ...'

'Is rising,' said the Prince. 'Or so you keep telling me.'

'It is indeed rising. Now Prince Friedrich has always behaved sensibly and soberly. He, if anyone, will prevent that tide from overwhelming us. As Crown Prince he will be a model of good behaviour.'

Prince Friedrich nodded happily. 'That's right. I always do what I'm told,' he said. Dr Stockhausen spared him a flinty smile.

'That's just what's wrong with him!' declared Anni.

Dr Stockhausen ignored the remark. 'Prince Friedrich is

admittedly a little more distant from the Crown than Prince Rudi,' he said. 'A cousin rather than a nephew. But suppose now that he were to marry the Princess Annetta here ...'

'*What?*' shrieked Anni. 'You think I'd marry *Friedrich*? You can take a running jump at yourself!'

'With respect, Princess ...' the Prime Minister began.

The Prince Laureate had been growing visibly angry. 'That'll do, Prime Minister,' he said. 'I've always thought of Rudi as my heir, and now he's back in Essenheim I expect him to settle down. I never did want to replace him with Friedrich, and there's no reason any longer why I should. And I'm not aware that it's part of your duties to marry off my niece.'

'I beg you, sir, to consider ...'

The Prince banged a fist on the tablecloth, making several glasses jump.

'I am not having this kind of thing at my dinner-table!' he proclaimed. 'In the presence of ladies, too; and with Rudi's guest here. Disgraceful! And incidentally, I think it's time the ladies withdrew. We shall join you shortly, ladies.'

'I wouldn't like to be in old Stockhausen's shoes for the next ten minutes,' said Anni happily as she went with Kate and Mrs Stockhausen into the adjoining room. 'Uncle Ferdy'll chew him up, and serve him right! And now, if you'll excuse me, I'll go away and play some of the records my terrible brother brought me.'

Kate was left alone with Mrs Stockhausen. It was not a particularly taxing half-hour, as Mrs Stockhausen was prepared to make all the conversational running. She spoke English, French and German equally badly, and moved apparently at random from one to another of them, but disdained to express herself in Essenheimisch. 'Of course, I would use it when talking to a peasant or a servant,' she remarked, 'but it is not a diplomatic language, not a language for educated people. It is better suited to potato soup than to politics.'

She informed Kate at some length about her travels to international capitals and her encounters with the wives of world leaders. Then with a change of tone she declared that she and Dr Stockhausen had never sought their present eminence; her husband would have been quite happy to keep a little shop and she herself sometimes yearned to be an ordinary housewife. Kate almost asked her, mischievously, for a recipe for potato soup, but thought better of it.

Kate noticed however that Mrs Stockhausen kept well away from any sensitive question. Perhaps the Prime Minister's wife was more shrewd than might at first appear. But this was a sleepy reflection, for the combined effects of a long day, a heavy meal and the steady turgid flow of Mrs Stockhausen's conversation were increasingly soporific. She was jerked into awareness by the arrival of the male members of the party.

Whether or not Anni's prediction had been correct, they

seemed now to be on much better terms than at the dinner-table.

'I knew you would be sensible in the end,' the Prince was saying to the Prime Minister in a tone which suggested that he'd brought up his big guns and secured a decisive victory. 'And I'm sure Rudi now fully understands his responsibilities. It is an excellent outcome.'

Having seated himself heavily in his armchair – a signal to everyone else to be seated – he beamed at Kate and said once again, half to himself, 'Charming. Quite charming.' In a louder voice he remarked to Dr Stockhausen, 'And, my dear Prime Minister, we must celebrate the return of the prodigal. We'll open up the Great Hall and have a reception to mark Rudi's return as Crown Prince. It's high time some light and life were let into that place.'

'The cost . . .' murmured Dr Stockhausen.

'No, no, don't tell me about that. I do so little public entertaining these days. People will be complaining that they never see their Prince.'

'We could combine it with the anniversary of your coming to the Throne,' the Prime Minister said. 'That's on Thursday week. Rather short notice, but we can manage it.'

'Good heavens, has that come round again? How many years is it now? Thirty? And it feels like yesterday!' The Prince sighed deeply. Then he went on, more briskly, 'Very well. Please make sure that every member of your family and mine, however remote, is invited, and everyone else in the Principality who is of the least importance.'

'Of course, Prince,' said Dr Stockhausen. 'That shall be done.'

'And see that old Beyer gets the proper story in that dreadful news-sheet of his. Poor fellow, he's really getting too old for the job. I hope he'll retire as soon as that apprentice of his is trained. Not that I've any room to talk about people being too old for the job.' He sighed again.

The huge clock went into action.

'Gracious heavens,' said the Prince when its clamour had

died down, 'it's ten o'clock already. Nearly bedtime.' He turned to Kate.

'I keep early hours, my dear,' he told her. 'And Dr Stockhausen is a busy man who tends to work far into the night. So our dinners usually break up early.'

He paused and Kate, feeling it was expected of her, said the time had flown and it had all been very enjoyable.

'Of course, for people of your age the night is young,' the Prince said. 'Why don't you adjourn to the second sitting-room? You will be well entertained there. It has its own television set, which receives Serenia quite well.'

That didn't sound to Kate like riotous living.

'You'll have gathered that we don't yet run to a TV service of our own,' the old man added apologetically. 'And now you may kiss my cheek.'

Still trying to do what was expected, Kate kissed the Prince's worn cheek, and curtseyed as well for good measure. He was still smiling approvingly on her when they left the room.

Outside, Kate turned to Rudi and said crisply, 'You've a lot of explaining to do.'

Rudi said, 'Well, er, yes.'

'In fact the amount to be explained gets more and more and I feel as if I know less and less. Come on, now, Rudi, give!'

'Kate,' said Rudi, 'I will see you in the morning. But tonight there is something I must do most urgently. Please forgive me.'

'You mean you don't want to answer my questions!'

Rudi turned on the smile, though Kate was too tired for it to have its full effect.

'Dear Kate,' he said, 'I don't mean that at all. There is somebody I have to see, and I cannot delay it. Now, what do you wish to do? Would you like to watch the famous Serenian television? It is probably some American or British serial, with subtitles in four languages.'

'I think I'd rather go to bed,' said Kate. 'But first I'd like to telephone my father. How do I do that?'

'There's an instrument in your room. Just lift the earpiece

86

and tell the exchange what you want. If it's Adela and the system's working, you'll get through. If it's Rosy, she's not so helpful. But earlier this evening it was Adela. Good-night, now.'

He kissed her lightly. Kate hoped this wasn't becoming a routine.

In her room, she undressed before tackling the telephone. She was rather awed by the venerable instrument. But she got through instantly to the exchange.

'Hello, castle!' said a cheerful feminine voice. It continued in Essenheimisch, 'There hasn't been anyone in *that* room for quite a while. What can I do for you?'

'Can you get me a call to London?' Kate inquired.

'If I'm lucky I can. Who is it? Is that Rudi's new girl-friend?'

'Everybody seems to think so,' said Kate. She gave the operator the number of the *Morning Intelligence*, and asked for a personal call to Mr Milbank.

'All right. Hang up, will you? I'll call you when I have the number.'

It wasn't as long as Kate expected before the operator rang back. 'I've got him for you,' said the cheerful voice. 'Here he is.'

'Hello,' came Edward's voice.

'Hello, Dad.'

'How are you?'

'Fine. How are you?'

'Fine. Having a good time?'

'Yes.'

'What's been happening?'

'Nothing much.'

'How long are you going to stay?'

'I don't know yet. A few days, maybe.'

A pause.

'What's the weather like there?'

'Oh, not bad.'

Another pause. Kate yawned.

'Well,' said Edward. 'Nice to speak to you. Take care of yourself. Have fun. Sleep well. Good-night.'

'Good-night, Dad,' said Kate, and got into bed. She was exhausted. But she couldn't sleep. The ordinariness of her conversation with Edward, though reassuring in a way, hadn't stopped excitement and puzzlement from swirling around inside her. She wished she knew what Rudi was up to; felt she ought to distrust him, since he'd admitted that the kidnapping story was untrue; yet, curiously, found that the mysteries of his personality and behaviour seemed to add to his attractions. There were no mysteries about George. George was solid and reliable, but far less interesting.

She lay first one way then the other, but her body felt full of itches and fidgets. She got up, had a drink of water, and tried again. Still it didn't work. She'd packed in such a hurry that she hadn't brought anything to read. She looked out of the window for a while, but there was nothing to see except a pattern of lights at the various levels of the hilly town. She felt an urge to wander round the castle, though she was well aware that she'd only seen a tiny corner of it so far, and no doubt it was big enough to get hopelessly lost in. Still, she had to be doing something. She put on her dressing-gown and pushed the bedroom door open.

From somewhere along the passage she could hear the sound of an early Beatles number being plucked out uncertainly, with many mistakes, on a guitar. She followed the sound. It came from a room which Rudi had pointed out to her as containing the television set. But the set wasn't on at present. Pushing open the door, Kate saw Prince Friedrich, sitting on a cushion with his back against the wall and frowning with concentration as he tried, slowly and painfully, to find the right notes. It was a minute or two before he noticed Kate. Then he put down the guitar and scrambled apologetically to his feet.

'Don't let me stop you,' Kate said hastily.

'You're not s-stopping me. I was going to stop anyway. I don't seem able to get it right tonight.' He added anxiously,

'I c-can play it better than this sometimes. I think I'm a b-bit off form.'

'Nobody's *always* on top form,' said Kate, trying to reassure him. Friedrich smiled gratefully. There was a brief, awkward silence. Then he said, with some effort, 'I h-hope you'll like it in Essenheim.'

'I expect I shall,' said Kate.

'I'm not c-cross about Rudi coming back, you know,' Friedrich told her. 'The Prime Minister wants me to be C-crown Prince, but I never wanted it for myself. I know I'm not clever.'

Kate couldn't think of anything to say to that. Friedrich went on, in a burst of confidence, 'What I'd really like is to play with a group. But being a p-prince makes it a bit difficult.'

It seemed to Kate that Friedrich's skill on the guitar wasn't enough to get him into any group, whether he was a prince or not. But it wasn't for her to say so. She smiled sympathetically. The silence prolonged itself. After a while Friedrich said shyly, 'I l-like you, Kate. You have a nice smile.'

'Thank you,' said Kate.

'I've never had a girlfriend myself. They do try to find one for me, but she'd have to be s-suitable, of course. And the suitable ones think I'm a bit slow. Well, you c-can't blame them, can you?'

Once again Kate couldn't think of anything to say.

'Of course, there's C-colonel Schweiner's daughter. He's the army chief. He'd be glad to f-find any man for Elsa, she's so ugly.' Friedrich giggled. 'He asks me to dinner sometimes, and Elsa tries to hold my hand.' He added, confidentially, 'Maybe they won't be so keen when Rudi's been reinstated. I understand more than some of them think, even if I'm not very clever. If you ask me, the c-clever people should be keeping an eye on Colonel Schweiner. He'd like to be boss in Essenheim. He thinks he could boss *me*, just like Dr Stockhausen does.'

Poor Friedrich, thought Kate.

'M-mind you,' Friedrich went on, 'Elsa fancies Rudi really,

not me. But she knows she hasn't a chance there. *All* the girls fancy Rudi.'

The awkward silence was resumed. After a few minutes Friedrich asked hesitantly if Kate minded having the television on.

'It's "S-soap",' he told her. 'I don't really understand it. But it p-passes a bit of time.'

Kate didn't mind. But she hadn't been following the programme herself and didn't feel like watching it now. Before long she went out, intending to return to her own room. There was a window open at the end of the corridor, and she heard from outside a murmur of voices and a low laugh. It was the laugh that caught her attention.

She turned and went to the window. It was narrow, and set deeply into the original castle wall, apparently at the back. The view was not the same as from her own room. A brief gleam of moonlight showed, below her and not far away to the right, a paved and ornamented terrace on the edge of a sheer drop. There were seats on the terrace, and on one of them were a man and a woman, sitting very close together. She couldn't see their faces or hear what they were saying, but the voices sounded intimate and familiar with each other, and she thought she recognized one of them. When the low laugh came again, she was sure she did.

Rudi.

12

Kate was awakened by the sharp strident sounds of a raised masculine voice from somewhere below her window. It was broad daylight: after eight o'clock, and a sunny day. She went to the window in her nightdress and looked down into the court-yard below. A squad of some thirty soldiers was drilling under the eye of a massive, erect and impressive figure, as big as any two of them, with a flat cap, red face and bristly moustache, and the loudest voice Kate had heard in her life.

Her vocabulary in Essenheimisch didn't include military terms, but there was no mistaking the meanings of his commands: quick march, left turn, right turn, about turn, halt. The squad moved like clockwork, with the exception of one unfortunate in the back row who was forever getting out of step or mistaking the order. He came in for special attention from the instructor, who bawled at him repeatedly and event-ually separated him from the flock and drilled him mercilessly for five minutes on his own. Kate felt increasingly sorry for him.

There was a tap on her shoulder.

'Hi!' said Anni. 'Sleep well?'

'Fine, thanks.'

'That's our army down there.'

'All of it?' asked Kate.

'Half of it. There's sixty men altogether. It's enough, I guess. You should hear old Stockhausen complain about the cost. But my uncle won't have it disbanded. He commanded it himself in the war.'

'Was Essenheim in the war?'

'Sure it was. We declared war on Germany two weeks before the war in Europe ended. And Japan, too, but I guess we couldn't get at Japan from here.'

'And what did the army *do*?'

'It was rounded up by a German patrol. Uncle Ferdy wasn't the brightest of commanders. But Germany surrendered soon afterwards and Uncle Ferdy got the Essenheim Grand Cross for Gallantry from the Prince of that time – his dad – so he was quite happy about it. He's still the commander in theory, with Rudi as his second. But in practice Schweiner's in charge.'

'Schweiner?'

'That's Schweiner down there, drilling them. Colonel Schweiner, promoted from Top Sergeant. Keep clear of him, Kate, he's a bastard.'

Kate watched for a few more minutes as the squad marched to and fro. Then they were halted, and Colonel Schweiner turned to meet someone walking across the courtyard towards him. It was Rudi, also in officer's uniform, looking trim, slim, and extremely handsome.

Schweiner brought the Essenheim Army smartly to attention and saluted. Rudi responded with a casual flip of the hand. A few words were spoken which Kate couldn't hear. Then Schweiner dismissed the squad. The men disappeared round a corner of the castle wall at high speed, as if afraid their commander might change his mind. Rudi and Schweiner walked slowly across the courtyard, turned and walked back, deep in conversation. Schweiner was twirling a swagger-stick. Confidence and self-satisfaction were expressed in every movement he made. Kate recalled Prince Friedrich's remark that those he called 'the clever people' should be keeping an eye on Colonel Schweiner. Was Rudi doing just that, she wondered?

'Come and have some breakfast,' said Anni. 'Tell me what's happening in London. I keep expecting a letter from my friend Betsy, but it doesn't come.'

Kate did her best, realizing her knowledge of the London that interested Anni was limited. But although she felt inadequate in this respect, she saw that Anni was developing an attachment to her.

'It's great to talk to you,' Anni said over the coffee and rolls. 'Like having an older sister.'

'Oh?'

'Not *much* older, of course,' Anni said hastily. 'I'd hate to be twenty, wouldn't you? I couldn't *bear* to be twenty.'

'I expect you will be, some time,' said Kate. 'It comes to all of us in the end.'

'Yeah, I guess so. How disgusting.'

Rudi didn't appear at breakfast. Kate felt some reaction after the previous day's events, and needed to hear a voice from home. She went to her room and tried to call George. But the telephone operator had changed. Instead of the cheerful Adela of the night before, it was now Rosy. She was slow and unhelpful, and on being asked for the Ritz-Albany Hotel informed Kate that she'd never heard of it. Kate remembered that it had formerly been Frau Schmidt's boarding-house, and after a brief battle was reluctantly put through. The person who answered the call spoke only a dialect of Essenheimisch which Kate found hard to understand. The one thing that was clear was that this person was unable to put George on the line.

Frustrated, Kate collapsed on her bed. It was still only mid-morning. She felt low-spirited and homesick. She was tempted to try to call her father again, but she knew he'd still be in bed after his night's work; besides, she didn't want another tussle with Rosy.

It was then that Rudi tapped at the door and came in. He was still in military uniform.

'I apologize for the fancy dress,' he said.

'It suits you,' said Kate; and it did. He was tall and athletic-looking, and more beautiful than any young man had a right to be. She knew him to be aware of it, and knew by now that he traded on it, but it made no difference. She didn't know how to resist a charm like that.

Rudi took her in his arms and kissed her slowly, deliberately, meltingly. The knowledge that it was an expert performance, perfected no doubt with a good deal of practice, didn't prevent it from having its effect.

With a huge effort of will Kate rescued herself from the clinch and took a step back.

'Now,' she said. 'At last. You are going to tell me just why you brought me to Essenheim and how long you want me to stay. And also, just what you have told your family.'

Rudi sighed. 'Kate, dear,' he said, 'I will tell you all. Come with me for a walk in the grounds.'

The day was clear and becoming warm. They left the modern-ized corner of the castle by a small back door and strolled across a lawn which was wide and interspersed with flowerbeds, though not particularly well maintained by the standards of London parks. Looking behind her, Kate saw the tower that soared skyward from the opposite corner; it was so high that she had to bend her head back to see to the top.

'You can climb right up there,' Rudi observed. 'It means going up innumerable spirals of stone steps, but the view is marvellous. You can see the whole Principality from up there. Do you wish to do so?'

'Yes, please.'

'Very well. One day while you're here I will take you. But not, I think, now. And see, Kate, we are approaching the cliff edge.'

Kate recognized the place. It was the paved terrace she'd seen from the window the previous night. Below them was the lower part of the town, clinging bravely to the slopes and looking as if it might fall at any time into the river below. On their right, a great arched bridge crossed the chasm. Opposite was more of the town. 'And beyond that,' said Rudi, 'is another steep valley. It's the valley of the Wandel, which flows into the Esel at this point.'

He sat down, and drew Kate towards him. She pulled herself away.

'*Now* tell,' she said. 'Now, now, *now*.'

'Yes, Kate,' said Rudi. 'From now on I must trust you completely.'

'Well, I should hope you can.'

'You know, of course, that I am engaged to be married.'

'Yes. You told me.'

'To my distant cousin, the Princess Margaretta of Lubenstein. If Germany were to break up into the cluster of principalities and dukedoms from which it was assembled, she would be the heiress to a throne and to vast estates. That won't happen, of course. But she *is* the heiress to a famous name and what's left of an enormous fortune. Both these things cut a great deal of ice with Uncle Ferdy. Especially the fortune.'

'He's hard up, isn't he?' said Kate.

'Desperately so. My great-grandfather mortgaged his estates to the hilt to pay for this castle, of which we use only a tiny corner. Great-Uncle Willy, who succeeded him, didn't help matters by having a weakness for chorus-girls and visits to Monte Carlo. By comparison, Uncle Ferdy is a model of rectitude. He's never had the money to be anything else. His idea of living it up is to sit and watch Serenian television. But he does have one ambition, and that's to retrieve the family fortunes.'

'Through your marriage,' said Kate.

'Yes.'

'I think it's terrible. And what about this poor little girl? Having a husband wished on her while she's practically in the cradle! It's an outrage! She mightn't like you at all when she grows up!'

'Oh, I expect she will,' said Rudi confidently. 'They usually do. But that's not quite the point. The point is that, as I told you before, she is just ten years old. There can't be any marriage for another six years.'

'Hard luck!' said Kate sardonically.

'Meanwhile, my uncle thinks I'm footloose and irresponsible.'

'I gather there's something in it,' Kate said.

'Well, maybe so. Just imagine how boring it is to be Crown Prince of Essenheim, with nothing to do but open bazaars!'

95

'I'd have thought you could find other things to do if you tried.'

'I can, actually. That's what Uncle Ferdy's worried about. He wants me to settle down. With a nice young woman.'

'But ...' Kate began, and then stopped short. 'Oh!'

'You see, to people of his upbringing and generation, it's the obvious thing to do. If you can't marry for a few years, you take a mistress.'

'And you're thinking of that as a job for *me*?' Kate asked incredulously.

'Well,' began Rudi. For once, he sounded embarrassed. 'Well, not exactly.'

'Because if you were, you might have told me. And it's not on, anyway. Rudi, I'm still at school, and I'm going to college, and my career plans don't include being a prince's mistress.' She added crossly, 'It sounds like a corny musical.'

'Not so fast,' Rudi said. 'It is my uncle rather than myself who, at the moment, is thinking of you in that capacity.'

'You must have led him to.'

'I admit it, Kate. You see, suitable young ladies are not easily found. In Essenheim the aristocracy, such as it is, consists of my own family. I have seventeen female cousins, all titled. But it would not be proper to seek an irregular relationship there. The professional and administrative classes consist of Dr Stockhausen and *his* connections and relatives. A liaison in that quarter would be even more improper; in fact, Dr Stockhausen wouldn't stand for it. And the rest of the nation is nothing but shopkeepers and peasants. How could a person of such origins be installed as the accepted consort of the Crown Prince?'

'So you have to go outside.'

'Well, I myself am not enthusiastic about the idea at all. But yes, it has long been my uncle's view that I should look outside Essenheim. He doesn't think it necessary, or even desirable, that my associate should be an aristocrat. At the same time, he wouldn't wish me to bring a rough, uneducated young woman to Essenheim. And he certainly wouldn't want an actress or any such person to be virtually his daughter-in-law. So a girl of respectable bourgeois parentage would be ideal ...'

'And you thought *I'd* do!' Kate was furious. 'Well, you have another think coming. I'm not having anything to do with it. Please arrange to have me flown out of Essenheim as soon as possible!'

'Wait a minute, Kate, please. We still haven't come to the real point. How old do you suppose my uncle to be?'

'I don't know. I haven't thought.'

'He is seventy-six. He has been Prince Laureate of Essenheim for thirty years. His health isn't good; he's overweight and he has trouble with his back and with his breathing. Above all, Kate, he is weary. He has had enough of being Prince. He would like to retire; that is, to abdicate. And to abdicate in my favour.'

'Why doesn't he, then?' Kate asked. 'It would give you something to do.'

'Why doesn't he? Partly because of Dr Stockhausen's opposition. As you heard last night, Dr Stockhausen doesn't approve of me.'

'But your uncle's an absolute ruler. Surely he can just *sack* Dr Stockhausen.'

'That's more easily said than done. Dr Stockhausen has his hands on so many of the levers. Uncle Ferdy did sack him once, but he ignored being sacked, and eventually Uncle thought better of it. However, it's not only Dr Stockhausen. The fact is that Uncle himself doesn't trust me. He *likes* me but he doesn't *trust* me.'

'I can understand that,' said Kate.

'The obvious time for him to abdicate would be when I marry. But that's six years away. He'll be eighty-two, if he's still alive. He doesn't want to wait that long. Also, he's afraid that I'll kick over the traces again and that next time Cousin Friedrich really will be put in my place. So ...'

He hesitated, then went on. 'So I have made an arrangement with my uncle. At next week's reception, being now satisfied that I am on the point of settling down, he will not, as Dr

Stockhausen expects, merely announce my reinstatement as Crown Prince. Instead he will announce his own abdication in my favour!'

Kate gasped.

'Dr Stockhausen will be helpless. It will have been done in the full view of everyone who is anyone in Essenheim. The entire aristocracy and professional hierarchy will be there; so will young Moritz from the radio station and old Beyer who owns the newspaper; so will your friend George from the British press. No argument will be possible; I shall be Prince Laureate. And although I intend that democracy shall follow, I shall for the moment be the absolute ruler. If Stockhausen objects, I can have him thrown into jail!'

Rudi was clearly delighted with himself. Kate was temporarily speechless. He took her hand.

'You see how much I am trusting you,' he said. 'Dr Stockhausen is not to be underrated. If word of this intention got to him, he might yet manage to frustrate it.'

'But listen! Don't you understand? I'm not *going* to settle down with you.'

'I promise you,' said Rudi, 'that I shan't insist on any extra-marital rights, so to speak. You will have your own room; I shall not set foot in it uninvited; and as soon as my succession is an accomplished fact you can go back to London at any time.'

Kate said, 'You mean, you need me so you can convince your uncle that you're a safe, reliable successor. A married man in all but name.'

Rudi beamed. 'Yes, you understand perfectly. And once I am Prince Laureate, your presence is no longer needed. Unless of course you *wish* to stay. You would be very welcome, not least by me.'

Kate was silent for a moment, working up to an outburst. Then it came: 'You want me to deceive that poor old man!' she declared. 'And *you've* been deceiving *me*! Telling me that story about being kidnapped! What were you really doing all that time?'

98

Rudi looked uneasy. 'Well ...' he said.

'Is it true that you were seen in a London night-club with a millionaire's daughter?'

Rudi jumped.

'How did you ... ?' he began; then, reluctantly, 'Yes, Kate, it's true.'

'She was the first choice for the job you're offering *me*?'

'That's an unkind way to put it, Kate. But yes, I was willing to make a sacrifice for my country. Those oil millions would have transformed our prospects.'

'So what happened?'

'She went off with somebody else. A singer.' Rudi recovered his self-possession and went on, 'But I was not sorry. She was not the person I really sought. That was always *you*, Kate.'

'So you say now. But I don't believe you. It was my father you wanted to meet in the first place, because of his job, not me. And when he wouldn't take the Essenheim story from you and insisted on putting his own reporter on to it, you lost interest in him and the *Morning Intelligence*. That's the truth of the matter, isn't it?'

'It was a little like that,' Rudi admitted. 'But I *did* like you, Kate, from the beginning. You must believe me. Why else should I seek you out and bring you to Essenheim?'

'Because you hadn't anyone better at the time, I expect. Well, I've told you, Rudi, I won't have anything to do with this scheme. I absolutely refuse. I shall tell Prince Ferdinand the truth!'

'My poor uncle,' Rudi said sadly. 'You could make him so happy if you wished. The deception would be so unimportant, the equivalent of a small white lie, and his relief on abdicating would be so great. He has waited so long for an excuse.' He sighed. 'You are hard, Kate. I didn't think you would be so hard.'

'You know what, Rudi?' said Kate with sudden conviction. 'You're the most devious person I've ever met. And I'm beginning to think you're the biggest phoney!'

Rudi looked at her with appealing brown eyes. He seemed

hurt. Suddenly she wanted to run her hand through his hair She couldn't believe she'd just said he was a phoney. Part of her was convinced that he was, but another part of her was saying she must be misjudging him; he was in a difficult position, and probably his actions were all for the best.

'I beg you to reconsider, Kate,' he said. 'My plans are dependent on you. *I* am dependent on you. You *will* help me, won't you, Kate?'

'I don't know.'

'Please think about it,' Rudi said. 'Just think about it, that's all I ask.' He smiled winningly. Kate remembered Anni's remark that Rudi could persuade anybody to do anything. She felt sure he was confident he would get his own way. She didn't feel equally sure that he wouldn't get it.

13

'Kate, my dear,' said the Prince Laureate after lunch, 'come and talk to me for a few minutes.'

Kate followed him into the little private sitting-room. The television was on; a couple of cartoon animals did terrible things to each other but recovered in the next second. Prince Ferdinand hobbled to the set and switched it off.

'It is my drug,' he said. 'Keep me off it for a while.'

Kate helped him into his armchair and seated herself on a stool close by it. He was a nice, harmless old man, she thought; harmless and lonely.

He looked at her with evident approval. 'Now that I see you by daylight,' he said, 'I like you even more. Perhaps Rudi has good taste after all. When he said he had brought a lady home, I must admit I wondered what sort of a lady it might be. But you, my dear, an unspoiled English girl of ordinary family ...'

The Prince smiled. There was a hint of Rudi in his smile; but it was a sweeter smile and in an odd way more innocent.

'The only thing that worries me,' he said, 'is that you may be too good for Rudi.'

Kate stared.

'Don't look so surprised,' he said. 'I am fond of my nephew. It is my dearest wish that he should succeed me. But he's a little wild, a little unreliable. He gets his way with people rather too easily, and has been known to let them down. I should not wish that to happen to you.'

'I don't really know Rudi well,' Kate told him. 'I met him in London at a party, and then he came to my home. I got interested in Essenheim and learned a bit of the language. I didn't see him for a while, and then he suddenly arrived a few days ago and invited me on Anni's behalf to come and stay. So here I am.'

'And you are not ... ?'

'No, I'm not.'

'Oh, well, there is time,' said the Prince benignly. 'I am not sorry. I did not care to think that Rudi might have taken advantage of a girl who is really rather young.' He patted her hand. 'I like you very much, my dear,' he said. 'And you are of course *fond* of Rudi, I don't doubt.'

'Well, yes,' said Kate, not knowing how to tell the Prince that Rudi's physical presence almost made her swoon but that she still wasn't sure she liked him.

'Of course. Young ladies are always fond of Rudi. He is so very handsome. He has the family looks.' The Prince beamed complacently. 'And whatever anyone may tell you, he's a good boy at heart. So I trust you will come to next week's reception.'

'If you really want me to, I will,' said Kate, making up her mind on the spot. 'But,' she went on, embarrassed, yet determined, 'I wouldn't like the guests to be given the wrong idea.'

'Don't worry, Kate. I shall introduce you as a dear friend, not only of Rudi but of all of us. I hope I may call you *my* friend, and Anni has already developed a great liking for you.'

Kate suspected that such an introduction wouldn't prevent people from drawing their own conclusions. But the Prince's expression was so kindly she hadn't the heart to demur.

'I understand you will not be staying long in Essenheim,' he said. 'A pity. But I hope you will come again soon, and come often. And perhaps later on, when you are ready ... you would certainly be a charming associate for Rudi. It's a pity you're a commoner, my dear, and without fortune. If your origins were suitable, I should not in the least mind Rudi's marrying you. But that, of course, cannot be. You understand, I am sure.'

'Oh, yes,' said Kate drily.

'But perhaps with good luck we will achieve the next best thing, eh? In time, of course; in time.'

Anni bounced into the room. 'I want the two good horses this afternoon!' she declared. 'I want Kate to ride with me. You do ride, don't you, Kate?'

'Not really,' said Kate. She'd once had a few lessons, but she hadn't ridden much.

'Of course you do!' Anni said. 'And it's a lovely afternoon. We'll take a ride up the Wandel valley.'

'Just the thing, my dear,' said the Prince approvingly; and, to Kate, 'That will put some colour in your cheeks. I mustn't keep you sitting here talking to an old man.'

He got up with some effort and stumbled over to the television. The cartoon had finished and a film was in progress. Two cars hurtled along a highway, screaming past other traffic, missing head-on collisions at the rate of two a second, the people in the pursuing car firing at the leading one, and a bridge ahead of them blowing up as they approached. Prince Ferdinand Franz Josef III of Essenheim settled placidly into his armchair and began watching.

'You look pleased with yourself, Rudi,' Anni remarked. 'What have you been up to while we were riding?'

'None of your business,' said Rudi cheerfully. 'But I'm taking you out to dinner, both of you.'

'Me as well?' Anni sounded surprised.

'Yes, you as well.'

'Why do I get to come? Has Uncle Ferdy insisted on a chaperon?'

'You could be right.'

'I bet I *am* right.' Anni turned to Kate. 'In Uncle Ferdy's world there are two kinds of girls. Good girls and bad girls. Good girls get chaperoned. I guess you're a good girl, Kate.'

'Uncle Ferdy lives in the past,' said Rudi. 'Except for the television. He'll be glad to have us out of the way this evening, so he can have a quiet supper in front of it.'

Rudi was attentive to both girls. He drove them through the cobbled streets and squares of Essenheim, lined with small shops, colour-washed houses and little pavement cafés; then through the country to the Spitzhof, an extremely smart and expensive-looking restaurant perched on a crag overlooking the Esel river. The manager greeted him with a casual 'Evening, Highness'; the barman inquired, 'The usual, Highness?' on serving drinks before dinner. Kate experimented with a special Essenheim drink which tasted like toothpaste-flavoured kerosene, and was relieved to replace it with mineral water. If she had wondered what had become of the pâté, smoked salmon and caviare that she'd seen flown into Essenheim, she needed to wonder no longer; they were all on the menu.

After dinner and her exertions of the afternoon, Kate felt sleepy. She hardly noticed when Anni slipped away to talk to someone she knew. But she came awake when a stranger approached their table. He was a short man in late middle age, plump in a sleek, shiny way, as if he owed it to years of eating excellent food. His face was pink and round, without a wrinkle; his eyes were smallish, shrewd and blue; his hair blond but greying, and very short. His suit was impeccably cut and obviously expensive. He clicked his heels when Rudi introduced him to Kate as Herr Finkel.

'Delighted, gracious young lady,' he said, and bowed.

'Herr Finkel has been closely associated with my family for many years,' Rudi said.

'I have indeed had that honour,' said Herr Finkel.

At Rudi's invitation, he took the chair which Anni had left. Gravely, in excellent English, he interrogated Kate about her family, her interests and occupations, her work at school, her intentions for the future. He listened with courteous interest to all she said. Kate, like many other people, found herself a fascinating topic, and when encouraged was very willing to hold forth. For the next quarter of an hour she enjoyed herself, talking ever more freely. Then suddenly she became aware of a calculating mind behind Herr Finkel's shrewd eyes and realized that he'd been interviewing her, almost like a prospective employer. She became wary; and, as if he'd noticed this, Herr Finkel got up to go.

'It has been a great pleasure to meet you, Miss Milbank,' he said. 'I should be happy if his Highness could find it possible to bring you for a meal at my home some time soon.'

Kate said nothing to that. Rudi said, non-committally, 'That would be very pleasant.'

Herr Finkel said, 'Your servant, Highness. Your servant, gracious young lady,' clicked his heels again, and withdrew.

Anni was talking animatedly with a party of youngish people two or three tables away. Rudi had an opportunity to speak to Kate unheard.

'Well?' he said. 'Have you decided what you're going to do?'

'Yes,' said Kate. 'I'm not too happy about it. But the Prince is so nice, and I didn't take to that Stockhausen man, and I quite see that if your uncle doesn't get you installed soon there could be a disaster and it might be poor Friedrich who became Prince Laureate. I have a funny kind of feeling as if things were coming to a head. So I'll do as you want. But you must promise, Rudi, that after next week's reception you'll fix a flight out for me as soon as I want it.'

'Of course,' Rudi said. 'You may trust me, Kate.'

'I wouldn't trust him *too* much, if I were you,' said Anni cheerfully, returning to the table. 'What's he on about, Kate?'

'Nothing that concerns you!' said Rudi in an elder-brother tone of voice.

'I noticed you were talking to the paymaster,' Anni remarked.

'The paymaster?' Kate asked.

'That was old Finkel, wasn't it? The richest man in Essenheim. Owns this restaurant, among much else. He owns *us*, lock, stock and barrel. Great-grandfather borrowed from Finkel's grandfather to build the castle, and since then we've never once been out of debt to the Finkels. Have we, Rudi?'

'That's correct,' Rudi said coldly.

'Now if we're talking about trusting,' Anni said, '*there's* a man not to trust. I'd trust old Finkel about as far as I can throw a grand piano. With one hand.'

'Herr Finkel is all right,' said Rudi. 'He has shown himself a good friend from time to time.'

'Sure,' said Anni. 'By lending us still more money at still higher interest.' Then, 'Do you want to be rid of your chaperon for an hour or two?'

'No, thank you, Anni,' Rudi said. 'In fact it is time we were returning to the castle. I said we would not be late. It is important that Uncle should feel he can trust us all.'

'Trust, trust, trust,' said Anni. 'I reckon people you can really trust don't go on about trusting all the time. Hey, Rudi, aren't you getting a bill?'

Rudi seemed a shade embarrassed. 'It is not the custom to give me a bill here,' he explained. 'Herr Finkel has ordered it so. He says he doesn't expect his friends to pay for a meal in a place that belongs to him.'

'Friends!' said Anni. 'Some friend, if you ask me!'

'Don't talk of what you don't understand!' Rudi told her crossly. And then, to Kate, 'Come on, Kate dear. I think you're tired. You could do with a good night's sleep.'

'Yes, I think I could,' said Kate. She was almost asleep already.

14

Kate wasn't one of those people who worry their lives away. She lived mostly in the present; she expected to enjoy herself and usually did. She'd been puzzled or anxious from time to time since setting out for Essenheim, but it wasn't her nature to dwell on her puzzlement or anxiety. Her instinct was to put them out of her mind and to get on with the activities of the day.

She woke up the next morning feeling cheerful and optimistic. She decided she didn't at all mind staying until after next week's reception, when it would be fun to see the installation of Rudi as Prince Laureate and the discomfiture of starchy Dr Stockhausen. She'd been assured that she would be put on a flight home as soon after that as she wanted. In the meantime she was in Essenheim on holiday, and she meant to make the most of it.

And in fact she was at the beginning of a pleasant interlude. The weather in Essenheim was clear and warm but not oppressively hot. And Rudi, in spite of his occasional unexplained absences, was attentive. He had a small, not new but decidedly zippy sports car which was kept in the extensive former stabling of the castle, and he drove Kate round most of the narrow winding roads of the Principality. The royal launch *Lorelei* was cleaned up and serviced, to the reported annoyance of Dr Stockhausen, who considered it an unnecessary expense; and the Royal Essenheim Navy, consisting of Commander Himmelwein and

Able Riverman Flusswasser, took Rudi, Anni, Kate and a couple of royal cousins on a languorous all-day river trip between the villages and vineyards that lined the banks of the Esel. Children ran down to the water edge to wave and shout 'Hello, Highnesses', and Kate felt rather like royalty herself.

She realized that the Prince Laureate and Anni were becoming increasingly fond of her. The Prince would call her in for little chats, and pay her the high compliment of turning off the television. His conversation consisted largely of reminiscences of his boyhood in the old Austrian Empire, and of his godfather the Emperor Franz Josef who'd reigned over it for nearly seventy years. Sometimes it was less than fascinating, but Kate liked the old man and didn't grudge him the pleasure of having a willing listener.

Anni took her out riding, or swimming in a pool that belonged to one of the cousins, and informed her of her tastes in music, movies and pop stars. They discovered one afternoon that they were the same dress size.

'Thank goodness!' said Kate. 'I didn't bring anything to wear at receptions and such goings-on; I had to pack in such a hurry. Could you lend me a dress, Anni?'

'Help yourself,' said Anni.

Kate riffled through the long line of dresses in Anni's wardrobe. There were dozens of silk and taffeta confections in shiny bright colours, all covered with frills, sashes, lace and sequins.

'Aren't they terrible?' said Anni gloomily. 'I have to use the court dressmaker. Same one as in my granny's day, and she was old-fashioned then. What I wouldn't give for one hour's shopping in London!'

'This one's OK,' said Kate at last, finding a totally plain, off-the-shoulder, rather clinging black silk thing. 'It's very nice, in fact.'

'It's a nightdress,' said Anni.

'Just the same, I shall wear it,' declared Kate, holding it against herself in the mirror.

'Well, if you're wearing that, I shall wear *this*,' said Anni, producing an exactly similar nightdress in white. 'But you wouldn't dare!'

'Watch me and see,' said Kate.

It began to seem like a good time: not quite real, yet enjoyable and relaxing. On alternate evenings Kate rang her father and told him what she'd been doing; she never had any difficulty in getting through, and Edward was always calm and matter-of-fact.

The one thing that surprised Edward, and surprised Kate herself when she came to think about it, was that she didn't see anything of George. He didn't present himself at the castle, where no doubt he assumed he would be unwelcome and might risk being turned out of the country. Kate's attempts to telephone him were frustrating; he was never available and no one ever knew where he was. Eventually she rang Frau Schmidt's at a time when George himself answered the telephone, and was surprised to find that he hadn't been told about her calls and had himself made just as many unsuccessful attempts to telephone *her*.

George had rented a car and was obviously carrying out his duties in a responsible and George-like fashion. He had learned much more about the social and economic structure of Essenheim than Kate knew, or really wanted to know. When however she asked if he was filing any news stories, the answer was that he wasn't; he was preparing a series of features to be published when he got home. There wasn't any day-to-day news in Essenheim, he said. And yet, assessing the political situation, he thought there might be before long.

'What do you mean?' Kate asked. But George wouldn't say.

'I don't think there's any privacy on the telephone here,' he told her. 'And there's a fellow who I think is watching me. I keep seeing him across the street or waiting outside, and I'm sure that when I go out he follows.'

'What sort of a fellow?' Kate asked.

'A big blond man with cropped hair and the look of a bouncer.'

It sounded rather like Karl, whom Kate had seen in London.

'I'll ask Rudi about it,' she said.

'Oh, Rudi ...' said George, without enthusiasm. Then he added unwillingly, as if professional need were conquering personal reluctance, 'All the same, now I have some background, I ought to have a talk with Rudi, if I could do it without attracting attention.'

'I'll ask him about that, too,' said Kate. And on Sunday morning she mentioned George to Rudi.

Rudi sounded just as cool about George as George had sounded about him. George's problems, he said, were none of his business. Kate wondered for a wild delicious moment if he and George were jealous of each other on account of her, but she wasn't quite vain enough to believe it.

Later in the day, Rudi seemed to change his attitude.

'I've arranged for George to come and see me tomorrow morning,' he told her. 'I'm giving him an interview on the basis that he doesn't publish anything until after next Thursday's reception. Then, when I've taken over, he can put the story of Uncle Ferdy's abdication through to London with the interview as background. That should be a bonus for him *and* your father, shouldn't it?'

He smiled the winning smile. Kate felt the familiar melting of her insides.

'And I've got old Stockhausen to take Karl off George's tail,' Rudi added.

'That's more than you could do for yourself, isn't it?' said Kate in some surprise. But Rudi didn't seem to want to talk about it.

'What's more,' he said, 'as I have a busy day tomorrow, I've suggested that after the interview he might like to take you out with him. I've fixed up a visit to the university, which will be useful for George and interesting for you. You can meet my friend Klaus Klappdorf there.'

'How do you know George wants to take me with him?' Kate asked. 'And what does your busy day consist of?'

Rudi smiled teasingly. 'You ask too many questions, dear Kate,' he said.

When she was in bed that night it occurred to Kate that Rudi might wish to get herself and George out of the way, while knowing where they were. But she put the thought out of her mind. She was getting too suspicious, she told herself. Surely the explanation was simple; Rudi couldn't give her his own company, so he thought it would be nice for her and George to make an excursion together. It was kind of him. She'd been in danger of misjudging Rudi, thinking he was always devious and always had ulterior motives. Perhaps he was kind, really, and straightforward.

But the fact is that Kate had to deceive herself in order to think this. In her heart she knew that Rudi, though he might on occasion be kind, was never straightforward.

'Well,' said George next morning. 'So there you are.'

'Yes,' said Kate. 'So here I am.'

There was a pause.

'It's nice to see you,' said George.

'It's nice to see *you*,' said Kate, though actually she wasn't excited at the thought of an outing with George. She suspected she would be bored and possibly irritated.

'Are you having a good time?' asked George.

'Yes, thank you,' said Kate. 'Are you?'

'Yes, thank you,' said George.

Another pause.

'I spoke to your father last night,' said George.

'So did I,' said Kate.

Pause.

'He seemed to be quite well,' said George.

'Yes, he did,' said Kate.

Pause.

'I've just been talking to Prince Rudi,' said George.

'I know,' said Kate.

'He's fixed for me to go to the university,' George said. 'And for you to go with me.'

'Frankly, it sounds a bit dull,' said Kate. 'Also, it's raining.'

'I don't suppose you need go if you don't want,' said George, a little huffily. 'Actually I can get on better by myself. But seeing it was Rudi's suggestion, and seeing you're Edward's daughter and I respect Edward . . .'

'You thought you'd manage to put up with me,' said Kate.

'Well, if you care to put it that way,' said George.

'It certainly *sounds* like that,' Kate said. 'So maybe you'd better go off like a good little boy and do as you're told.'

Logically, at that point, they should have turned on their heels and stalked off in different directions. But in fact they remained where they were, staring at each other. Then George said, 'Kate, we shouldn't *be* like this. What would your dad think?'

And Kate, who knew quite well what her dad would think, and who was also faced with the alternative of a day of little chats with the Prince and Anni, said, 'Sorry, George. I didn't mean to be rude. May I come with you after all?'

George said, 'Please do, Kate.' They got into the rented car and drove down the tree-lined avenue, across the bridge, through the hilly streets of the little town and out into the country.

'Rudi said the university's in the old pickle factory,' George told Kate. 'He said we can't miss it, and he promised he'd ask his friend Klaus Something-or-other to look out for us.'

And in fact they couldn't and didn't miss the old pickle factory. It was all in red brick and was the biggest building Kate had seen in Essenheim apart from the castle. The legend FINKEL'S PICKLES had been built into the façade irremovably by the use of differently coloured bricks, but a painted sign over the main gateway now said UNIVERSITY OF ESSENHEIM.

They were barely inside the yard when they were stopped by a young man and a girl who planted themselves firmly in front of the car. Both were in dirty jeans. The young man had a big black greasy beard; the girl's blonde hair straggled over her shoulders and down her back. They looked like students who hadn't been told the 1960s were over.

'Where are you going?' the young man asked, in aggressive Essenheimisch.

'Into the university,' George said.

'They're forcigners,' said the girl. 'What accent is that?'

'You Germans?' asked the young man.

'No.'

'Good. We don't like Germans. You French?'

'No.'

'Good. We don't like the French.'

Several other young men and girls had gathered round.

'You Swiss? Italian? Czech? Serenian?'

It appeared that they didn't like any of them.

'British,' said George eventually.

'Oh, British.' It seemed that Britain was too far away to generate much feeling either for or against.

'Beatles,' said somebody uncertainly. 'Beatles are British.'

'John Lennon's dead,' said somebody else, in a tone implying that this might affect the issue.

'May we come through?' George asked patiently.

'What do you want to come through for? What are you doing here?'

'Press,' said George. 'We have an appointment.'

'We don't like the Press.'

'Spies!' called someone from behind.

'If I were you,' the bearded young man advised George, 'I'd back out through that gate and head back into town. Quickly.'

The girl was less hostile. 'There's nothing personal about this,' she explained. 'It's just passive resistance.'

'Passive resistance to what?' George asked, surprised.

'You ask too many questions!' said the first young man. 'Watch it! Some of us believe in *active* passive resistance!'

Then somebody came bustling through the crowd. Way was made for him. He was a tall thin man with a small ginger beard. He waved the students away.

'Well done, boys and girls!' he told them. 'A good professional show, but enough's enough.' Then he cried, beaming, 'George! Kate! Welcome to the University of Essenheim!'

He reached through the open window of the car and pumped

George's hand vigorously. 'Rudi told me you were on the way!' he declared. 'It's good to see you!' He turned and addressed the students.

'Demonstration over!' he proclaimed. 'These are friends. They come from Rudi. Let's give them a welcome!'

Someone in the crowd picked up the cue and began a chant which swelled rapidly: 'Rudi! Rudi! Rudi!' On the fringes, two or three people shouted, 'Rudi out! Rudi out!', but after some mild scuffling they were silenced.

The ginger-bearded man got into the back of the car.

'You can go ahead now,' he told George. 'Drive on to the main block.'

George edged the car forward. The crowd parted to make way. Everyone was smiling. The chant of 'Rudi! Rudi!' continued until the car had gone past.

'Allow me to introduce myself,' the ginger-bearded man said. 'I am Klaus Klappdorf, Dean of the Faculty of Arts, Sciences and Other Studies. And a friend of Rudi's. We are all friends of Rudi here, I hope. Except,' he added, frowning, as two or three students broke away and followed the car yelling, 'Rudi out!', 'except for a misguided few, who will certainly fail their examinations. I'm sorry you were held up, but it's passive resistance practice this morning. We encourage them to take a practical approach and to prevent penetration of the campus. I didn't receive Rudi's message in time to stop them. Actually I must say they did it rather well.'

George stopped the car at the main block.

'And now,' said Klaus, 'let me take you to see the President!'

Round the corner from the entrance lobby was a door with its upper part glazed and the words BOTTLING DEPARTMENT engraved in the glass. On this door hung a card with the words

PRESIDENT OF THE
UNIVERSITY
Professor-Doctor Ehrenwald

Klaus tapped on the door. A deep, weary-sounding voice called 'Come in!'

The President of the University of Essenheim stood up with some effort as they entered, then sank back into his chair. He had an enormous mane of silver hair and a ravaged, deeply furrowed face. He looked very old.

'Oh, yes. British,' he said when Klaus had introduced Kate and George. 'I have always loved England, though it's some years since I was last there. I used to know Churchill, long ago. And my early books were published there.'

'You wrote a very well-known book before World War II, didn't you?' George asked him.

'Yes, indeed. It made my reputation as an economist. It was called *Prosperity Without War*.' The President sighed. 'That was my prediction in 1929. Alas, it was followed by the slump and World War II, and people thought I had got it wrong. Yet my forecasting was excellent; it was merely that actual events took a different course.'

Klaus Klappdorf said swiftly, 'That was a great work, if I may say so, sir.'

The President inclined his head gravely. 'It was,' he acknowledged. 'It has been unjustly underrated. And now you see me here as President of what can only be called a minor university in a minor country, when it might so well have been Harvard or Oxford.'

'That is Harvard's and Oxford's loss, sir,' said Klaus.

'It is indeed,' said the President, 'and I deeply regret it.'

'Perhaps you could tell me something about the curriculum,' George suggested.

'Ah, yes, the curriculum.' The President sounded a little bored. 'Actually I leave all that kind of thing to Klaus.'

'Well, it's not as extensive as it might be,' said Klaus. 'The faculty consists of myself as Dean of Arts, Sciences and Other Studies, and Sonia Zackendorf, who's just come back from abroad, as Deputy Dean of Arts, Sciences and Other Studies. And of course there's the schlagfuss coach. Schlagfuss is our national game.'

'And there's that poet fellow,' said the President.

'Oh yes, there's Aleksi Wandervogel, the poet-in-residence.'

'We've met him,' said Kate.

'Have you? Nice fellow. *He's* back from abroad, too. He's offered to run a seminar on Essenheim literature, but as there isn't any Essenheim literature except his own work he's a bit restricted. I'm afraid the seminar hasn't actually started. It's held up at the moment by lack of students and lack of material to study.'

'So what classes are actually running?' George asked.

'Well,' said Klaus, 'we felt we ought to have our own speciality. Something this university could become known for, which wasn't done anywhere else. And we hit on Studentship Studies.'

'Is that what we saw going on outside?'

'Yes. We feel it's the most relevant subject we can offer. These young people are students for three of the most formative years of their lives. What ought they to be studying? The answer is obvious, isn't it? They should be studying the thing that most concerns them, namely, being a student. So we've established Studentship as an academic subject.'

He paused, impressively. No one made any comment.

'It's a two–part course,' Klaus went on. 'Part One, theoretical Studentship. Part Two, practical Studentship. At the end of that, if they've carried out their assignments and passed their exams, they get the degree of B. Stud.'

'And does that qualify them for any jobs?' asked Kate.

'Oh, no. That's not the point at all. We believe in study for its own sake. In *relevant* study for its own sake, of course.' Klaus paused and added, 'In the world of today.'

'Well, anyway, it keeps them out of mischief for a while,' said the President.

'And you are satisfied with this curriculum, sir?' George asked the President.

The President's furrowed cheeks became yet more deeply grooved in a weary smile.

'Frankly,' he said, 'I don't care if they study nutcracking, so long as I can draw my salary and work on my book.'

116

'The President,' said Klaus reverently, 'has been busy for some years on a work to be called *Why No Prosperity? Why War?* It will justify his predictions and explain the process by which the facts failed to match them.'

'That should be useful,' said George.

On the way out, they passed what looked at first sight like a football field. On it two teams of burly male students opposed each other in a game which appeared to be a mixture of soccer, hockey and street warfare. Participants armed with stout sticks aimed blows indiscriminately at a ball and at any accessible part of their opponents' bodies. Reserves waited in readiness to take the places of any who were carried off injured.

'That's schlagfuss,' Klaus observed with satisfaction, as two players, shouting abuse and taking swipes at each other with their sticks, were separated by the referee at some risk to his own life and limb. 'It's not an elegant sport, but it's good training. One of these days it may turn out to have been very useful.'

'Now for the Mayor,' said George as they drove away from the University of Essenheim.

'Rudi didn't say anything about seeing a mayor,' said Kate.

'I didn't fix it through Rudi,' said George. 'Rudi doesn't know *everything* I'm doing. I hope.'

'I hadn't even realized there was a mayor,' Kate said. 'Is he very important?'

'I don't think he seems very important to the powers-that-be,' said George. 'But he's the only representative of the ordinary people, so I feel I ought to see him.'

Essenheim Town Hall was a modest, squarish stone building behind the marketplace. Mayor Feldbach received them instantly. He was a shirt-sleeved, clean-shaven man in late middle age. His thick dark hair was greying, his eyes sharp, his expression shrewd – if a little worried. His physique was powerful, and he looked as if he could defend himself, given half a chance.

'It's not often I see any foreign press,' he remarked. 'Does the Prime Minister know you've come to see me?'

'I don't know,' said George frankly. 'I thought the Prime Minister didn't even know I was in the country. But I realized the other day that someone was following me. However, there's no sign of him today.'

'Rudi got Dr Stockhausen to take him off,' said Kate.

The Mayor shot her a sharp glance but made no comment on this.

'There are others in Essenheim besides the Prime Minister who might be very interested in your presence here,' he told George.

'Oh? Who?'

'Well, there's Colonel Schweiner for a start. His ambitions rise far above the command of a little army like ours. And although the force he controls must seem derisory to you, it could be formidable in our small peaceable country.'

Kate shuddered. She hadn't liked the look of Colonel Schweiner at all.

'And there's another power in the land,' the Mayor went on. 'Come to the window. Look. You see the big white house on the hillside over there?'

'A mansion!' said George. 'Is that a private home?'

'It is indeed. It has thirty-nine rooms.'

'The owner must be rich.'

'He *is* rich. Very rich.'

'I can guess who it is!' Kate exclaimed. 'Herr Finkel!'

'You are right,' said the Mayor. He sighed.

'It sounds as if you didn't like the fact,' observed George.

'I will be frank with you,' said the Mayor. 'So far as the people of Essenheim are concerned, Herr Finkel is the burden we have to bear. I stand up to him as best I can, but it is difficult. He would have me in the bargain basement if he could.'

'You mean the castle dungeons?' George asked.

'Yes. At present, fortunately, he has no power to put me there. Essenheim is still, precariously, a free country. Dr Stockhausen is a bureaucrat and inclined to be authoritarian, but he isn't a dictator. And the old Prince is a strong restraining influence. If

Stockhausen goes too far, the Prince can still put him in his place. But if anything happened to the old Prince, I don't know what would become of us all. I suspect that Herr Finkel would make his presence felt.'

'Tell me why he's such a burden,' George said.

'He owns most of the Principality. We are peasants and wine-growers and a few shopkeepers. In hard times, Herr Finkel has advanced money to almost everyone. He is the only source of money in the Principality. He owns the bank, he owns the radio station, he owns the only large store in the town, he owns the Spitzhof restaurant.'

'Princess Anni said he almost owns the castle,' said Kate.

'So I believe. Well, we ordinary folk don't care much what happens to the castle, so long as it leaves us in peace. But we're squeezed by Herr Finkel. He owns the winery, you know. The growers used to press their grapes in their own cellars, but now they have to send them to Herr Finkel for pressing.'

'And if they don't?'

'He has his strong-arm men. Unpleasant things happen to those who resist him. I can defend myself better than most, but even I have been beaten up in my time. I knew it was Herr Finkel's men, but I couldn't prove it.'

'If Rudi succeeds the present Prince,' said Kate, wishing she were free to tell the Mayor that the succession would be almost immediate, 'surely he'll stop all that kind of thing.'

'Perhaps,' said the Mayor doubtfully. 'He would not find it easy to steer a course between those two, Schweiner and Finkel.'

'I have the impression,' said George, 'that Prince Rudi is steering a very complicated course already.'

15

On Tuesday morning, with the weather sunny again, Kate went out early by herself and made her way to the little paved terrace looking out across the deep gorge that divided the town of Essenheim. She leaned over the white-painted wrought-iron railings and studied the morning scene. Beneath her were the red roofs of the Low Town, and farther down still the river, with the landing-stage at which she'd embarked for that day trip, and boats that looked from here like tiny toys. Across the gorge was a scatter of cottages, dominated by the great white mansion of Herr Finkel; farther downstream she could glimpse the less precipitous vine-clad slopes.

Essenheim seemed peaceful and lovely this morning. Kate found herself daydreaming. She lived here; the terrace was hers, and she would have her coffee and rolls brought to her here on such a day as this. Rudi would sit opposite . . .

'Oh, come off it, Kate!' she said to herself disgustedly, aloud, and set off back towards the castle. As she approached the rear courtyard she heard staccato commands and the movement of boots on gravel, disturbing the morning peace. It sounded like Colonel Schweiner drilling his men. But when she rounded the corner she saw that it wasn't the whole Essenheim Army; it was one unfortunate soldier, the gangling fellow who'd been getting everything wrong the other day. With a heavy pack on his back he was racing at the double, back and forth, left-turning, right-turning and about-turning as Schweiner roared orders at him.

His face was red with effort and pouring with sweat, and his heavy panting could be heard in the brief intervals between the commands. Schweiner, intent on the drill, didn't notice Kate at first, and she was horrified by the look of gloating enjoyment on his face.

But when Schweiner saw her, his face straightened instantly and he shouted a 'Halt' order. The soldier, in a state of near-collapse, stood saggingly at attention. He was young, with a blank round face and frightened eyes.

'To your quarters, dismiss!' Schweiner snapped; and as the young soldier tottered thankfully away the Colonel, formerly Top Sergeant, turned with an ingratiating smile to Kate.

'Punishment drill, gracious young lady,' he explained, wiping sweat from his own beefy face.

Kate didn't feel it was up to her to ask what the young man's crime had been, but her expression must have shown she was disturbed, for Schweiner went on to add, 'It doesn't do them any harm, a good workout. These poor physical specimens *need* hard exercise. He'll live to thank me for it.'

He looked Kate up and down in considerable detail, and seemed to like what he saw. Kate, unused to being surveyed in such a way, recalled Rudi's early remark about Essenheim standards of feminine beauty. Perhaps, she thought, here in Essenheim she was glamorous. But that didn't save her from feeling deeply repelled by the evident interest of Colonel Schweiner. She tried to move on, but the Colonel detained her by dropping a hefty paw on her arm.

'Allow me, gracious young lady,' he said, 'to welcome you to Essenheim in the name of the army.'

'Thank you,' Kate said faintly, and tried to detach herself. The Colonel's grip tightened.

'It is a great pleasure to us all,' he said, 'to have someone so young and beautiful in the castle.'

Kate made no response. Colonel Schweiner perceived that his remarks were not being warmly received.

'You must forgive me, gracious young lady,' he said, 'if I

seem over-familiar. I am, alas, a widower. I have a daughter of about your age, and paternal feelings come naturally to me.'

It seemed to Kate that the look in his eye was not at all paternal. And he didn't show any fatherly delight when at that moment a young woman came into the courtyard and addressed him as 'Papa'.

'This is my daughter Elsa, gracious young lady,' he said stiffly. And to Elsa he said, 'You have the honour of meeting Prince Rudi's friend, of whom we have heard so much.'

Kate thought that the description of Elsa as about her own age was not quite accurate. She looked about thirty and was remarkably homely, with a long thin nose, small close-set eyes and an angular figure.

The ingratiating smile returned to the Colonel's face. 'I hope I am not presumptuous,' he said, 'but I would find it pleasant if you two young ladies could become friends, great friends. I am sure you have much in common.'

Kate smiled tentatively, but was startled by the look of sheer hostility that flashed from Elsa's eyes. Then she recalled a remark by Prince Friedrich and wondered if what they had in common was an interest in Rudi. She didn't think, somehow, that Elsa Schweiner had much chance of attracting Rudi, but that of course wouldn't prevent her from suffering the pangs of love. And jealousy.

There was an almost audible silence. Kate sought for some harmless remark with which to break it. The smirk froze on the Colonel's face. It was an awkward moment, broken by the arrival of Rudi himself, who didn't seem to notice anything amiss.

'Ah, there you are, Kate,' he said. 'Come and have some breakfast.'

Colonel Schweiner sprang to attention and saluted. Elsa curt-seyed stiffly. Both of them stood stock-still as Rudi bore Kate away. She didn't look round. But she could feel the eyes of the two Schweiners still on her and, for different reasons, she felt uncomfortable about both of them.

*

'We will go,' said Rudi at breakfast, 'down to old Beyer's printing shop, to collect the invitations for the reception. I must go for them myself, to be sure he's got them right. And it may interest you to see our news-sheet, the *Essenheim Free Press*, which Beyer owns. It appears twice a week, and one of the editions will be going to press just about now. I'm afraid it's not quite like the *Morning Intelligence*.'

Herr Beyer's printing shop was in the market square, a few doors away from the town hall. It smelled of ink and hot metal. Herr Beyer himself was setting headlines by hand in a compositor's stick when they arrived. His apprentice sat at the keyboard of an ancient stuttering typesetting machine, painfully picking out the letters. The front page of the *Essenheim Free Press* lay, partly assembled in metal, on a table in the middle of the floor.

'That hole in the page is where *you're* going, Highness,' said Herr Beyer. He was a small, thin, wizened man, wearing an exceedingly dirty once-white apron. 'It's the main story this week, of course. All about you coming back, and the reception on Thursday. And about you, too, gracious young lady.'

The apprentice called in Essenheimisch from his keyboard, 'How do you spell "castle", master?'

Herr Beyer tut-tutted and told him.

'Half illiterate, Highness, that's what he is,' he complained to Rudi. 'If I want something doing properly I have to do it myself.'

'Then I hope you did the invitations yourself,' Rudi said.

'Of course, Highness,' said Herr Beyer. He wiped his hands on his apron – though it was hard to see how either hands or apron could be improved by this operation – and led the way to a corner of the printing shop, where a pile of large, handsome deckle-edged cards was stacked. Herr Beyer picked up the top one, stamping it with a big black thumb-print.

'It's all right, Highness,' he observed, noticing Rudi's eyes on this. 'I've printed plenty. A few spoils are allowed for.'

The cards were printed in Gothic type. They read:

His Illustrious Highness, Prince Ferdinand Franz Josef III,
Prince Laureate of Essenheim,
Duke of Teufelwald, Count of the Two Rivers, Baron Schatztal,
Field Marshal, Admiral of the Fleet,
Commodore of the Royal Essenheim Air Force. . .

'I didn't know Essenheim had an air force,' Kate said to Rudi.

'You didn't look on the other side of the plane the other day, did you?' said Rudi. 'It says "Essenheim Airways" on one side and "Royal Essenheim Air Force" on the other.'

'Oh,' said Kate, and went on reading:

presents his humble compliments to

_____

and begs to request the pleasure of his/her company at

A GRAND RECEPTION

to welcome the Prince Rudolf Wilhelm on his return
to the Principality,
to proclaim the reinstatement of the said Rudolf Wilhelm
as Crown Prince,
and further to celebrate the visit to Essenheim
of
the Lady Catherine of Hammersmith.

R.S.V.P.

Kate stared at the last item. 'Who on earth,' she asked, 'is the Lady Catherine of Hammersmith? I live in Hammersmith myself and I've never heard of her.'

'It's you,' said Rudi. 'Uncle thought it sounded better and would make sure the royals treat you with proper respect.'

'Oh,' said Kate again.

'Well, are you satisfied, Highness?' Herr Beyer asked.

'Very nice,' said Rudi, 'but I don't entirely like the spacing.' They fell into a technical discussion. Kate wandered round the printing shop, examining the presses and the cases of type. Everything looked extremely old; the typesetting machine, clanking and chattering away in a corner, was the most modern feature. She paused to watch the apprentice at work. He was a curly-haired lad with a freckled nose and an open, innocent expression.

'Gracious young lady!' he whispered, then cast a glance across the room at his master and pressed two or three keys by way of keeping his machine at work. 'Gracious young lady!'

Kate signified that she was listening.

'You're at the castle, gracious young lady?'

Kate nodded.

'Do you see the ... the Princess Anni?'

'Every day,' said Kate.

'Isn't she ... oh, isn't she ... isn't she *great*?'

The lad blushed crimson and rattled out a machine-gun burst of typesetting.

'There, I got it full of mistakes,' he said. 'I'm sorry, gracious young lady, I hadn't any right. I just couldn't help myself. I *had* to speak to somebody who speaks to Princess Anni.'

'Hey, Hansi, what's going on over there?' called Herr Beyer from the other end of the room.

'I just asked the gracious young lady how to spell "reception",' said Hansi.

'You've no business asking the gracious young lady anything!' said Herr Beyer crossly. 'If you want to know how to spell "reception", you ask me. You ought to know how to spell it anyway. I beg your pardon, gracious young lady. I'm afraid he's a simpleton.'

Hansi looked down, abashed. Kate thought he was rather nice. She wondered if he was the boy whom Anni liked but couldn't have anything to do with because he was only an apprentice. She was sure he wasn't such a simpleton as poor Prince Friedrich.

*

'Last of all,' Rudi said as they got back in the car, 'I must take you to the radio station. They'd like you to go on the air for a few minutes, just to say hello. After that there won't be anything more to do. You can relax until the reception. And then, if you *must*, you can go home.'

Rudi sighed deeply and flickered a glance at her from under his long eyelashes.

'I shall have to begin my reign without you,' he observed sadly.

'I'll have served my purpose, won't I?' Kate said, with such sharpness as she could muster. Really she wanted to run her fingers through his hair.

'Oh, Kate, Kate!' said Rudi. He took a hand from the wheel to hold hers, and held it intermittently all the way to the radio station, which was on the southern heights a little way out of town.

'It belongs to Herr Finkel,' Rudi told her.

The façade was ultra-modern and neon-lit; plate-glass doors slid apart and the lobby was carpeted. But obviously funds had not been unlimited. Behind the lobby, Radio Essenheim dwindled rapidly to a couple of rooms and a studio. The station director, who was waiting for them and was also producer and studio manager, was apologetic. 'It is all due for rebuilding on a larger scale,' he explained.

Finger on lips, he led Kate into the studio, which was very small, and seated her opposite the programme presenter, a bespectacled young man in a multicoloured shirt who offered her a welcoming grimace. A pop record which had figured in the charts some eighteen months ago was just coming to an end. The presenter followed it with some extremely fast talking, in tones of mixed delight and astonishment, about the virtues of a potion which cured rheumatism, headaches, diseases of the nervous system and influenza, and which ended indigestion, cleared the skin, brightened the eyes and conferred abounding health on all who imbibed it. It was available at modest expense from every chemist's shop in Essenheim.

Then, in the voice of one who could hardly believe himself to be so immensely privileged, the presenter announced that a distinguished visitor to Essenheim was here in the studio with him. He addressed Kate in halting English. She replied in moderately fluent Essenheimisch. This was a great success. The presenter became almost incoherent with enthusiasm. He congratulated Kate three times over on her excellent accent, repeated his appreciation of the honour conferred on him by her presence, and asked her what she thought of Essenheim. Kate replied that she liked it. The verdict was received with rapture, and the interview proceeded from height to height. Kate herself began to feel that her arrival at Radio Essenheim was a milestone in its history. After seven minutes, with an eye on the studio clock, the presenter thanked Kate effusively, announced that there would be a live broadcast of next week's reception, finished talking on the dot of the hour, and activated a time signal that sounded uncannily like a door-chime.

'And now, Essenheimers,' he went on, 'your world news bulletin.'

Kate listened, wondering which items of world news would most interest the people of Essenheim. It seemed in fact that their world was a small one. There wasn't anything about international affairs. The bulletin began with an item about a peasant who'd fallen into a stream on his way home from a wine-cellar and ruined his Sunday suit. It continued with news of a crime wave which appeared to have hit Essenheim. The Town Magistrate had sent two people to prison for five days each, on separate charges of creating public disturbances. They were Aleksi Wandervogel, poet, and Countess Sonia Zackendorf, university teacher. The bulletin continued with two or three further local items before the presenter sounded his door-chime again and began to extol the virtues of Willi Bamberger's Used Car Lot, just behind the Town Hall.

The station director came into the studio, finger on lips again, and led Kate away. The presenter gave her a thumbs-up sign as she left.

'He seems very enthusiastic,' she said to the station director.

'Moritz? I should hope he does. That's what we pay him for. He has a foul temper when he gets off the air, though.'

'Remember,' Rudi told him as they left, 'all staff on duty on Thursday. And we don't want anyone pulling the plug out at a crucial moment, like they did last time you had an outside broadcast.'

'That won't happen again, Highness, I assure you,' the station director said. 'Herr Finkel would have me shot, so to speak, if it did.'

'I don't want anybody shot,' said Rudi. There was a dryness in his voice, as if the remark had more significance than met the ear. Kate directed a searching look at him, but it didn't get beyond his profile. He looked pretty good in full face, she thought, and in profile he was simply devastating.

'Did you hear,' she asked him on the way back to the castle, 'about the arrests?'

'What arrests?'

'Aleksi and Sonia. Sent to prison for five days for causing public disturbances.'

Rudi swore in Essenheimisch. 'They'll still be there on the day of the reception,' he said. 'And I know that pair. They'll yell the place down. You can hear shouting from those cells all over the castle.'

'You mean they're in the castle dungeons?' asked Kate.

'Oh, yes. The dungeons serve as lock-up for the whole Principality. They're the best part of the castle, really. The architect would have liked to convert them into our apartment, but Uncle Ferdy said he wasn't a prisoner yet, thank you very much, and had the first floor done instead.'

'Are there many people shut up there now?'

'Oh, no. Except at festivals and the wine harvest, when we get a few drunks, the cells are mostly empty.'

When he'd parked the car, Rudi took Kate in through the side door by which she'd first entered the castle – long ago, as it now seemed – but instead of going through to the modernized princely apartment he turned off through the echoing old kitchens and led the way down a flight of spiral stone steps. At the bottom a stout wooden door blocked the way.

'I'll call Maxi to open up,' Rudi said. 'Maxi's the jailer and also the cellarman. There's enough wine and brandy down here to keep the entire population drunk for a decade.'

Shouts from the prisoners could already be heard. A loud declaiming male voice was being perpetually interrupted by a furious and even louder female one.

'Maxi!' yelled Rudi above the uproar. 'Maxi!'

Maxi appeared in a cobwebbed doorway near the foot of the steps. He was a small thin middle-aged man with an ingratiating smile.

'Highness?' he said, bowing.

'What are you going to do about that horrible din?'

'Highness, there's nothing I *can* do, short of hitting them on the head, and the Prince wouldn't like that.'

'I suppose not,' Rudi admitted grudgingly. 'The policeman should have had more sense than to arrest them at a time like this. Creating a public disturbance, wasn't it?'

'Yes, Highness. Aleksi was reciting his stuff in the marketplace. Annoying the passers-by, the policeman said. That probably means he was annoying the policeman. Those two don't get on together at all. Somehow poetry and policing don't mix.'

'And Sonia?'

'She was parading the High Street with a sign saying "Down with the Fascist Prince!" '

'Why should she be arrested for that? It's supposed to be a free country.'

'Yes, Highness, but she'd taken the sign from Frau Schmidt's front garden and painted her slogan on the back of it. It was a nice new sign saying "Ritz-Albany Hotel". Countess Zackendorf said she'd only borrowed it, but the Magistrate sent her down just the same.'

Maxi led the way along a stone-flagged passage to a row

of cells. Kate shivered in the dungeon chill. The faces of the two prisoners could be seen at the tiny openings in the doors of the first two cells.

'Jailer!' shouted Aleksi. 'Bring me a pencil and paper!'

'Not allowed,' said Maxi.

Aleksi saw that Rudi and Kate were with the jailer.

'Hey, Highness!' he urged. 'Tell him to bring me a pencil!'

'What for, Aleksi?'

'I've made up a great poem to mark this occasion. The poet imprisoned by his unappreciative fellow-citizens. I must get it down on paper before I forget it. Listen to this bit!'

'Stuff it, Aleksi!' yelled Sonia from the next cell.

Aleksi ignored her and declaimed in dramatic tones a passage which Kate translated from the Essenheimisch as 'Prisons are constructed without any stone in the walls, and cages without iron bars.' She tried to puzzle out what it meant. Then it dawned on her. 'Stone Walls do not a Prison make,' she said aloud, 'Nor Iron bars a Cage.'

'That's right, gracious young lady!' called Aleksi delightedly. 'Richard Lovelace, the Cavalier poet. One of the influences on my work.'

'I don't think you've quite understood the poem,' Kate said.

'Cavaliers!' shouted Sonia in disgust. 'Aristocrats! I spit on them!'

'We must get these two out of here,' said Rudi. 'I know what I'll do. I'll just slip upstairs to Uncle and get him to write out a royal pardon. I won't be a minute.'

'In the meantime, please step into my humble abode, gracious young lady,' Maxi said to Kate.

Just off the passage was a cheerful room with a big stone fireplace, in which burned a much-needed coal fire. In front of the fire sat a buxom girl of about twenty with black hair, red cheeks and bold dark-brown eyes. From a room beyond, presumably the kitchen, emerged a massively built woman of similar colouring, obviously the girl's mother. She was not so much fat as immensely muscular; she dominated Maxi completely and made her buxom daughter look slim. She curtseyed with heavyweight agility.

'I'm *his* wife,' she informed Kate, with scornful emphasis on the word 'his', as if to make it clear that in reality possession was the other way round. 'Bertha's my name. And this is my daughter Bettina. You wouldn't think a little fellow like him could be responsible for a fine girl like her, would you? Well, he was. Lively as a monkey he was, in his youth.'

'Now, now, Mother!' protested Maxi.

'You were, you know you were. A disgusting little fellow. Well, that's all over now and you needn't think you're going to start again ... I beg your pardon, gracious young lady, we're plain folk here and I have too free a tongue, I admit it, but you know what men are, they have to be kept in their place.'

Kate didn't doubt that she was capable of keeping Maxi in his.

The girl was looking at her with interest and some slight hostility.

'So you're Rudi's new girlfriend,' she said.

'*Prince* Rudi to you, my girl!' her mother told her. 'Don't be familiar with your betters!'

'It's a bit late to tell me that!' the girl retorted.

'And you just watch what you're saying! You'll be giving the gracious young lady some wrong ideas. We're only the jailer's family, and don't you forget it!' Bertha turned to Kate. 'Take no notice of her, my dear. She gets ideas above her station, and then she imagines things. Things that aren't so. Trouble is, her father hasn't disciplined her the way he should.'

'I'm not Rudi's girlfriend,' Kate explained patiently. 'Just a visitor.'

There was a knock on the door and Rudi came in. He had a piece of paper in his hand, presumably a pardon from the Prince Laureate. Kate wondered whether there was a swift exchange of glances between him and Bettina, or whether she was drawing wrong conclusions. She felt a moment's jealousy of Bettina.

Maxi accepted the piece of paper and went along to the cells, jingling his keys. But it seemed that the prisoners didn't want to leave. They were quite comfortable, they declared. Sonia accused Rudi of trying to evict them without notice, in a manner typical of a fascist state. When Kate and Rudi left the dungeons, the cell doors were open but Aleksi and Sonia were still inside, respectively declaiming and complaining, while Maxi appealed to them in vain to come out.

'They'll leave before long,' Rudi assured Kate as they climbed the stone steps. 'They're making plenty of fuss, but now they've been pardoned there won't be any food for them. They'll go home when they're hungry.'

16

The afternoon before the reception, it occurred to Kate that she still hadn't been up the tower. Rudi had disappeared on some of the unexplained business which from time to time took him away from the castle. Kate proposed the ascent to Anni, who was not enthusiastic.

'Those steps go on for *ever*,' she said. 'I went up once. I was *dizzy* and I was *exhausted*, and there's nothing when you get there except a view of Essenheim. And you want to know what views of Essenheim do for me? Nothing, that's what they do for me. Nothing. I'd rather have a view of the King's Road.' It was clear that she would prefer to play her records while Kate did the climbing.

'Send for Maxi,' she advised Kate. 'He has all the keys. He's the jailer.'

'I've met Maxi,' said Kate.

Maxi was summoned, and arrived jingling his bunch of keys. He led Kate through the Great Hall and along two or three corridors until they came to a massive wooden door, bolted and barred. Maxi raised two bars, drew two massive bolts, chose and inserted a key and opened the door.

'Shall I come with you, gracious young lady?' he asked. 'It's gloomy in there. There's no light in the tower except what comes in through those tiny windows. Ladies usually need a man with them, so as not to be frightened.'

'*I* don't need a man with me, thank you very much,' said Kate sharply. 'I'm not easily frightened.'

'Very well, gracious young lady. There are 197 steps from here to the top. If you count them on the way down, you'll know you're back at the right floor. And here, if you're on your own you're going to need a key.'

He detached one from his bunch. 'It's a spare,' he said, 'but don't forget to give me it back. It opens this door, and the one at the top of the tower on to the roof, and the door into the basement from the old kitchens. So anyone who has this key can get into the dungeons and wine-cellars. Take care of it, gracious young lady, please. And be careful on those steps!'

The door swung to behind Kate with a solid-sounding clunk. In spite of what she'd said about not being afraid, she felt a moment's unease.

'Don't be silly, Kate!' she told herself.

She was on a small stone landing, from which a flight of spiral steps led upwards and another down into the depths. A little light filtered in through a slit window. Maxi hadn't exaggerated when he said it was gloomy.

Kate set off on the upward climb. The staircase was fairly wide at first; there was another slit window at each turn of the spiral, and periodically she came to a landing like the one she'd started from, with a locked door to some other level. Then the landings ceased and the spiral became so tight that she had to place her feet sideways and began to suffer from vertigo. Obviously she was now in the high narrow part of the tower.

It took a long time to climb the 197 steps, and Kate was both tired and dizzy by the time she reached the top. The stairway ended at a locked door. Straining her eyes in the half-light, Kate found the keyhole, inserted the key that Maxi had given her, opened the door and stepped out into blinding sunlight. There was just room to stand between the parapets.

Kate blinked. When her eyes became used to the light, she could see that the view was indeed spectacular. Directly beneath her was the sheer east wall of the castle, plunging to the river gorge far below. Across the gorge, the Low Town clung crazily to such precarious ledges as would accommodate streets and buildings. From the western parapet she saw the more recent quarters of the town, the high street, the market square, the bridge across the chasm, the airstrip, the masts of the radio station. And from north and west the two rivers, the Esel and the Wandel, flowed to their confluence immediately below. Beyond the town on all sides were the hills and valleys of Essenheim, and beyond those again the high mountains which cut the Principality off from the world. Two or three small clouds, accompanied by their shadows, sauntered across the landscape.

Alone on this high tower, Kate had a sudden sharp sense of isolation. She didn't want to stay up here long. She went inside again, locked the door behind her, and in the dim light from the slit windows made her way cautiously down the spiral staircase. Halfway down she realized that she'd forgotten to start counting the 197 steps, but she didn't feel like going back to the top and beginning again. She thought she knew roughly where she'd got to.

But she was deceived by the difference between the toil-some ascent and the easier descent. She was just beginning to think she must be getting near her point of entry to the tower when she realized that light was reaching the staircase from an open door. She had come too far and was only a few steps from the bottom. The door, through which she could see a stone-flagged passage lit by a small electric light bulb, presumably led into the basement where the dungeons and wine-cellars were.

Kate wondered for a moment whether to go back up the steps and look for the door at which she'd come in. But she didn't know how far up it was, and felt a strong disinclination to return to the gloom of the staircase. Surely if she went out into the basement she would soon find Maxi's quarters. She could give him back his key and return to civilization through the old kitchens.

She walked out of the tower and along the passage. On either side of it were rows of empty cells, all with closely barred windows and heavy doors ajar. Silence lay thick as dust and was hardly disturbed by Kate's feet in their soft shoes.

Eventually the passageway branched. Each branch was similarly lit by low-powered bulbs; there was nothing to indicate which would be more likely to take her to a way out. At random she took the left-hand branch, and soon found she was in among the wine-cellars. Room after room, though empty of people, was full of barrels: hundreds of barrels, barrels beyond counting. Prince Ferdinand Franz Josef III of Essenheim might be a poor man but he seemed to have a wealth of wine and brandy. Enough to keep the entire population drunk for a decade, Rudi had said. She could believe it.

Kate went back to the point at which the passage had branched and took the other direction. Here there were more empty cells. She shivered, feeling the dank stone chill of the place and regretting her decision to leave the staircase. Then, ahead of her, she thought she heard clicking, scraping and rattling sounds and – faint as a rustle of leaves – human voices. She went on, hoping this was a sign that she was approaching Maxi's quarters. It wasn't.

The sounds were coming from a room on her right. The room had no door into the passage; it had a small window which, unlike those she'd passed earlier, had glass in it. The glass was extremely grimy. She peered through and saw that the door to this room was in the opposite wall, reached from some other part of the castle.

The room was an armoury. There were racks of rifles, there were ammunition boxes, there were items of weaponry and equipment that Kate, being inexpert in such matters, couldn't identify. And the armoury was in use; was indeed the scene of activity at this very moment. Soldiers were coming in, one at a time, and being issued with weapons under the eye of Colonel Schweiner, whose unmistakable back was towards Kate. As she watched, three men received revolvers, then two with stripes on their arms got submachine-guns.

Kate was surprised; somehow she hadn't thought of the Essenheim Army as actually carrying arms. Perhaps this issue was for security at tomorrow's reception, though she wouldn't have imagined there was a need for submachine-guns. She could have tapped on the glass, made her presence known and asked the way out, but she felt reluctant to do so; she didn't want to bring herself to the notice of Colonel Schweiner. She tiptoed away and continued to the end of the passageway. It ran into another one and, turning left, she realized thankfully that she'd come to a part she had been in before. She was passing the row of cells of which two had been occupied by Aleksi and Sonia. They were empty now.

She continued and came to the door which she was sure belonged to Maxi's apartment. It was closed. She tapped on it confidently. Nobody came. She knocked more loudly. Still nobody came. Well, she could find her way out from here. She banged on the door once more, just for luck. And this time somebody came and opened it.

Rudi.

His expression was startled. He seemed on the point of closing the door in her face. Then, holding it just a little ajar, he addressed her from the opening.

'Kate!' he said. 'What *are* you doing down here?'

Kate began to explain, but hadn't even finished a sentence when a rough feminine voice came from inside the room.

'Oh, let them in, whoever it is!' the voice called.

Rudi spoke a cross word in Essenheimisch and reluctantly opened the door wide. As before, there was a blazing fire in the room. In her seat at the chimney corner was Maxi's daughter Bettina. She looked slightly dishevelled. And Kate knew as well as if she'd seen it that Rudi and Bettina had been embracing.

Bettina looked sour but not embarrassed. 'Oh, it's you, gracious young lady,' she said. On her lips the phrase sounded like an insult. 'Well, you've found your boyfriend, haven't you? And now you're finding that he's mine as well!'

Rudi said to Kate, uneasily, 'Take no notice of Tina, she's a joker.'

Bettina said, 'Oh, yes, sure, it's all a joke. You can hear me laughing, can't you? Kiss and make up, that's Rudi, and he always gets away with it. But I'll give you a warning, gracious young lady. The less you get involved with him, the less you'll get hurt!'

Kate said coldly, 'I got lost, Rudi. I was in the tower and I came down too far.'

'I'll show you the way to my uncle's apartment,' Rudi said.

'It's all right. I can find it for myself.'

'Let me come with you, all the same.'

'Don't believe any tale he tells you!' Bettina advised her.

Out in the passageway, Rudi said, 'There's a simple explanation.'

'I expect there is,' said Kate. 'But don't bother to give me it.'

'Oh, Kate!' He tried to take her hand, but she pulled it away.

'I know just where I am, Rudi,' she said. 'In more senses than one. I shall stay over Thursday so as not to embarrass your uncle. And then I'm going.'

'I'm sorry . . .' Rudi began.

'That's all right,' said Kate with all the dignity she could muster. 'You don't have to apologize. It's your life. But I'm not playing any more part in it. *Please* don't come with me now. Stay with Bettina.'

She walked away from him. Later she wondered if she ought to tell him about the issue of weapons from the armoury. But she decided she wouldn't. She didn't want to talk to Rudi any more if she could help it. And she didn't understand these things. Probably it was all perfectly normal and she should mind her own business. She wouldn't say anything to anybody.

17

There was heavy rain in Essenheim on the morning of the reception. But everyone assured Kate that it wouldn't last; and it didn't. In mid-morning the thick cover of cloud drew slowly back across the sky like a great curtain, revealing a brilliant expanse of blue. Streets and roofs shone in the sunlight; the trees along the avenue that led from castle gate to market square glistened green in the newly freshened air.

Kate and Rudi hardly spoke to each other that morning. Once or twice he looked at her with mute appeal; at other times he seemed tense and preoccupied. The old Prince however was in good spirits. After lunch he took Kate to the window of his private room, which had a balcony looking out over the main forecourt and the avenue into town. Flags were flying and streamers hung across the street saying LONG LIVE OUR PRINCE and HAPPY ANNIVERSARY and 30 GLORIOUS YEARS. People were already gathering on the open space before the castle, and the Principality's little squad of police were all on duty controlling them. As Kate watched, a shout of 'Prince! Prince! Prince!' was set up.

'I must go out and wave,' the Prince Laureate said.

Cheers rose from the crowd as he went out on to the balcony. He turned and beckoned to Kate to join him. Doubtfully she went out, to be greeted with more cheering. Everyone seemed to know who she was; no doubt it was all in the paper.

'Where has Rudi got to?' the Prince muttered crossly. But Rudi had disappeared on more of his mysterious business.

There were tears in the old man's eyes, when, after repeated waves from him and shouts of acclaim from below, he finally limped inside.

'They still love their old Prince,' he said. 'I'm not a great man, you know. I was born to this job; I didn't get it on merit. But I've done my best. They'll miss me when I'm gone.'

Kate found herself kissing his cheek. 'There, there,' she said. 'You won't be gone for years and years yet.'

'You can't deceive me, my dear,' the Prince said. 'I'm not in good shape.' He shot a sideways glance at her. 'I believe Rudi told you of our plans.'

'Yes,' said Kate.

'He shouldn't have done, really. But I'm sure I can trust you.'

'I haven't told anyone,' said Kate.

'Of course you haven't. I should have preferred to stay on the throne until Rudi married. He is still wild and unpredictable. Marriage would settle him, or even a suitable and lasting relationship with the right person.' The Prince looked wistfully at Kate. 'But it seems that is not to be. And I must make sure without delay that he succeeds me. I cannot risk being outmanoeuvred once more by Dr Stockhausen and having poor Friedrich thrust upon my unfortunate people.'

Kate said nothing to that.

'My dearest wish is to see Rudi safely married and an heir born. But I don't suppose I shall live long enough for that.' The Prince sighed. 'Now if only *you*, my dear ...'

He paused. Kate still said nothing. The Prince went on in a hopeful tone, 'Suppose I were to ennoble your worthy father? Then perhaps it would not be impossible for you to be an acceptable bride.'

'What about Princess Margaretta?' asked Kate. 'His fiancée?'

'That would be a complication. But the Hohenbergs and

the Lubensteins have sorted out such questions before. There are plenty of suitors for little Etta, with a fortune like hers. The trouble is, to be frank, that you would bring no dowry.'

'That's not the only problem,' said Kate. The unlikely picture of herself as Princess of Essenheim and wife of an adoring Rudi flashed briefly before her eyes. She replaced it rapidly with one of her semi-detached home in Hammersmith and another of Rudi the previous day emerging from the embrace of the jailer's daughter. 'It's not possible *at all*,' she added firmly.

'I suppose not, my dear,' the Prince agreed sadly. 'Well, I must rest for an hour or so, if I am to carry out my duties this afternoon. And I advise you to do the same, Kate. You will find the occasion rather demanding.'

Kate hadn't taken afternoon rests since she was in kindergarten, but when she got to her room the bed seemed suddenly tempting, and she decided she'd lie on it for ten minutes, though she wouldn't go to sleep. The next thing she knew was being shaken by Anni.

'Wake up, wake up, Kate. They're starting to arrive!'

Kate sat up, blinking.

'And we haven't changed!' she said. Anni was still in jeans.

'We won't be needed in the first hour,' Anni told her. 'I've been to these affairs before. Rudi as heir to the throne and Dr Stockhausen as Prime Minister welcome the guests; that's the way they do it here. Then they all tuck into the food and wine; it's what most of them come for anyway. Uncle Ferdy appears later on the dais and makes his little speech. All it amounts to is "Hello, folks", but they all applaud like it was the greatest show on earth. You and I come on as the supporting cast. Uncle introduces us, as if they didn't all know who we are already. And then we and Uncle circulate, saying polite nothings to everyone in sight. All you have to remember is not to swear and not to say anything that matters.'

'I can't swear in Essenheimisch anyway,' said Kate.

'Remind me tomorrow and I'll teach you. And now, Kate,

come with me and watch them arriving. I know a perfect spy-spot. Don't change yet; you're going to get dirty.'

Anni led the way into her own room, a couple of doors away from Kate's. She opened a tall cupboard which stood against the castle's outer wall, and casually slid aside a panel in the back of it.

'What on earth ... ?' began Kate.

'Don't look so startled,' Anni said, taking a flashlight from a shelf. 'It's only a secret passage. The castle has lots of them, and I know more than anybody else. They come in handy sometimes.'

Kate squeezed her way along the passage behind Anni. It was only just wide enough, and she had a fantasy of being hopelessly stuck there in the dark. They went round a corner and continued for some distance before Anni signalled Kate to a halt. They were at a superb vantage-point. On one side of the passage, a slit window in the castle's outer wall gave an excellent view of the main forecourt; at the other side the interior of the Great Hall could be seen through a narrow opening in a dusky recess, invisible to anyone on the floor of the hall. Guests could be seen arriving in the forecourt, and observed again a few minutes later as they entered the hall.

Kate watched with fascination, helped by a running commentary from Anni. Some thirty royal cousins and other aristocracy arrived in carriages drawn by large, plodding horses. 'They usually pull the winery drays,' Anni explained. The gentlemen wore knee-breeches and embroidered velvet coats; the ladies were in full, brocaded silk gowns, some with bustles. The finery had a slightly dusty look, suggesting to Kate a period play put on by an amateur dramatic society with limited funds. The professional guests were sharply distinguished from the aristocracy: the men wore mostly black coats and striped trousers and the women long evening dresses. Some arrived in chauffeur-driven cars, some drove their own, and the handful of decrepit town taxis made several appearances. On one of these trips, a soberly suited George was disgorged. A minority of the humbler guests arrived on mopeds, bicycles and on foot. Altogether there seemed to be about two hundred.

'Everybody who's anybody in Essenheim is here now,' Anni remarked. She didn't seem particularly impressed by the thought.

From the opening in the other wall of the passage, Kate could see the guests being received. As they were announced, they were greeted by Rudi at one side of the door and Dr Stockhausen at the other. Kate caught her breath on first beholding Rudi, who looked more splendid than ever. His dress upstaged everyone else's. It was a little later in period than the rest: he wore a crimson cutaway coat and tight-fitting white trousers which fastened at the ankle. Kate, who knew her Jane Austen, thought he looked like a younger and sprightlier Mr Darcy. As he bent over the hands of curtseying ladies, she was sure they were all in love with him.

Gradually the forecourt emptied and the hall filled. The guests headed eagerly for the food, which did indeed look very good. Essenheim Airways had made two or three extra flights to bring in more delicacies. Most of the castle staff had been pressed into service as waiters or waitresses, and circulated gracefully or gracelessly according to their abilities. There was an air of faded splendour about the scene, the twilight of the once-great Hohenbergs.

Kate was musing on this when Anni dug her in the ribs and said, 'Come on. Our turn now.' They stumbled back along the passage. An anxious chamberlain in knee-breeches (he was the dark-suited official she'd seen on her first arrival at the castle, and from time to time in the intervening days) was waiting to hurry them up and glancing, White Rabbit-like, at his watch; and the little round-eyed maid Lilli hovered between Kate's room and Anni's, trying to help them dress. It didn't take them long to put on the white and black silk nightdresses. Kate had a moment's dreadful doubt about the suitability of these, but Lilli seemed to admire them.

In his private sitting-room the old Prince was waiting for

them. His ceremonial army uniform didn't flatter his sagging form; he looked a little pathetic and his spirits had drooped.

'Well, it's the last time,' he said with a kind of mournful satisfaction. 'Rudi says when he's Prince Laureate he'll stop the dressing up.'

'I bet he won't,' said Anni. 'Costume suits him too well.'

The Prince grunted. Then, looking from Anni to Kate and back, he grew more cheerful.

'You look beautiful, my dears,' he told them. 'Beautiful. You could marry emperors and do them credit, both of you, if only there were a few emperors left.'

He offered his right arm to Anni and his left to Kate. Preceded by the chamberlain, they moved from the private apartment along a gallery and down the main staircase, which Kate had not previously used. She had a momentary wild impulse to detach herself from the Prince and slide down the balustrade; she wouldn't actually have done it but she thought Anni might. For the moment however, Anni was demure and dignified. A few guests had wandered from the Great Hall and respectfully watched their descent. At the foot of the staircase Rudi and Friedrich joined them. Gentlemen bowed and ladies curtseyed as they passed.

The chamberlain went ahead through the double doors into the Great Hall. The band struck up the national anthem, 'Heaven Help Essenheim', set to a mournful tune by Kammer-jungfer which contrived to suggest that heaven would have its work cut out. The chamberlain went to the microphone.

'It's working,' whispered Rudi. 'Hurrah!'

'His Illustrious Highness, Prince Ferdinand Franz Josef I I I,' the chamberlain announced. He intoned the Prince's titles: Prince Laureate of Essenheim, Duke of Teufelwald, Count of the Two Rivers, Baron of Schatztal, and two or three others there hadn't been room for on the invitations. The Prince himself shambled forward, to spontaneous applause. Dr Stock-hausen approached him, bent a knee, and read a loyal address in his dry accountant's tones. The Prince went up to the micro-phone amid cheers. Somebody adjusted it for him.

'My dear people,' he began. There was renewed cheering. 'It is a great joy to come before you once more, after thirty years spent in your service as Prince, to say how deeply I am touched and honoured by your loyalty.'

The Prince reminisced for a few minutes about some of the principal events of his reign. Rudi, standing beside Kate at the back of the dais, looked anxious and impatient; at one point he muttered so that only Kate could hear, 'I wish he'd get on with it!' She wondered for a moment whether it was possible that the Prince, moved by the applause, would change his mind and not abdicate after all. But finally he half turned and motioned Rudi forward to join him.

'You will all know,' he said, 'that my nephew Prince Rudolf has lately returned to the Principality. It was my intention today to proclaim his restoration to the position of Crown Prince, heir to the throne of Essenheim.'

There was a little scattered applause, which the Prince halted with a gesture.

'I have, however,' he said, 'come to a different decision.'

Kate, watching Dr Stockhausen's face, saw a startled expression come to it, and was sure he hadn't known.

'I am an old man,' the Prince went on, 'a tired man. The time has come to say that I have done enough. I now announce to you my abdication with effect from this moment, and the succession of Prince Rudolf to the Crown.' He turned and said in a firm voice, 'Rudolf, step forward.'

Rudi went and knelt before him. The Prince raised him to his feet. 'Rudolf Wilhelm Hohenberg,' he said, 'I renounce my throne to you, and proclaim you from this moment Prince Laureate of Essenheim.' In his turn he knelt down. 'And I declare myself your loyal subject.'

There was a stunned silence all through the Great Hall. The ex-Prince struggled painfully to his feet. Then suddenly Dr Stockhausen was at the microphone.

'I cannot allow it!' he declared in sharp, ringing tones. 'The constitution of Essenheim does not provide for abdication. The law must be changed before anything like this can happen!'

Rudi grabbed the microphone from him. Dr Stockhausen tried to get it back, and Rudi pushed him away.

'The monarch is absolute!' Rudi proclaimed. 'He can do as he wishes. He *has* done as he wished. I speak to you as your Prince Laureate. I expect and demand your loyalty!'

There was an outbreak of loud excited talk all over the hall. No one seemed to know what to make of events. Dr Stockhausen picked himself up and returned to the attack.

'You are not Prince Laureate!' he told Rudi. 'Not yet!'

Then the bulky form of Colonel Schweiner stepped from the floor to the dais. There was a pistol in his hand. He strode up to Dr Stockhausen, placed the pistol at his head and fired. The explosion, close to the microphone, was deafening. It looked for a moment as though Schweiner had shot the Prime Minister. But Stockhausen didn't fall to the ground. He stepped back a pace, unsteady with shock, and stared unbelievingly into Schweiner's face.

'That,' said Schweiner, 'was a blank. Another time, it would not be a blank. Heinrich von Stockhausen, you are under arrest!'

Soldiers were swarming on to the dais. Two of them seized Stockhausen by the arms. He seemed too startled to resist.

'Colonel Schweiner!' Rudi's voice was loud and indignant. 'What are you doing? I don't require that kind of help from you! It is disgraceful!'

'You too are under arrest, Rudolf Hohenberg!' said Schweiner; and then, into the microphone, 'The army has taken over!'

There were cries of outrage among the royal guests, and a surge towards the dais, but the movement lost impetus when suddenly it was seen that Schweiner's men were everywhere. The entire sixty-strong Essenheim Army appeared to be in the hall, and every man had a gun. On the galleries surrounding the Great Hall were stationed men with machine-guns. One of them, from design or accident, fired a burst into the ceiling.

'Stay where you are!' Schweiner ordered the guests. 'Anyone who moves will be shot.'

More and more soldiers had mounted the dais. Two of Schweiner's men seized Rudi. He struggled, and one of them hit him on the head with the butt of his gun. Rudi slumped to the ground. Two more men dragged a kicking, screaming Anni from the dais. The ex-Prince, the Prime Minister and Prince Friedrich had already been hustled away. And rough arms went round Kate from behind.

'This way, gracious young lady!' said a soldier's voice in her ear. 'You too are under arrest. You are to be taken to your room until further orders from the Colonel!'

A hand was slapped across Kate's mouth. She tried to bite it, but was so tightly held that her lips couldn't move. As she was marched from the dais and away through the double doors she heard shouting from the hall, followed by three or four more single shots and then Schweiner's voice again at the microphone.

'It is no good resisting,' he was telling the assembled guests. 'The party is over. Those of you who wish to leave the room alive will swear loyalty to me and then go quietly to your homes. I, Hermann Schweiner, am the ruler of Essenheim!'

18

For five or ten minutes after the door of Kate's room had closed behind her the shouting continued. There were several more shots, one alarming scream cut off in the middle, and the tramping of a good many feet. And then there was silence, a total silence which soon began to seem uncanny. Kate sat on her bed, shocked and bewildered and unable quite to believe what had happened, though her lips and cheeks still hurt from the pressure of a soldier's hand.

One of the men who brought her there had vanished. The other – the raw recruit who had been given such a hard time on the parade-ground – stood just inside the door, watching her. Her legs felt like water, but after a few minutes, with enormous effort, she got up and made as if to leave the room. The soldier stopped her.

'I'm sorry, gracious young lady,' he said, 'but you aren't allowed to go. It isn't me that says so, it's orders. Colonel's orders.'

'What's happening?' she asked him.

'You heard the Colonel's announcement, gracious young lady. *He* is happening. He has taken power. It was his patriotic duty. He told us so.'

'And was it his patriotic duty to have me locked up?' she demanded indignantly. But the soldier made no reply to that.

Kate crossed to the window. It was too high to jump from, and there was no foothold on the wall below. Even if she hadn't been guarded, there was no escape that way. She picked up the telephone, and the sour voice of Rosy announced with apparent satisfaction, 'No outgoing calls today!'

Kate went back to her bed. She sat for a few minutes, still suffering from shock, then felt she had to do something, whether useful or not. She went into the tiny bathroom, thankful to have this amount of privacy, and changed into everyday clothes. Then she put the radio on. It was playing the usual elderly pop music. She left it on at low volume and sat down once more on the bed. She was now recovering rapidly, and feeling frustrated as much as shocked.

The music on the radio stopped. A rough male voice could be heard in altercation with the announcer. Kate turned up the volume. The male voice, triumphant, said, 'Everybody stay at home. Wait for instructions. The army is in control.' The pop music returned. Two more records were played. Then the voice of Moritz, the presenter she'd met on her visit to the radio station, came through in the usual tones of bright excitement and cheerful salesmanship.

'Essenheimers,' he said, 'it's a great day for the Principality. The former Principality, I should say. Freedom has come to Essenheim. The dead hand of the Hohenberg monarchy has been removed from the people's throats. Colonel Schweiner has taken control. The future of the nation is no longer at risk. Peace and prosperity lie ahead of us. To ease the transition there will be a curfew in Essenheim town until dawn tomorrow. Anyone who goes out will be shot.'

Moritz presented this last piece of information as if it was an amazing bargain offer, not to be missed.

'So stay at home, folks,' he continued, 'and rejoice quietly where you are. Colonel Schweiner will broadcast to you all at nine o'clock this evening. Make a date with Radio Essenheim for nine o'clock, and hear the new leader of the nation!' And he went on to announce another Rolling Stones record.

The young soldier had been listening with her. Kate asked him, 'What about the Prince? And Prince Rudi and Princess

Anni and Prince Friedrich? And Dr Stockhausen? What's happened to them?'

'I don't know, gracious young lady. I don't know any more than you do. I just do as I'm told.'

Kate sat down yet again on the bed. There were still a couple of hours to go before nine o'clock. She reviewed her own position. Surely she herself could not be detained for long ... or could she? What about George? Had he been arrested, too? Even if he was at large, could he get the news out of Essenheim without any help from the telephone exchange?

'Come on, Kate!' she told herself. 'Don't just sit here. Think what you can *do*!' The trouble was that she couldn't think of anything to do except await developments.

Just before eight in the evening, another soldier appeared with food for her. It was a plate piled high with hors d'oeuvres, crackers, peanuts, canapés, cocktail sausages and other leftovers from the reception. Kate hadn't any appetite, but when you didn't know what was going to happen next it seemed a good idea to eat while you could. She finished every scrap.

Shortly before nine, she switched the radio on again. Moritz was delivering a commercial. It all sounded just as usual. But then came the door-chime time-signal, followed by the ponderous semibreves of 'Heaven Help Essenheim'. Moritz announced 'The President of the Revolutionary Council, Saviour of the Nation and Leader of the People of Essenheim, His Excellency, Colonel Hermann Schweiner.'

A pause. And then the pompous, overbearing tone which brought her a sudden, repellent recollection of the man's physical presence.

'Essenheimers,' it began, 'the revolution is complete. I, Hermann Schweiner, have led it to success. I, Hermann Schweiner, promise you that the old, dishonoured régime of the Hohenbergs is at an end. I, Hermann Schweiner, will revive the nation as I have revived the army. Essenheim, though small, will be great.'

And so it went on. The announcement was all about the power and glory of Schweiner. It seemed he had taken over the posts of Prime Minister, Foreign Minister, Minister of Defence and Commander-in-Chief, and had promoted himself to the rank of Field Marshal. At the end of his broadcast, almost as an afterthought, he said that the two Pretenders, Princes Rudi and Friedrich, and the former Prime Minister, Dr Stock-hausen, would be put on trial for crimes against the state. The nature of these crimes was not stated, but Schweiner assured the people of Essenheim that after a fair and impartial trial they would all be found guilty and severely punished. The ex-Prince Laureate would be spared because of his age, and would be flown out to Serenia.

'Essenheimers,' he concluded, 'put your trust in Hermann Schweiner! Accept the new régime! Anyone who fails to do so will face the consequences!'

'That,' said Moritz in the tones of one introducing a unique new product, 'was the leader of our nation, Colonel Hermann Schweiner.'

'Field Marshal!' rapped out the voice of Schweiner.

'Field Marshal Schweiner,' said Moritz hastily. He added, with patriotic fervour, 'Heaven help Essenheim!'

The opening bars of the anthem were repeated. Kate switched the radio off. In another minute she'd have been throwing things at it. Her resentment against Rudi had evaporated and she was white-faced with fury.

'Tried for crimes against the state!' she echoed. 'Oh, Rudi!' She turned on the young soldier who was guarding her.

'What's your name?' she demanded.

'Willi, gracious young lady. Private Willi Braun.'

'Let me out of here, Willi Braun! At once! Let me out, I tell you!' She put all the passion and authority she could into her voice. The young soldier trembled. But he didn't give way.

'Colonel's orders!' he said. 'Field Marshal's orders, I mean.'

Kate felt like kicking or punching him as the only available substitute for the odious Schweiner. But it wasn't his fault, of course. Instead she hurled herself on to the bed and beat with her fists on the pillow. A minute later she found herself sobbing violently, and Willi was trying awkwardly to comfort her while at the same time remaining on guard in case she turned on him.

After half an hour she had sobbed herself into a frustrated silence. Then suddenly the door burst open and Schweiner himself strode in. The young soldier sprang to attention.

'Out!' ordered Schweiner. 'At the double!' Willi went. Schweiner turned to Kate.

'Get up, get up!' he told her.

Kate got to her feet. Schweiner misinterpreted her look of loathing.

'Don't be afraid,' he said. 'I'm not going to eat you.'

'I'm not afraid,' said Kate. 'Where are the people you arrested?'

'The old Prince is in the cells until we fly him out. Rudi, Friedrich and Stockhausen are also in the cells, awaiting trial. Princess Anni like you is confined to her room until I decide what to do with her. But never mind them. I didn't come here to talk about them. They are yesterday's people.'

'And *you* are today's? Heaven help Essenheim!'

Schweiner wagged a finger at her. 'Now, now, gracious young lady. Calm yourself and be respectful. You are talking to the ruler of the country. Everything is under my control. A few stupid people out in the town resisted and had to be shot, but it's all quiet now. The change is irreversible. Firm rule and unquestionable authority is what the people need, and I, Schweiner, will give it them.' Then a smirk came to his face.

'As for *you*, gracious young lady, you may care to know that I have a soft spot for you. It could even be said that I, Hermann Schweiner, *like* you.'

Kate felt the urge to throw his liking straight back in his face, but restrained herself and said, 'Then let my friends go.'

'I am not discussing that,' said Schweiner. 'But gracious young lady, it is more than possible that you yourself have a future in this country.'

'I don't think so,' said Kate.

'Young lady, you are no doubt aware that the former royal family did not propose to treat you honourably.'

At last, Kate was silenced.

'You were not to be Princess. You were to be Prince Rudi's mistress.'

'I never would have been,' said Kate.

'Perhaps not. But that was the intention.'

'The old Prince thought so at first, I believe. But he changed his mind when he got to know me. They both knew I was only here as a visitor.'

'Let me tell you something more, young lady. Unlike those of the former royal family, the intentions of Hermann Schweiner are entirely honourable.'

'What do you mean?' Kate asked, startled.

'I am a widower, gracious young lady. A widower, Kate. I am considering remarriage.'

'That hasn't anything to do with me.'

'It could have,' said Schweiner. He looked at her with a benevolent expression which almost turned her stomach over. 'I am no longer, perhaps, in my first youth. Indeed, I confess that the age of fifty now lies behind me. But I am still a fine figure of a man, in the prime of life!'

'Are you proposing to me?' Kate asked, aghast.

'Not quite. Not yet. Do not jump to conclusions. Do not, as we say in Essenheim, count your eggs while they are still in the chicken. But it is a possibility.'

'Oh no it's not!' said Kate.

Schweiner didn't understand that she was expressing horror at the idea. He seemed to think she couldn't believe her luck.

'In the Essenheim of Hermann Schweiner,' he said, 'all things are possible.'

'Colonel Schweiner,' said Kate. 'I mean, Field Marshal Schweiner. One thing that is *not* possible in Essenheim is to hold foreign subjects prisoner. You must let me go or you'll have to answer to my government.'

'Your government?' Schweiner repeated. He laughed heartily.

'Will your government launch a war against Essenheim? Did the American government go to war with Iran over the hostages? I don't give a squashed grape for your government. You are at my mercy, dear young lady. It's fortunate for you that Hermann Schweiner is a man of shining character.'

His smile again became benevolent. 'Young ladies are sometimes coy,' he said, 'but they usually get some sense into their pretty heads in the end. I shall give you time to grow accustomed to the new situation and to consider the glorious future which may lie ahead of you. But now, for the moment, I must deprive you of my company. We Heads of State are busy people.'

He took Kate's shoulders in his big, hairy-backed hands, and made as if to kiss her. She turned away.

'Very well,' Schweiner said, and added archly, 'It won't always be like that, I'm sure. Good night, dear Kate. Sleep well.'

He called the young soldier back into the room and said as he went out, 'Watch her. She's not tamed ... not yet. Don't give her any chance to escape. If she did, there'd be a dead body in this castle. Yours! Understand?'

'Yes, sir,' said Willi. He was almost too frightened to bring himself to attention.

Kate lay awake for a while but eventually slept by fits and starts. At two in the morning she woke to hear snores from the direction of the door. Willi had fallen asleep, but he was sitting on the floor with his back to the door. It was impossible to get past him without waking him up, and the door was almost certainly locked anyway.

For a long time she couldn't get back to sleep. There didn't seem any way out of her present situation except by persuading Schweiner, which seemed unlikely, or by marrying him, which was unthinkable. She didn't know what had become of George; it hadn't seemed wise to mention him to Schweiner. But even if he was free she couldn't think of anything he could do except get out of Essenheim and publish his story. And if George left Essenheim she would be truly, totally alone.

In the end she slept again. When she woke up she found that the guard had been changed; Willi had gone and there was a dark, scowling young man who didn't answer her greeting. Her breakfast however was fresh coffee and rolls, and later she was brought a decent lunch of cold meat.

Her link with the outside world, such as it was, was the little radio on her dressing-table. Kate didn't know how long its batteries would last, and used it cautiously. The programmes from Radio Essenheim seemed once again deceptively normal. But soon after noon Moritz interrupted himself with a special announcement. In order to pay for Essenheim's coming prosperity, it said, all taxes would be raised by half.

In the afternoon, she thought she heard shots fired outside. She switched the radio on again and heard a news bulletin repeating Field Marshal Schweiner's earlier declarations about coming greatness and quoting him as saying that a little more to pay in taxes was a small price for so rich a reward. Nothing was said of any resistance, and the bulletin was followed by the inevitable succession of pop records.

In the early evening the new guard went off duty and Willi returned. He smiled sheepishly at Kate, but when she asked him what had been happening in the town he couldn't tell her anything: nor did he have any information on the royal prisoners or on whether the ex-Prince had left for Serenia.

'Don't press me, gracious young lady,' he urged her after a while. 'What if the Colonel – I mean the Field Marshal – came along and found me talking to you like this? He'd have my guts for garters.'

Kate had no appetite for her supper, which was a thick Essenheimisch stew. And after supper Schweiner appeared once more and banished the trembling Willi to the far side of the door.

Schweiner seemed to have puffed himself up to even greater and more frog-like proportions. He wore a familiar-looking uniform, covered with medals and insignia of rank. Seeing Kate's eyes on this, he remarked, 'Yes, it's the old Prince's. Too tight in the chest and too slack in the stomach for me, of course; old Ferdy hadn't my figure. But it will do for today, while the tailor makes me a new one.'

'But ... the Prince was wearing it at the reception.'

'Yes. He's in his underpants now. There's nothing like taking away a man's dignity if you want to keep him quiet.'

'That's horrible. And anyway, I thought he was being flown out to Serenia.'

'Perhaps, young lady, perhaps. I'm having second thoughts about that. There have been new developments since last night. One of them was unfortunate.' He frowned. 'Somebody got into the dungeons and let Dr Stockhausen and Prince Friedrich out.'

'I'm glad,' said Kate.

Schweiner ignored her. 'We suspect it was that henchman of Stockhausen's,' he said. 'The tough, fair-haired fellow. Karl. We should have arrested him with the others. Anyway, he and Friedrich and Stockhausen have vanished, and Mrs Stockhausen's disappeared from her home. There's no trace of any of them anywhere.'

'Good for Karl!' said Kate.

'They'll be found, gracious young lady, there's no doubt about that. We're watching the frontiers and searching all the likely places. It's only a matter of time. However, let's not dwell on that minor annoyance. I have far more important news for you, Kate. Prepare to congratulate me. I am to become the father of a princess!'

'You're *what*?' said Kate, staring.

'I am to be the father of a princess. And father-in-law of a prince.'

'But ... how?'

'By marriage, dear Kate. That is the other development since last night. A happy one. Prepare to be surprised. Prince Rudi is to marry my daughter Elsa!'

'You're joking,' said Kate faintly.

'I am not joking. Elsa went to see him in his cell this

156

morning. He proposed to her and she accepted him. Now he has been released. He will not be tried after all. He is to remain Prince Laureate, and the Princess Laureate will be Elsa. Their engagement will be announced on the radio tomorrow and in the *Essenheim Free Press* on Tuesday.'

'You mean,' Kate said incredulously, 'that Rudi has bought his freedom and his title back by agreeing to marry Elsa?'

'I don't like your way of putting it,' said Schweiner, frowning. 'He will get a good and suitable wife. Elsa is a fine girl, fit to bear future princes.'

'And *you* will rule the roost!'

'I shall govern Essenheim,' Schweiner agreed. 'Essenheim needs me. But I have no personal ambition. I am a man of outstanding modesty. I am not taking the title of Prince Laureate for myself. Rudi will keep that, and I may indeed confer a greater title on him in addition. No doubt you have heard of the Holy Roman Empire, founded by Charlemagne and lasting for a thousand years. There has been no Holy Roman Emperor since early last century. The Counts of Luxemburg were once Holy Roman Emperors; why not then the Princes of Essenheim? In due time, my dear Kate, I plan to proclaim my son-in-law Holy Roman Emperor!'

'You're mad!' said Kate, and added to herself in English, 'He's barmy. Bonkers. Bananas. Round the twist!' Then a thought struck her and she asked, 'What about the old Prince and Anni? Aren't they included in the deal?'

'There is no deal,' said Schweiner. 'I would not have done a deal with Rudi over his relatives even if he had asked me. That would have been sordid. Besides, since Rudi has been freed and Stockhausen and Friedrich have escaped, I need someone to put on trial. It may have to be the old Prince.'

'You *have* to put someone on trial?'

'Of course. It is the mark of a new régime. We must expose the villainy of the old one. So you see, Kate, when you ask for Prince Ferdinand to be freed you are asking a great deal. What do you offer in return?'

'Nothing,' said Kate.

'Nothing? In this world one doesn't get anything for nothing.' Schweiner looked knowingly at Kate. 'There is a way in which you can save the old Prince and Princess Anni. And I think you know what it is!'

'Not ... ?'

'Yes. By marrying me!'

Kate said bitterly, 'You told me you were a man of honour!'

'I *am* a man of honour. What Hermann Schweiner does is always honourable. But it is my conduct that determines honour, not honour that determines my conduct. In Essenheim from now on there can be no other standard. Honour and Schweiner are the same thing!'

'You are appalling,' said Kate.

'You would not speak like that if you had fully understood your position,' Schweiner said. 'Very well, I shall not hurry you. You shall have until this time tomorrow to decide.'

He looked at her with an air that was already almost proprietorial.

'Let me put it bluntly, dear Kate. You can secure your own future and the release of your friends by saying "Yes" to Hermann Schweiner. Or you can behave like a child and say "No" to Schweiner. In that case I do not know what would happen to Anni and the Prince, but if I were you I would fear the worst. What's more, I do not know what would happen to *you*. It is even possible' – and here he positively leered at her – 'that Hermann Schweiner will not take "No" for an answer!'

19

Five minutes after Field Marshal Schweiner left the room, there was a tap at the door. Willi stood aside to admit Rudi, now wearing officer's uniform.

'Oh. It's you,' said Kate.

'Don't look so disapproving, dear Kate,' said Rudi. He smiled his most disarming smile. Stunned as she was by his reported conduct, Kate felt once more that treacherous inner melting at the sheer beauty of him.

'I've come to see what I can do for you,' Rudi said.

'You mean your prospective father-in-law sent you?' Kate asked. 'Well, I'll tell you what you can do. You can get me out of here, and your uncle and Anni as well, and you can put us all on a plane for Serenia. And that's *all* you can do for me.'

'Kate,' said Rudi reproachfully, 'you misunderstand me. Sometimes I think you have *always* misunderstood me.'

'I understand,' said Kate, 'that you are going to marry Elsa Schweiner. That's quite enough to have to understand for the moment. And I suppose you're encouraging the unspeakable Schweiner to come and make passes at me.'

Rudi reacted indignantly to the latter remark.

'I didn't put Schweiner up to that,' he said. 'It's all his own idea. He fancies you. I can't help it.'

'Well, I don't want to talk about who fancies whom. Just let me go, Rudi, please. For good.'

'It's not as simple as that. You must try to realize that

Schweiner's in charge, I'm not. The army obeys him, not me.'

'Then why are you playing his game?'

'The Schweiner coup has happened, Kate. It's no good wishing it hadn't. My aim now is to have a restraining influence. There's no telling what he might get up to on his own.'

'So you've done it all for the best, I suppose?'

'Well, yes, actually,' said Rudi. He put on his most appealing look. Kate yearned to believe him, and almost achieved it. But she hardened her heart.

'And you have your reward,' she said. 'The title of Prince Laureate. Also a charming bride. I wish you joy of Elsa Schweiner.'

Rudi winced. 'I hope it won't come to that,' he said. 'I shan't let the wedding day be fixed for very soon, I can assure you. And in the meantime I have other cards to play. I don't really see myself as son-in-law to Schweiner. I don't see you as Schweiner's wife, either.'

'Thank goodness for that.'

'But I think that for the present you should go along with him. Let him believe that if he persists he'll succeed in the end. In short, you must play for time. I know Schweiner. If you reject him, he'll turn nasty, perhaps very nasty. That's my sincere advice, Kate.'

'And what,' asked Kate, 'would be your sincere advice to Elsa Schweiner? And to your dear friend Bettina?'

'Kate, neither Elsa nor Bettina means anything to me at all. I'm involved with them, in different ways, but I feel nothing for them. You're the only one who matters to me. I love you, Kate.'

'Then *let me out*!'

'I've told you, it is beyond my power. If I told this clumsy clot here' – he jerked a contemptuous thumb at Willi, who was standing nervously by – 'to release you, do you think he would? Of course not! He takes his orders from Schweiner!'

'In that case,' said Kate, 'it seems the only thing you can do for me is go away and leave me alone.'

Without another word, Rudi turned and let himself out of the room. Willi placed his back to the door in case Kate showed signs of following. Kate didn't know whether, if Rudi had stayed another few seconds, she'd have hit him or have thrown herself weeping into his arms. As it was, she went to sit once more on the bed and thought hard for a long time.

One of the subjects of her thoughts was Willi. At some stage he had brought a little stool from the bathroom, and he now sat on it just beside the doorway, looking blankly at nothing in particular. She got up and went over to him. As their eyes met, he gave her an uncertain smile.

'What do *you* think of all this, Willi?' she asked him. 'All these goings-on in the castle.'

'I don't think about them, gracious young lady. I'm not paid to think. That's what the Colonel – I mean the Field Marshal – tells us all every day.'

'You let him do the thinking for you?'

'Yes, gracious young lady. Well, he's in command, isn't he? Thinking's his job. We just do as he tells us.'

'And does the army have confidence in him?'

'Oh, *yes*, gracious young lady. Colonel Schweiner is a great man. He says so himself, and he *knows*. He wouldn't have been put in charge of us by the old Prince, would he, if he hadn't been a great man? I mean, Prince Ferdinand, being the father of his people as they say, wouldn't have put any *ordinary* person in that position.'

'But now he's imprisoned the old Prince. What do you make of that?'

'I don't know, young lady. Like I say, it's above my head, that kind of thing. But the Field Marshal knows what he's doing.'

'And the army's not likely to rebel against him?'

Willi looked shocked. 'Oh, *no*, gracious young lady. Certainly not!' He added thoughtfully, 'Though I must say, some of them are a bit disappointed.'

'Oh!' said Kate with interest. 'What about?'

'Well, they'd got it into their heads that when the army took power they'd be allowed into the castle cellars to drink all they wished. There's supposed to be thousands of litres of good Essenheim wine and brandy down there.'

Kate recalled the barrels she'd seen, and could well believe it. 'And what actually happened?' she asked.

'The Field Marshal said they'd misunderstood him. He never intended to let them loose in the cellars. And I must say, considering what some of them are like when they're in drink, I'm not surprised. So the cellars have stayed locked. The Field Marshal says they'll get a bottle each on their next pay day, to drink his health with, and that will be all.'

'O-ho,' said Kate, suddenly recalling the key she'd been asked to give back to the jailer. She'd forgotten all about it, and it was still in her jeans pocket. A thought occurred to her and she changed the subject.

'How do you get on with the others, Willi? I saw the Field Marshal giving you a hard time a few days ago.'

'Well, I'm the new recruit, young lady. And I admit, I'm not all that smart. It takes time for things to sink in with me. So they do make fun of me a bit. They'll accept me in the end, I dare say, but maybe I'll have to wait until I'm a bit older or there's a newer recruit. At least, I've had a bit of luck in getting *this* job, guarding you.'

Willi smiled his tentative smile. 'I expect the Field Marshal knows he can trust me,' he said. 'There's some that he wouldn't care to put in charge of a beautiful young lady.' He blushed. 'Of course,' he went on, 'you wouldn't know what I mean, having been brought up ladylike.'

'I think I might guess,' said Kate.

Willi blushed more deeply. 'For me,' he said earnestly, 'it's a privilege to be here.' Kate was taken aback by the look of devotion in his eyes. She turned away, to spare them both embarrassment. But she didn't feel that the conversation had been a waste of time.

*

Willi fell asleep before Kate. Once again he sat with his back to the door and his snores rasping out like a saw cutting into a tree-trunk. She thought she couldn't possibly go to sleep amid such noise and with so much to think about, and was tempted to make a further effort to get past him, if only to wake him up and get some respite from the snoring. But while she was considering this possibility she herself dozed off, lying fully clothed on the bed.

She was awakened by a touch on the cheek, and shot up in alarm to a sitting position. Somebody was stooping over her. In the dark she couldn't see who it was, but a voice spoke to her in a barely audible whisper, 'Kate! It's Anni!'

'Anni!' Kate's whisper was equally soft, and full of wonder.

'Is there a guard in the room, Kate?'

'Yes,' whispered Kate.

'Come with me. Quiet! Can you see?'

'Not much.'

'You'll get used to it. Ssssh!'

Willi stirred, and his snoring altered its note. Both girls stood still and silent for a minute. Then Anni took Kate's hand and led her to the wardrobe in the corner of the room. Kate's eyes were getting accustomed to the dark. She could just see Anni burrowing soundlessly among hanging clothes. Anni disappeared briefly from view; then a hand reached out from between two dresses and drew Kate after it. She realized she was being led into a passage, probably the one along which Anni had taken her to watch the guests arriving for the reception.

Anni left Kate for a moment while she closed the wardrobe door and presumably a panel in the back of it, then shone a flashlight to show the way. After a few yards the passage ceased to be pitch-black; moonlight was coming in through a tiny slit window. Anni doused the light and shone it again when they were past the opening. They picked their way over rubble which lay in the narrow passageway. Anni switched off the light again at the next window and at the one after that; and then they heard ahead of them the sound of voices raised in altercation.

'Oh, the fools, the fools!' hissed Anni. She quickened her pace and positively ran along the dark narrow passage. Kate followed as best she could. The passage opened into a tiny narrow chamber, set no doubt in one of the many mysterious recesses of the castle. A similar passage led out of the chamber at the other end.

'Be quiet!' Anni commanded the occupants. Kate had thought she recognized the voices, and she was right. They were those of George and Sonia. Sonia was telling George in no uncertain terms that his duty was to combat oppression, which in the present circumstances meant fighting Schweiner. George was telling Sonia with equal conviction that it was a journalist's job to report the news, not to make it. But when Kate stumbled into the chamber, he broke off in mid-sentence, hurried across and took her in his arms.

'Oh, Kate, Kate!' he said. 'Oh, am I glad to see you!'

He kissed her on the lips, again and again. It was startling, as George hadn't ventured any such intimacy before. But it was quite enjoyable, and the relief of being with George was tremendous. She found herself kissing him back, in a friendly way.

'I too was locked in my room,' Anni explained, 'but for me it was easy to get out of the castle and into town. It is a little perilous, Kate, as you may soon discover, but I've been doing it since I was a child. Then I went in search of your friends, and here they are. Not the poet – I couldn't find him; but I think it is not the services of a poet you need just now.'

'This is a time for revolutionaries, not for poets!' Sonia declared, her voice rising excitedly.

'Quiet, quiet!' Anni repeated; and then, 'It is for Kate and George to decide, but it seems to me they should leave Essenheim.'

George said, 'Kate, I'm going to get you out of here. And we must go at once. This minute. They might find any moment that you're missing.'

Anni said, 'That's right. And you must be in Serenia by dawn. Do you still have the rented car, George?'

'Yes, it's at Frau Schmidt's.'

'It will take you fifteen minutes to get there, and you'll have to evade the guards on the bridge. And you mustn't take the main road to Serenia along the river bank. You'd be caught at the frontier post if not before.' Anni paused and considered. 'There are lesser roads, and I know of one – not much more than a track – which crosses the frontier at an unguarded point. But whether you could find it is a different question.' Then she smiled brilliantly and added, 'Unless I come with you!'

'You!'

'Why not? What is there for me in Essenheim? I don't want to be a princess, I just want to be a teenager before it's too late. I can find Uncle Ferdy in Serenia and get some money. Then off to London to join my friend Betsy!'

'Anni,' said Kate, 'didn't anyone tell you? The old Prince isn't in Serenia. Schweiner changed his mind. He's still held in the castle!'

Anni exclaimed fiercely in Essenheimisch. Sonia said, 'Anyway, you would go off and leave the fascist pig Schweiner in control? That is truly royal, to run away! We must have another revolution and throw the bastard out!'

'Oh, yes?' said Anni. 'A revolution led by whom?' And then, 'Kate, I didn't know they still had Uncle Ferdy. I can't escape and leave him behind.' Suddenly her self-possession seemed to be crumbling, and she spoke to Kate as if appealing to an older sister: 'Kate, what shall we do?'

'*I* can't go and leave your uncle a prisoner, either!' said Kate firmly.

George said, 'Kate, *you* must but *I* can't. I'll see you to the frontier and give you a story you can phone through to the paper from Serenia. But as for me, I shall come back here to Essenheim. You can tell your father I'm following up the story. Remember, I'm a newspaperman, and that's what I'm paid to do.'

Kate said, 'George, you can understand plain English. I am not, repeat not, leaving Essenheim until Prince Ferdinand is free!'

George said, 'That's ridiculous. I'm telling you you must go!'

Kate said, 'Who do you think you are to tell me things? Just because you're male, you think you're the boss. Well, you're not!'

George said, 'I promised your father I'd look after you. He'll be tearing his hair by now.'

Kate said, 'No, he won't. He knows I can look after myself. And he doesn't get ruffled about *anything* except trouble with the plumbing.'

George said, 'You can't do anything to help the old Prince here. The best thing is for you and Anni to get away, and for the world to hear about Prince Ferdinand's imprisonment.'

'Nothing doing!' said Kate decisively. And Anni reached out for Kate's hand, as if for that of an older sister. 'I stay too,' she said.

'There you are, you feeble male bourgeois Press lackey!' said Sonia scornfully to George. 'As always, the women have the guts, the so-called man is a flinching coward!'

'What do you propose, Sonia?' George inquired mildly.

'We will overthrow Pig Schweiner, of course! Then the royals can leave Essenheim, and good riddance! It is simple!'

'And who is going to defeat Schweiner's soldiers?'

'The students, of course!' said Sonia. 'What are students for? It will be their hour of glory. They will serve the people at last!'

'The soldiers have guns,' said George. 'What do the students have?'

'They have their schlagfuss sticks and their courage.'

'I'm afraid,' said George, 'that schlagfuss sticks and courage don't give much protection against bullets. You're not realistic, Sonia. If the soldiers are loyal to Schweiner, there's no way they can be overthrown.'

'I wonder,' said Kate. 'Listen to me. I've just had an idea.'

'It's a mad scheme!' said George ten minutes later. 'And it means putting your head in the lion's mouth. I can't let you be such a fool, Kate.'

'You can't stop me,' said Kate.

'That's right,' said Sonia. 'We women stick together. We are sisters. We are invincible!'

'Well, *I'm* not having anything to do with it!' said George.

'You don't have to, George,' said Kate. 'But you can get back to your car and run Sonia up to the university.'

'I said I wouldn't have *anything* to do with it.'

Kate said sweetly, 'Remember what you said about following up the story? That's all I'm suggesting you should do. You're going to be on the spot when things start happening.'

George sighed deeply. 'All right,' he said. 'Some fathers have dreadful daughters. I shall tell Edward so when I see him, if I ever do. Anyway, Kate, when your crack-brained plan fails, let's hope you get another chance to escape this way. I'll still be in Essenheim, waiting for you. I won't let you down.'

'I know you won't,' said Kate. This time it was she who put her arms around George. A minute later he went off with Sonia along the other passage, and she followed Anni back the way she'd come. She had a dreadful feeling that George was right in calling her plan crack-brained. 'Heaven help Essenheim!' she said to herself. 'Heaven help us all!'

20

'Good morning, Willi!' said Kate.

The guard rubbed his eyes. 'Good morning, gracious young lady,' he said.

'Sorry to disturb you, Willi, but I thought it was time you were awake. The other guard will be coming to relieve you soon, won't he?'

'Yes. Thank you very much, gracious young lady. Ludwig would probably have reported me for sleeping on duty.'

The look of devotion was on Willi's face again. A minute later he said, 'You know, it's very strange, gracious young lady, but I had a dream last night that you'd escaped. Oh, I was in such a panic in my dream. It's surprising I didn't wake up!'

'I'm glad you didn't,' said Kate truthfully.

The other guard came in with Kate's breakfast. He scowled at her and jerked a thumb at Willi. 'Off you go, rookie!' he said. 'Don't fall over yourself!'

The day dragged on. It was hot and seemed extremely long. Kate managed to doze a little after lunch. She was awakened by sounds of drilling outside her window. In spite of his successive promotions to Colonel and Field Marshal, there was obviously still a great deal of the Top Sergeant in Hermann Schweiner. He was exercising his men at the double. In the sweltering heat, the sweat poured from their faces. It seemed they were being given a harder time than ever.

'They'll be thirsty after that!' Kate said to Ludwig. He hadn't stirred from his post at the door, but he couldn't have helped hearing Schweiner's barked commands.

'They're not the only ones,' he grunted. 'It's thirsty weather.'

'Would you like a drink of water?'

'I'm not thirsty for water.'

'There's nothing else in here,' Kate said. The guard grunted once more. Sounds of drilling continued for some time to float in from outside. But eventually it seemed that even Schweiner had had enough, and she heard the men being dismissed. The long afternoon dragged on. Kate dozed a little more. Then at six o'clock Willi reappeared, carrying her supper on a tray. Ludwig went out without a word to either of them.

Kate ate her meal, though rising excitement and apprehension had affected her stomach and she didn't really feel like it.

'You weren't out drilling, then, Willi?' she asked.

'No, young lady. This is my duty at present. When I'm not in here, I'm supposed to be having my sleeping time.'

'You must need a lot of sleep, Willi,' Kate remarked.

Willi blushed. 'Well, I admit I did get forty winks last night,' he said. 'I'm glad I wasn't out in the heat today. The Field Marshal really did put them through it. They were all a bit fed up when they came in. And they weren't any nicer to me for having escaped it, I can tell you!'

'Would you like to make yourself more popular?' Kate asked.

'Course I would, gracious young lady. But how?'

'Well . . .' said Kate. She went to the wardrobe, took out her jeans and felt in the pocket. The key was still there.

Willi's eyes, round and wide, followed it as she brought it across the room. 'What is it, gracious young lady?'

'It's a key to the basement. To the wine-cellars.'

Willi gasped. 'Fancy you having that! The Field Marshal told the jailer not to let anyone go down there. There's been talk among some of the wilder ones of breaking the door down, but they won't do it. Schweiner would court-martial them and have them jailed for years!'

'What if I gave you this key, Willi? Then you could let them into the cellars. That would make you popular, wouldn't it? They'd think differently of you then.'

'Gracious young lady!' For a moment Willi's eyes shone. Then his face clouded over. 'I wouldn't dare!' he said. 'They'd all get as drunk as lords and the Field Marshal would be furious and the truth would all come out. And I don't know *what* he'd do to me then!'

Willi shuddered at the thought. Kate was dismayed. She'd persuaded herself that he would accept the key with alacrity. Her plan depended on it. It looked as though she'd failed. Then the door burst open and the other guard came in.

'You, rookie!' he said. 'I'm taking over for a while. The lads want to see you in the barrack-room!'

'W-what for?' stammered Willi, alarmed.

'You'll soon see! They felt sorry for you, missing this afternoon's drill. Thought you ought to have something to compensate!' There was a malicious grin on Ludwig's sour, swarthy face.

'B-but . . . the Field Marshal himself told me not to report for drill today. Because of being night guard for the gracious young lady.'

'Or so as not to mess it all up by falling over yourself, more likely,' said Ludwig. 'Your pals think you really need that drill, Willi. So they're going to give you a bit extra in the barrack-room. That'll be nice for you. A pity I have to miss it. I'm going to relieve you for the time being. Aren't you grateful to me?'

'Are they going to beat Willi up?' Kate asked in alarm.

'No. Just a bit of fun.'

It didn't seem from Willi's expression that he expected it to be fun for him. 'I'm on duty, Ludwig,' he said. 'I can't go without permission.'

'Oh yes you can!' said Ludwig. 'And the Field Marshal wouldn't mind if he did know. Come in, fellows!'

Two other grinning soldiers appeared. They seized the protesting Willi by the arms. Kate saw her chance. She began gently tossing the key from hand to hand.

'What's that?' Ludwig demanded.

'Wouldn't you like to know?'

'It looks like a castle key to me. You've no business having keys. Where is it for?'

'I'm not telling.'

The other two men, still holding Willi's arms, halted and watched with interest. Ludwig said, 'You'll tell me what that key is for. And hand it over!'

Kate said with pretended reluctance, 'I won't.'

Ludwig made a grab for the key. Kate held it out of his reach.

'You can't have it,' she said. 'It's the key to the cellars. I'm keeping it until I can give it back to Maxi.'

Ludwig made another grab, and this time got possession.

'You heard?' said one of the other men. 'The cellar key! Do you think it really is?'

'We'll soon find out!' said Ludwig. 'Let that fool go, and come on!'

A moment later, Kate and Willi were once more alone in the room. Willi looked apprehensive. 'If our chaps get at the drink . . .' he said.

'Yes, Willi? What?'

'Well, there's no telling, gracious young lady, there really isn't.'

'It's not your fault, is it, Willi?' Kate said. 'You've had nothing to do with it.' She looked at her watch, wondering if time was on her side. 'Do they drink fast, Willi?'

'If the drink's free,' said Willi, 'it'll go down faster than your eye could follow.'

Silence fell between them as they contemplated, from different viewpoints, the likely consequences. After an hour or so, Kate began to listen out, hoping to hear sounds of roistering; but that was too much to hope for. All remained quiet. And at eight o'clock promptly, Field Marshal Schweiner entered the room. He was resplendent in a magnificent new purple uniform, the chest of which was largely hidden by medal ribbons.

As before, Schweiner dismissed Willi brusquely, telling him

to wait outside. Then he turned to Kate with his ingratiating smirk.

'Well, young lady?' he said. 'Well, Kate? Have you now thought about your future prospects?'

'I've thought about nothing else,' said Kate.

'And have you arrived at a conclusion?'

'Not quite.'

'Not quite?' Schweiner seemed surprised. 'I don't understand you. How can you still hesitate?'

At home in Hammersmith, Kate and Edward often engaged in conversational duels: games of verbal skill. Kate now began the subtlest and toughest such game she had ever taken part in. Her task was to resist Schweiner yet at the same time convince him that victory was at hand if he went on trying. And she had to keep him trying for as long as possible. She brought facial expression to her aid, and combined coy reluctance with a good deal of come-hither.

After some twenty minutes, Schweiner put an arm round her waist. Kate managed not to recoil.

'Oh, Field Marshal, you shouldn't!' she protested, giving him a sideways glance from under lowered eyelids which strongly hinted that he should. Schweiner, encouraged, went on at some length on the subjects of his own desirability as a husband and the further glories which he intended to achieve as father-in-law of the Prince of Essenheim and Holy Roman Emperor. This took his mind from the immediate pursuit of Kate, and for a while he made no more advances. Then, returning to the business in hand, he leaned towards her and planted a slobbery kiss on her cheek.

'Field Marshal! How dare you?' Kate cried with easily simulated indignation. She wondered if she could give herself the pleasure of slapping his face, but decided that was more than she could get away with.

'Kate! Dear Kate! Let me assure you once more that my intentions are wholly honourable. Accept me and you shall be the wife – the lawful wife – of Schweiner. Of Hermann Schweiner himself!'

This prospect didn't appeal to Kate any more now than it had done in the past. She steeled herself to keep the game going. Eventually Schweiner, with both arms clamped around her, was kissing such parts of her face and neck as he could get at, while with some difficulty she kept her mouth away from him. The smell of his breath – garlic sausage, at a guess – assisted her in this endeavour.

'Dearest Kate, say yes to me!' Schweiner urged, in a hoarse rasp which was the nearest he could get to an amorous whisper.

Kate disengaged herself. 'Give me just one more minute!' she begged. 'It is so important a step, I must try to think coolly.'

'Of course, my sweet. I won't take advantage of the ardour that my embraces must have kindled in you. By all means think coolly. But please, Kate, think quickly as well. I have many duties and cannot stay much longer.'

Kate went to the window, moving slowly and absent-mindedly as if deep in thought. And when she looked out her heart leaped up and it was all she could do not to cheer. A posse of students was proceeding in a straggling column up the narrow service road that led to the castle's side entrance. It was led by Klaus Klappdorf and Sonia, marching side by side. Many of the students were waving schlagfuss sticks; most of the rest had home-made weapons of one kind or another. Nobody seemed to be impeding their approach. And, thank goodness, somebody must have impressed on them the need for silence. They weren't making a sound.

At that moment however sounds began to be heard. They were from inside the castle, not outside. Loud, drunken voices, laughter, a crash of something being broken. Schweiner, whose eyes had been fixed on Kate in fond reverie, snapped rapidly out of it. He jumped to his feet and took four or five paces towards the door.

Kate thought fast. There might still be time for him to rally his men. She rushed to intercept him and flung her arms round his thick red neck.

'Field Marshal!' she cried. 'Hermann! My Hermann!'

That stopped him. Her face was inches from his and her bosom pressed against his medal ribbons. He would have had to throw her out of the way to make any progress. And anyway he was obviously overcome with delight.

'Kate! Kate, darling!' he said. 'So it is yes?'

From somewhere beyond the door, voices could be heard raised in furious argument. Schweiner made as if to move, but Kate clung tightly to him.

'Hermann!' she breathed. 'How could I resist?'

Her eyes gazed into his bloodshot ones. 'How could you indeed, my dear one?' he said. 'How could *any* girl resist Hermann Schweiner?' And then there was another, much louder crash, followed by a burst of cheering. Schweiner broke determinedly from Kate. 'I'm sorry, dearest,' he said. 'I must find out what's going on.'

Before he could reach the door, it burst open in his face. The two soldiers who had earlier been with Ludwig reeled into the room. Both were carrying bottles. Schweiner recoiled a step. They were too drunk to be afraid of him.

'Have a drink, shargeant!' said one, waving his bottle and spilling wine down Schweiner's immaculate new uniform.

'He'sh not a shargeant now, he'sh a field marshal!' the other pointed out.

'It doeshn't make any difference! He'sh shtill good ol' Shargeant Schweiner! Drink, Shargeant, drink! And you too, gracioush young lady!'

Willi peered in from the doorway, terrified. From beyond him, more raised, raucous voices could be heard. Schweiner, outraged, roared a fierce Essenheimisch oath and buffeted each of the two drunken men in turn. One of them fell straight to the floor; the other staggered in a circle and fell on top of him. Schweiner kicked them both.

Then other sounds were heard: shots, a different kind of shouting, a rush of feet. Schweiner, startled, stepped over the fallen men and towards the door. There were more shots, more shouting, a bellow of pain.

Before Schweiner had reached the door, someone pushed Willi roughly out of the way, strode into the room, and confronted Schweiner face to face. Somebody in uniform. Somebody tall, lean and handsome. Somebody sober. Rudi.

Schweiner dived for his gunbelt, which he'd taken off and laid on Kate's bed. Rudi got to it before him. Schweiner threw himself at Rudi, tripped over one of the fallen soldiers and staggered. Rudi caught him off balance and sent him crashing to the ground on his back in a corner of the room. As he struggled to get up, Rudi drew his own revolver and pointed it at him.

'Hermann Schweiner, you are under arrest!' he declared.

Schweiner rose ponderously to his feet. Rudi said quietly, 'Make one more move and you're a dead man.'

Other people were filtering into the room: Klaus Klappdorf, Sonia, three or four students, and a pace or two behind them George, who seemed not merely to have followed the story but to have caught up with it.

Rudi yelled, 'Maxi! Maxi! Where's Maxi?' The shout was taken up in the doorway and echoed along the corridor outside: 'Maxi! Maxi!' Schweiner half stood, half crouched in a corner of the room, breathing hard, still with Rudi's gun on him. More people crowded into the doorway, including Anni, peering over people's shoulders as she tried to see what was going on. Then the jailer appeared, pushing his way between them and carrying handcuffs. But he could hardly bring himself to go within arm's length of Schweiner.

Rudi, speaking quietly again, said, 'Schweiner, put your wrists together in front of you.' Gingerly, Maxi put the handcuffs on him. And Schweiner seemed to be deflated by this action to two thirds of his former size.

'Take him to the cells,' Rudi said. A little knot of students bundled Schweiner away; others dragged the two drunken soldiers from the room.

'Well, that's that,' said Klaus with satisfaction. 'It's all over bar the shouting. Our lads took the soldiers by surprise and they were too drunk to resist. Only a few shots fired, and nobody hurt that I know of.'

The crowd in the room had thinned out. Rudi went over to Kate and stood in front of her, smiling. He put his hands on her shoulders and made as if to kiss her.

'Rudi!' she said faintly. 'I thought you'd gone over to Schweiner!'

'I was never Schweiner's man,' said Rudi coolly. 'That was pretence. The students, led by my friend Klaus here, came straight to me for support, and I gave it them instantly.'

Kate was silent, baffled. She was full of admiration for Rudi's handling of Schweiner in the past few minutes. Yet she couldn't help remembering that the plan which had toppled the would-be dictator had been devised by her, in association with Anni and Sonia. If it hadn't been for that plan, would Rudi still have been backing Schweiner and intending to marry his daughter?

It was impossible to tell. As so often, Rudi's motives were obscure to her. But he did seem to have a talent for emerging on the winning side.

Five minutes later she wasn't so sure on this last point.

'Now,' said Klaus Klappdorf, 'we'll adjourn to the Prime Minister's office to decide what happens next.'

'Is that necessary?' Rudi asked lightly. 'We've restored the position, except that Dr Stockhausen is still missing, and *that* isn't any great loss. As Prince Laureate I must find a new Prime Minister, of course, but at this time on a Saturday night there isn't any hurry. Monday morning will be soon enough.'

'Restored the position?' said Sonia coldly. 'Prince Laureate? Who says there is to be a Prince Laureate?'

Rudi looked from her to Klaus. Klaus was apologetic.

'Well, Rudi,' he said in a conciliatory tone, 'the old Prince has gone, Stockhausen's gone and Schweiner has gone. It does look rather as though it's time for a new start.'

'I'm giving you a new start,' said Rudi with a touch of impatience. 'That's been my intention all along. Don't worry about it, just leave it to me.'

There was a brief silence, broken only by distant cheers and shouting from the direction of the dungeons.

'I don't think you quite understand, Rudi,' said Klaus. 'The students are in control. Sonia and I brought them here from the university. They expect a lead from *us*.'

'They will do as *we* tell them,' Sonia added. 'Yours is one voice among many. Think yourself fortunate if we listen to you at all!'

For a moment there was anger in Rudi's face. Then Kate, watching attentively, could see it being brought under control.

'Very well,' he said. 'I will meet you, and any students who wish to come, in Dr Stockhausen's office in half an hour's time. I shall be happy to thank them all for their assistance in getting rid of the Schweiner régime.'

'Assistance?' said Sonia. 'Assistance to *you*? You are living in a vanished world. Let us not talk of assistance to self-styled princes. This is the revolution!'

21

Dusk in Essenheim; lights going on in the castle. In the big comfortable office that had once been Dr Stockhausen's, Sonia was taking charge of the meeting. She sat on the former Premier's desk while students squatted around her on the floor.

Kate, George and Anni, none of whom had been specifically invited, sat discreetly and unobtrusively at the back. Sounds of roistering still floated up from below. It appeared that most of the soldiery, helplessly drunk, had been driven by students with schlagfuss sticks to the dungeons, though a few had managed to discard their army jackets and join their conquerors. Now the schlagfuss players in turn were helping themselves to the contents of the castle cellars.

'They'll be as drunk as the soldiers before long,' Klaus had remarked with contempt a little earlier. 'Never mind, it keeps them occupied. They're the sporty lot. Drinking and schlagfuss are all they're fit for. The serious students will come to the meeting.'

But now Klaus had disappeared from the scene. There was no sign of Rudi, either. Sonia looked with irritation two or three times at her watch, then called the meeting to order, ready to begin without them. At the last moment, however, Klaus and Rudi reappeared together, both smiling. Rudi had changed from his army officer's uniform to a T-shirt and patched jeans. He and Klaus went straight to the front and took a chair at each side of Sonia. She glared at them, then opened the proceedings.

'Fellow-members of the proletariat!' she began. 'The people have come to power in Essenheim. I propose that we now establish a revolutionary government.'

'Seconded,' said Rudi cheerfully.

Sonia stared. '*You!*' she said. 'Seconding *this*? What sort of revolutionary are *you*?'

'I have resigned my princedom. I am Rudolf Hohenberg, ordinary citizen and man of the people.'

'I do not accept you as one of us,' said Sonia.

Klaus intervened. 'Mr Hohenberg has the same rights as any other citizen,' he contended. 'That's so, isn't it, friends?'

Many of the students seemed disposed to accept Klaus's view. There were shouts of 'Yes! Yes!' and one or two of 'Rudi! Rudi!'

Sonia looked black but made no further objection. 'Very well. Does anyone oppose my resolution?' she asked.

Nobody did. It was carried with acclaim.

'Next we need a title for the régime!' said Sonia.

'The People's Republic of Essenheim,' Rudi suggested promptly.

This too was unanimously approved.

'Now,' Sonia continued, 'we require a President. Would anyone like to submit a nomination?'

She looked expectantly round the gathering. Somebody obligingly said, 'I would like to nominate Sonia.'

'Are there any other nominations?' Sonia asked; and then, very rapidly, 'No? In that case I reluctantly accept ...'

But she wasn't quite quick enough. Klaus said, 'I nominate Rudi Hohenberg.'

'That nomination is out of order!' said Sonia.

'Oh no it's not!' said Klaus. He signalled to his supporters among the students and they began a chant, 'Rudi! Rudi! Rudi!' It continued for some time. A group of Sonia's supporters set up a rival chant, 'Sonia! Sonia! Sonia!' The parties seemed evenly divided.

There was obviously not going to be any reasoned discussion.

When there was a lull in the chanting, Sonia called, 'We will take a vote!'

There was a show of hands. Sonia declared herself to have been elected. Cheers from her supporters and boos from those of Klaus were halted when Klaus claimed in a loud voice that there had been a miscount and the vote had gone in favour of Rudi. Now there were cheers from his side and boos from Sonia's.

A recount was demanded, and was proclaimed by a Sonia supporter to have resulted in an increased majority for her, and by a Klaus supporter to have produced an increased majority for Rudi. There appeared to be total deadlock. Both sides cheered and booed at random. Then a little band of schlagfuss players erupted into the room, waving their sticks and shouting, 'Klaus! Klaus! Come and drink with us! Now!'

An appeal from Klaus put them instantly on his side. The Sonia party looked apprehensively at the brandished schlagfuss sticks and gave way without further argument. Rudi Hohenberg was President of the People's Republic of Essenheim.

During the next half-hour a succession of Ministries was distributed. By way of conciliating Sonia, Klaus proposed her as Prime Minister, and she was elected unopposed. Klaus himself was appointed Minister of Defence, in which capacity he dismissed his little band of schlagfuss players back to the cellars with the grateful thanks of their country. Werner, the black-bearded student, became Minister of Information and was dispatched to the radio station to see that Moritz read out a suitable bulletin.

Eva, the girl with long blonde hair who'd been with Werner at the university gate, became Minister of Finance. She seemed unsure about her duties.

'What does a Minister of Finance *do*?' she inquired.

'Collect the taxes,' Klaus told her.

Eva pouted. 'I'd rather have something that made me popular,' she said. 'Nobody likes paying taxes. You should hear what my father says about it.'

'Abolish them,' suggested somebody from the floor.

Eva's face brightened. 'That's a good idea,' she said. '*Then* I'll be popular.'

Sonia remarked sourly, 'Somebody's got to pay the castle staff and the street cleaners and policemen and so on. How will you do that if you abolish taxes?'

Eva looked thoughtful for a minute. Then she asked, 'Who prints the banknotes here?'

'Herr Beyer, of course, at the *Free Press* office.'

'Well, then, there isn't any problem, is there? We'll send somebody along to tell him to print lots more. Then we can pay everyone without *needing* any taxes.'

'Isn't there a fallacy there?' asked one of the students uncertainly. But nobody else seemed to share his view. There was general approval.

Eva said delightedly, 'I can't think why they didn't do that before. High finance is *easy*, isn't it?'

Aleksi was appointed Minister of Culture, in which capacity he announced his intention to produce a revised version of 'The Red Flag', taking into account the fact that the flag of Essenheim was purple. This project, combining revolution with national feeling, was warmly welcomed. But by now several of the students, especially those who hadn't received Cabinet appointments, were beginning to fidget and look restless, as if they felt they could be better occupied elsewhere. And a minute or two later Rudi said, 'Well, we now have a full Cabinet, probably the most democratically elected there has ever been. I propose that this meeting should adjourn and that the Cabinet itself should meet here at nine o'clock tomorrow morning.'

Everyone applauded this proposal, which was carried unanimously.

'High time too,' remarked a student just in front of Kate. 'Now we can *all* go down to the cellars. Why should the schlagfuss thugs have all the fun?' They trooped out with alacrity. Sounds of revelry, ever louder, were floating up from the dungeons.

Rudi stayed behind for a brief conversation with Klaus and Sonia. George attempted to use the Prime Minister's telephone, but pulled a face and came over to Kate muttering, 'Still no outward calls.' Then he, Kate and Rudi headed towards the private apartments.

'Well, Mr President,' said George in a faintly ironic tone, 'are you satisfied with tonight's proceedings?'

'Oh, it was all a lot of nonsense,' said Rudi cheerfully. 'If I were you, George, I wouldn't be in any hurry to get my story through to London.'

'What do you mean?'

'Well, they're only playing at being a government. It can't last, you know. We need a proper régime that can take charge and that really means business.'

'And how is that going to come about?'

'You'll have to wait and see, George, won't you?'

'What about freeing your uncle, Rudi?' asked Kate.

'I'll see about that tomorrow. We can't release the poor old boy into all the turmoil there is down there at present. And now, Kate, here we are at your room. I suggest you lock your door on the inside, just in case of intrusive drunks, and go peacefully to sleep. I have a little business to do outside the castle.'

'And I'd better go back to Frau Schmidt's,' said George, 'or she'll be locking me out.'

Kate was left on her own. She didn't think she'd be able to sleep. She switched on the radio. Moritz was explaining in tones of happy excitement that it was another great day in the history of Essenheim, the first day of the People's Republic; also that Quick 'n' Safe Sure-Fire Superstar Elixir would cure everybody's ailments and that you could buy a good used car very cheaply at Willi Bamberger's lot, just behind the Town Hall. And then it was pop records again. Kate switched off, and the exertions of the past twenty-four hours had their effect on her. In spite of her forebodings she was soon fast asleep.

*

When Kate woke, it was almost nine in the morning, and the private apartments of Essenheim Castle were an empty world. The doors of Prince Ferdinand's, Rudi's and Anni's rooms were all open, and the beds had not been slept in. No staff were to be seen; no table was laid in breakfast-room or dining-room.

Leaving the private rooms, she wandered through the Great Hall and found twenty or thirty students asleep, fully dressed, on the floor. Some were snoring, some twisting and turning restlessly, some simply flat out. Clearly it was the morning after the night before. In the castle kitchens there were again no staff, but a handful of students, most of them only half awake, were foraging for whatever they could find. Someone had succeeded in making coffee, and without a word or smile pushed a cup across to Kate. A reek of alcohol floated in from the cellars, but there wasn't a sound. Probably there were people sleeping down there as well. Kate didn't feel like exploring. She did however want desperately to find Rudi and secure the old Prince's release and a flight out of the country.

Recalling the Cabinet meeting, now due to start, she pulled herself together and set off briskly for the Prime Minister's office in the other wing. Here surely she'd be able to get hold of Rudi. And here she found people up and alert, and Sonia once more looking in irritation at her watch. Klaus was there, and most of the members of the Cabinet elected last night, but Rudi hadn't arrived. Klaus and Sonia were obviously anxious to get the proceedings started and became increasingly impatient with Rudi.

Twenty minutes passed. Sonia said crossly, 'I knew all along he was a playboy. Rudi Hohenberg, man of the people, indeed! He is still the effete aristocrat. Probably he is waiting for someone to take him his breakfast in bed. We will start without him.'

She took her seat on Dr Stockhausen's desk and rapped on it for silence. Conversation died down. And at that moment there was the sound of heavy, regular footsteps. The door of the Prime Minister's office flew open. Two big solid men with very short hair, wearing clean and pressed blue-grey uniforms and with guns at their hips, strode into the room.

'I thought so! There's more of them in here!' said one to the other; and then, in a peremptory tone, 'Come on, out of it! This way!'

'This is a Cabinet meeting,' said Sonia with dignity. 'It is strictly private. Please leave the room at once, whoever you are.'

The men didn't trouble to reply. Roughly they herded everyone together, shoving or cuffing those who didn't move fast enough, and forced them out through the door. Kate found herself being bundled along with a bunch of people that included Klaus, Aleksi, Sonia and nine or ten students.

They were driven through the Great Hall, from which the sleeping students had now been cleared away, and down the stone steps into the reeking dungeons, then along one of the passages Kate had traversed when she was there before. She tried to speak to one of the men but he took no notice of her and continued urging the little group along. Cell after cell after cell was now occupied, and from some of them people were shouting. At length they came to a run of empty cells into which they were thrust, one at a time, with contemptuous indifference. Kate's door was slammed and locked, and the captors walked away. She was imprisoned in the dungeons of Essenheim.

22

It was the worst and longest day of Kate's life. She didn't know who her captors were, and there was no one she could ask. From somewhere along the line she heard from time to time the voice of Sonia yelling imprecations, among which the words 'fascist' and 'pig' could be distinguished, but this told her little; in Sonia's vocabulary it might have meant anybody. Occasionally a uniformed man, gun in holster, would stride along the passage, his progress marked by a wave of appeals and complaints from cell after cell as he went by; but no such guard ever stopped or said a word.

Around midday, a trolley was pushed along the line, and Kate in common with other prisoners received a bowl of greasy and gristly stew, which she could not touch. The man who gave it to her ignored her attempts to question him. In mid-afternoon she was given a basin – identical to the stew basin – for the relief of bodily needs, and to her intense disgust had to use it. It remained unemptied in her cell until the arrival in early evening of a second bowl of stew. This, repulsive as it was, she ate.

She didn't cry, though she could have done. She kept despair at bay by telling herself a hundred times that this imprisonment couldn't last long. And she was right. Towards nightfall – though nightfall in itself meant nothing, for the only light she had seen all day was that of a feeble electric bulb – she heard two sets of heavy, echoing footsteps approaching along the passage. The cell door was flung open. A guard with insignia of rank on his shoulder strode in, followed by the lesser one who had brought Kate her meals.

'You are the girl from London?' he inquired brusquely.

'Yes,' said Kate.

'You are to be released. Follow me.'

'But ... who *are* you?'

'That is not your concern.'

'I mean, what's your organization? Who imprisoned me? Who says I'm to be let out?'

'I am head of the Finkel Industries Security Service. The order for your release comes from Herr Finkel himself. That is all I know. This way, please.'

Kate was taken back to her own room.

'You are free within the castle,' the guard said. 'But you are requested by Herr Finkel to remain here until morning, when you will receive further instructions.' He added grimly, 'I advise you to do as Herr Finkel requests.'

Once more Kate was left alone. She had hardly had time to look around when the telephone rang. The voice was Rudi's.

'Kate!' he said. 'So you're safe in your room. Thank goodness for that! Please stay where you are. I'll be with you in the morning.'

'Rudi! What's it all about?'

'Never mind, Kate. Don't worry. Go to bed. Sleep well.'

'But Rudi ... Rudi! *Rudi!* ... Are you still there?'

It was no use. He had hung up. And when, hopefully, she asked for a call to London, she heard the familiar message in the sour tones of Rosy, 'No outgoing calls at present!'

After a confusion of dreams involving soldiers, students, Schweiner, guards, passages and cells, Kate was caught up in a nightmare of being imprisoned for life. She woke in perspiring panic and couldn't sleep again for hours. It was daylight before she drifted into a more peaceful half-sleep, from which she was awakened by a chinking of china. The maid Lilli was at her bedside with a tray of coffee, rolls and butter and honey, and a clean folded napkin.

'Lilli!' said Kate. 'I haven't seen you in days!'

'No, gracious young lady. We were frightened by the firing and all went home. But this morning I was telephoned and told to come in as usual. And everything seems normal, except' – her voice still sounded uncertain – 'except for all those people in the cells. Anyway, a few minutes ago I saw Prince Rudi and he said, "Lilli, take coffee and rolls to Fräulein Kate." So here I am.' She dropped a curtsey and went out.

As she ate, Kate put the radio on. It was the usual, invariable pop. Then a pause, the sounding of the chime, the announcement of Radio Essenheim, and the voice of Moritz.

'Well, folks,' he began, 'here we are on Day Two of the return to law and order. For those of you who missed the earlier bulletins, Essenheim has a firm government once more. You'll be delighted to know that the new Prime Minister is our leading citizen, Herr Konrad Finkel, proprietor of Finkel's Wineries, the Finkel Bank, the Finkel Mortgage Corporation, Amalgamated Finkel Industries and United Finkel International. Don't take time out to rejoice; just go about your work as usual in a clean, sober, responsible and obedient manner. There'll be further orders later today.' Moritz paused. 'And remember, folks, that whatever happens you can still rely on Quick 'n' Safe Sure-Fire Superstar Elixir. It's a Finkel product . . .'

Kate switched the radio off, dressed, and hurried from her room. And just outside the doorway she bumped into Rudi. In contrast to the period dress of Thursday, the army uniform of Friday and the T-shirt and jeans of Saturday, he now wore a neat collar and tie and a dark business suit. He held her by the shoulders and kissed her affectionately.

'Congratulate me, Kate,' he said. 'After a few hours as President, I am now once more Prince Laureate.'

'But . . . I can't keep up with it, Rudi. What's happened since Saturday night?'

'I told you I had business to do outside the castle, didn't I? Well, my business was to see Herr Finkel. I had always intended to do so as soon as I was freed.'

'So you were only pretending to play along with the students?'

'I had to do it, Kate. Otherwise I'd have been thrown into jail along with Schweiner.'

'Not surprisingly, Rudi, seeing you're engaged to his daughter.'

'Was, Kate, was. That is all off, I need hardly say. Anyway, it was clear to me that only a person of substance could take over effectively in Essenheim, and that the one person of substance is Herr Finkel.'

'And does *he* have a daughter for you to be engaged to?'

'You are too cynical, Kate. Herr Finkel has no daughter. But he has what was needed yesterday. He has the security staff who collect the produce from the peasants and the interest on his mortgages.'

'His heavies, you mean? His strong-arm squad? I heard about them from the Mayor.'

'Call them that if you wish, Kate, but they saved the Principality yesterday morning. They were far more than a match for the ridiculous students and their schlagfuss sticks. It was all over in a matter of minutes.'

'I know that,' said Kate. 'And I spent a day in the cells.'

'I'm sorry about that. It took me all day to work myself sufficiently into his favour to secure your release and my own restoration as Prince Laureate. He was inclined to be distrustful of me at first.'

'You can't blame him for that,' said Kate. 'Where's George?'

'George was ejected from the castle and will be thrown out of the country when he can be found. At the moment he's missing. Stockhausen and Cousin Friedrich are missing, too. Apart from that, everything is under control. The soldiers who were sober enough to know what they were doing have been sworn in again for the new model army under Debt Collection Executive Trinkgeld, and are now at the service of the new régime. The students will cool their heels in jail for a few days and then be sent back to the university. And I, as I've told you, am restored to the throne. There will be no more nonsense about dictatorships or republics or the revival of the Holy Roman

Empire. To be Prince Laureate of Essenheim is quite enough for me.'

'And for Herr Finkel, I suppose. You'll have to do what he tells you, won't you?'

'There will be no difficulty, Kate. Herr Finkel and I see eye to eye. Come, you must renew acquaintance with him. He is anxious to see and reassure you.'

The outer office of the Prime Minister's suite was guarded by a massively built man in the uniform of the Finkel Industries Security Service. He sprang to attention and saluted smartly as Rudi approached. In the office, two neatly suited male clerks and a typist in navy-blue costume and white silk shirt rose and bowed. Rudi and Kate were shown into the inner sanctum.

Herr Finkel, immaculate as when Kate had seen him before, sat at the enormous desk which had been Dr Stockhausen's. He rose to his feet and bowed punctiliously.

'Good morning, Prince,' he said. 'Good morning, gracious young lady.'

'Good morning, Prime Minister,' said Rudi with equal formality.

'I must apologize, gracious lady,' Herr Finkel said, 'for your ordeal yesterday. It resulted from failure at a low level of command to make a necessary distinction.'

'Oh,' said Kate. She wasn't inclined to be too forgiving, after the dreadful day she'd had.

But Herr Finkel didn't wait for her to comment. 'I am glad to tell you, however,' he went on, 'that after the unfortunate events of the past few days we have now mastered the situation and are ready to make progress. The Prince and I will together lead Essenheim into the twentieth century, as we intended.'

'Are you quite sure there won't be another revolution tomorrow?' asked Kate.

'Revolutions are no joke, gracious young lady,' said Herr Finkel coldly. 'We want no more such nonsense here. Calm, order and stability are what we require, and an atmosphere in which business can flourish.'

'Especially,' added Rudi, 'such progressive businesses as those of Herr Finkel.'

Kate recalled the comments of the Mayor on Herr Finkel and his enterprises. Suddenly it occurred to her that all the action of the last few days had taken place in the castle.

'What do the ordinary people think about all these upsets?' she asked.

'The ordinary people?' Rudi and Herr Finkel both stared.

'What has it to do with them?' Herr Finkel asked.

'Well ... I suppose they do live here.'

'Yes,' said Herr Finkel. 'They live here. They have their function. They till the land, keep the little shops, perform their menial duties. That is all we require of them. And if they behave themselves we shall see that they are well fed and housed. Just as a wise farmer looks after his animals, so a wise government will look after its common people. But the animals do not run the farm, nor should the common people run the government.'

Herr Finkel gave Kate his wintry little smile.

'However,' he said, 'it is not for young ladies to trouble their heads about such matters. The function of young ladies is purely decorative.'

'Even in the twentieth century?' Kate asked.

Herr Finkel frowned. 'I see that subversive ideas have found some foothold in your mind,' he said. 'However, I am sure we can eliminate them.'

'You don't need to operate on my mind,' Kate told him. 'I'm only a visitor. I don't intend to stay here, whoever's in power.'

'My dear young lady,' said Herr Finkel, 'why do you suppose that, on the first day of my Premiership, with a hundred urgent matters requiring my attention, I am receiving you here and have given instructions that we are not to be disturbed?'

'I haven't the least idea,' said Kate.

'I have come to a decision,' said Herr Finkel. 'Or rather, the Prince and I have come to a decision. It is that the Prince should marry as soon as possible.'

'That,' said Kate decisively, 'is nothing to do with me.'

'Don't be so sure, gracious young lady. Suppose the Prince were to marry *you*? By that I mean, suppose he were actually to *marry* you?'

Kate gasped. 'What about Princess Etta?' she asked faintly.

'Princess Etta is easily dealt with. Her family owes me as much money as the Prince's, and is in no position to make difficulties.'

'And Elsa Schweiner?'

'That was a mere sop to Schweiner until we could get him out of the way,' said Rudi. 'I never cared a squashed grape for Elsa Schweiner.'

'And Bettina?'

'She is only a jailer's daughter.'

'Heaven help Essenheim!' said Kate.

'Kate, dear,' said Rudi, with an air of great sincerity, 'I love you. I have loved you since the day I first saw you at that party in London. My uncle thought marriage with a commoner was impossible, but Herr Finkel sees no such objection. Isn't that splendid? Our happiness is assured.'

Kate looked into his face. In spite of all the events of the past few days, she almost believed him.

'Say you will have me, Kate,' Rudi said softly. 'Say you love me.'

Kate felt the words 'Yes, Rudi' rising to her lips. Her sense of self-preservation struggled for survival. She swallowed twice, then said defensively, 'Isn't this rather *public* for a proposal?'

'Gracious young lady,' said Herr Finkel, 'it is at my request that the Prince has put forward this merger scheme, which you will do well to accept. Marriage, I must remind you, is the most serious business transaction in life. You now have a highly advantageous opportunity.'

Kate was silent. Herr Finkel went on, 'Possibly you think Essenheim is too small and backward a country in which to invest your marriageability. Let me assure you that this will not continue to be the case. The Prince and I have far-reaching plans for Essenheim. Ours will be a truly businesslike régime. First we shall encourage tourism.'

'Hotels, for instance,' said Rudi.

'Yes, the Finkel Hotels and Restaurants Division will expand greatly over the next few years. And we shall have a tourist board. Before long I am confident that tourists will be as thick as flies.'

'That sounds nice,' said Kate drily.

'And there will be shipping registration,' Herr Finkel went on.

'*Shipping* registration?' Kate said, surprised. 'But Essenheim doesn't have a seacoast.'

'That matters not at all. Shipowners will register their vessels here to avoid high fees and burdensome safety regulations in the maritime countries. The ship itself doesn't have to come to Essenheim. And we shall have company registration on the same basis. Companies will be able to register here and avoid filing accounts in their own countries.'

'It sounds a bit dubious,' said Kate.

'Dubious? Not at all. It is business,' said Herr Finkel solemnly.

'And postage stamps!' added Rudi with enthusiasm. 'A country the size of ours can make its fortune out of postage stamps. Instead of dull little stamps with pictures of my uncle on them, we will portray the sights of Essenheim and celebrate the incidents in its history.'

'Such as?' asked Kate.

'Well, er . . .' Rudi hesitated. 'Essenheim has not had many interesting incidents in its history, I admit. But we can have a series of stamps to mark the establishment of our new régime.'

'Postage stamps are very profitable,' Herr Finkel agreed. 'If the common people knew what we planned to do to increase the country's prosperity, and thereby their own well-being, they would bless the name of Finkel. And of course that of Prince Rudi. And, dare I say, perhaps also the name of the Princess Catherine?'

Rudi added with renewed enthusiasm, 'We could have a royal wedding issue. How would you like that, Kate? A stamp with a picture of you and me on it!'

Kate was silent. Her sense of self-preservation was recovering from the shock of Rudi's proposal. She felt she was suffering from a surfeit of honourable intentions: first Schweiner's, now his.

'You hesitate, my dear young lady,' said Herr Finkel. 'Well, take your time. But not too much of it. Perhaps, Prince, you should continue the conversation with Fräulein Kate in private, and leave me to grapple with the affairs of state.'

It was a dismissal.

'Yes, indeed, Prime Minister,' said Rudi. 'Come, Kate, let us go now.' As they left the room, Kate noticed that a security guard in the Finkel uniform had attached himself and was following at a discreet distance.

'I'm tired of all this,' she told Rudi. '*Please* understand. I want to go home.'

'It will be easier for you to go home if you do so as my fiancée.'

'You mean?'

'I don't mean anything, Kate dear,' said Rudi. 'But Herr Finkel has set his heart on our marriage. Herr Finkel is a very determined man. And I too, Kate, have set my heart on it.'

'What about your uncle?' Kate asked. 'Where is he now?'

'Ah, yes, my uncle. I had almost forgotten him.'

'*Forgotten* him?'

'He is no longer of importance,' said Rudi. 'He is a spent force.'

'He's still your uncle,' Kate pointed out, shocked. 'He wanted you to succeed to the throne.'

'Yes. Well, he got his wish, didn't he? However, Schweiner put him in the dungeons, and so far as I know he's still there.'

'He's *still* there? Down in those dreadful cells?'

'It's only until we decide what to do with him,' Rudi said. He looked sharply at Kate. 'That's another matter which your decision might help to resolve. We have a lot to discuss, Kate. I should like to talk to you in your own room. Or we could walk in the courtyard.'

'If you want to talk to me,' said Kate firmly, 'you can take me down to the cells to see your uncle. And that comes first.'

'Oh, very well,' said Rudi. He sounded a little peevish. 'I can think of many more interesting things to do.'

Reluctantly he led the way to the dungeons. As they went down the stone steps, their noses were assaulted by a strong smell of disinfectant and their ears by shouts, groans and mutterings from several directions. Half a dozen women with scrubbing brushes and galvanized buckets were swabbing the stone floors. In charge of them was massive, muscular Bertha, the jailer's wife.

'Good morning, Bertha,' said Rudi affably.

Bertha dropped a minimal curtsey. She did not look at all pleased.

'It's not such a good morning for me, Highness, I can tell you!' she said sourly. 'First the soldiers, then the students, and one lot as bad as the other. You wouldn't believe the filthy mess they've made down here! First there was good wine and brandy sloshing around everywhere, then they started relieving themselves all over the place, then half of them was vomiting and drinking more and vomiting again, and then there was fighting and blood and men lying around that you couldn't tell whether they was drunk or injured or both.'

Bertha's naturally loud voice had speeded up and grown even louder with the excitement of her narration, but she now dropped it and looked cautiously around her.

'And then,' she went on, 'there's this lot of Herr Finkel's, beating them all up and kicking and locking them away. A right lot of thugs *they* are, I can tell you. In fact, Prince' – her voice was rising again – 'if you want to know, I've had enough of it all and I can't stand much more and neither can my women here.'

Several of the women had stopped scrubbing and were listening with interest.

'There, there,' said Rudi in soothing tones. 'It was just a passing phase. Things are settling down, I assure you.'

'Yes, well, I'm just telling you, Highness,' said Bertha, unpacified. 'If there was any more of these goings-on, I don't know *what* might happen.'

Rudi called to a guard to take them to the ex-Prince. They were led past scores of cells, mostly now occupied by soldiers or students. The soldiers were quiet, appearing to take their confinement philosophically as a hazard of army life, but the students had recovered from their earlier states of shock or hangover. They jeered and shouted abuse at the guards, and a few of them cheered ironically as Rudi and Kate went past.

The more important prisoners had now been put in a row of cells at the farthest remove from the steps to the outer world. Rudi and Kate looked in through the tiny barred window of each in turn. Schweiner, red-faced and sweating, was bawling demands for his release and calling down the wrath of heaven on those who had imprisoned the saviour of the country and prevented the revival of the Holy Roman Empire. Sonia in the cell next door shrieked abuse impartially at him and at Finkel, taking time out to howl 'Capitalist lackey!' at Rudi. In such lulls as arose, Aleksi next door to her plaintively recited his poem based on 'Stone Walls do not a Prison make'. He sounded rather less sure of this than on the previous occasion.

In the last cell of all, the old Prince was slumped on a bare bench, awake yet blank-eyed, taking no notice of anything that went on.

'Kindly release ex-Prince Ferdinand into my charge,' said Rudi to the guard. But the man was reluctant.

'My orders is that no one gets out,' he said.

Rudi drew himself up. 'I am the Prince Laureate of Essenheim. Mine is the highest authority in the land. I instruct you to unlock this cell.'

'I'll just check with the Prime Minister's office,' said the guard uneasily. He hurried away along the passage and came back a couple of minutes later.

'Herr Finkel says it's all right for you to see the ex-Prince in the interview room, and afterwards Prince Ferdinand can be taken under guard to his former quarters, but he's not to be released.'

Rudi frowned but said no more. The cell was unlocked, and the old Prince shambled between a couple of guards to a little bare room farther along the passage where he, Kate and Rudi sat round a scrubbed deal table. Here the Prince's blankness was replaced by distress, though his mind still seemed clouded.

'Rudi!' he muttered. 'Little Rudi, my favourite nephew! Can you bear to see your old uncle treated like this?'

'Your time has passed, Uncle,' said Rudi coldly.

There were tears in the old man's eyes. Kate put her arms round him and kissed his cheek. He smiled a watery smile.

'You're a good girl,' he said.

'If it pleases you to know, Uncle,' said Rudi, 'let me tell you that I propose to marry Kate.'

'Oh!' said the ex-Prince. The words seemed to concentrate his mind. He asked, in a brisker tone than he'd used before, 'Have you accepted him, Kate?'

'No,' said Kate.

'Not yet,' said Rudi.

'Kate,' said the ex-Prince, 'I should be happy to have you as the mother of my great-niece or great-nephew, if I live long enough to see one. And yet, for your own sake' – he put a hand on hers – 'I think you should refuse.'

'It is nothing to do with you, Uncle,' said Rudi.

'Prince Ferdinand ...' Kate began, but the old man stopped her.

'You must call me Uncle Ferdy,' he said.

'Uncle Ferdy, what do you want to do now? Where do you want to go?'

'I want to leave Essenheim, Kate. Rudi is right; my time has passed. I should like best to join my married daughter at her villa in Serenia. She has staff and no children. She'll not mind looking after an old man. It won't be for long.'

'Rudi,' said Kate, 'please fix it for Uncle Ferdy to be freed, and for him and me to fly to Serenia. As soon as possible.'

'I don't know whether that can be done,' said Rudi. 'Herr Finkel will want some return for letting my uncle go. I've already hinted at the way in which I think you can ensure it.'

Kate knew what he meant, and had to restrain herself from an indignant outburst. She turned to the old Prince.

'Uncle Ferdy . . .' she began. But the old man was looking vacant again. He obviously hadn't been listening to the conversation. 'Uncle Ferdy,' she repeated. It was no use. The ex-Prince's mind, or as much of it as was present, had wandered away from her.

'They have much better TV reception in Serenia,' he remarked. When the guard returned a minute later to take him away, he stumbled obediently along without making any protest or saying any farewells.

'Rudi,' said Kate when they were left alone, 'the truth is that Herr Finkel is boss, isn't he? He makes all the decisions.'

Rudi was embarrassed. 'At the moment,' he agreed, 'Herr Finkel does tend to make the decisions. But once I am established as Prince, I assure you that things will be different.'

'I wonder,' said Kate.

'Meanwhile, I admit it is not easy to go against him. And Kate, I should warn you of another possibility. Uncle may yet be put on trial.'

'What's he supposed to have done?' asked Kate, startled.

'Oh, that's neither here nor there. It's easy enough to find a few charges. Conspiring with Schweiner, perhaps.'

'But he *didn't* conspire with Schweiner. Far from it!'

'That doesn't matter. It would be a neat way of getting both of them on the same charge. The evidence can be arranged.' Rudi added with a half smile, 'Uncle Ferdy would be *much* less likely to stand trial if you accepted me.'

'Rudi,' Kate began, 'there are times when you are *unspeakable*!'

Then there was a tap at the door. They both looked towards it. The tap was repeated, more strongly.

'Come in!' Rudi called.

Elsa Schweiner appeared in the doorway. For a moment she stood, dramatically silent. To Kate she seemed more pathetically ill-favoured than ever. She had been crying; her hair was all over the place and her eyes red-rimmed, and her appearance wasn't improved by a large boil in the middle of her left cheek. She was wearing a long dress of brilliant green velvet, cut in an off-the-shoulder style which was spectacularly unflattering to her flat, angular figure. Rudi shuddered visibly at the sight of her.

After that brief silence, Elsa flung herself to the floor in front of Rudi and threw her arms round his knees.

'Rudi, my dearest one!' she cried. 'You are still at liberty! But what will become of us?'

She buried her untidy head in his lap. Rudi sat uncomfortably, as if he'd just been given some bulky awkward parcel to hold, and said nothing.

'I knew it was you I saw,' Elsa continued. 'And for the first time since my poor papa was overthrown! I had feared they were holding you, too. Rudi, my darling, tell me you will let nothing stand in our way! Tell me Papa will be freed and we can still marry! Tell me, tell me quickly!'

Rudi's voice in reply was full of a tenderness which at one time Kate would have taken to be genuine. He took Elsa's head between his hands and raised it towards his own.

'Dear Elsa,' he said, looking into her eyes, 'it cannot be!'

'But why, Rudi, why?' she wailed. 'Why can it not be?'

Kate felt a surge of sympathy. She was sure Elsa must know the answer which hung unspoken in the air: 'Because you're too ugly.'

Elsa went on, 'We are betrothed. Only death or imprisonment should keep us apart. You cannot betray your loving Elsa!'

Rudi said gently, 'Circumstances have changed, dear Elsa. Death and imprisonment are not the only things that can come between us.'

Elsa rose to her feet and turned to point an indignant finger at Kate. 'No, indeed!' she cried. '*She* has come between us!' She addressed Kate directly, 'Adventuress!'

Kate recoiled, then tried to collect herself in order to reply. She had never before seen such hatred in a person's face. It was shattering. She found herself trembling

'Believe me, Elsa . . .' she began. Then hurrying footsteps were heard outside and another person burst into the room. It was Bettina, the bold-eyed, red-cheeked daughter of the jailer.

'Nailed you at last, Rudi Hohenberg, you rat!' she proclaimed. 'You get an honest girl into trouble, and then you don't want anything more to do with her!'

'I didn't know . . .' Rudi began.

'Of course you knew! I haven't told my mother yet. She'll kill me. She'll kill you, too, I dare say, with her bare hands; and serve you right!'

'I'll see that you get an income . . .'

'Oh, yes? You'll pay me a pittance for carrying your bastard while you go on having fun? Making up to the foreign young lady, I suppose. Well, let me tell you, ducky' – she turned to Kate – 'you'll never be the only pebble on Rudi's beach! Ask him about Adela at the telephone exchange. And Susi at the candy shop. And Trudi at the wine-cellar. And plenty of others. As for *you*' – Bettina faced Elsa and declared contemptuously, 'You're not a lady. You're not anything!'

'Why, you little scrubber!' retorted Elsa. Her voice rose and coarsened, her posture was invigorated by anger. Unexpectedly, she looked as if she might be a match for Bettina.

'Your dad's the biggest slob in Essenheim and you're the ugliest bitch!' declared Bettina.

Elsa flew at her, with fingernails directed at her face. Bettina dodged and aimed a blow at Elsa's skinny chest. Rudi leaped between them and was caught in the cross-fire. Elsa's nails scored his right cheek, drawing a line of blood diagonally across it, while Bettina caught him a hefty thump just below the collarbone. All three stood still for a few seconds, breathing hard. Then the guard came back.

'What's all this?' he demanded. He turned on Elsa: 'Get back to the barracks, you!' And to Bettina: 'Off you go the other way and behave yourself!' And, finally, to Rudi: 'If I were you, Highness, I'd go back to my own part of the castle!'

It was as good as a command. Under the eye of the guard, Rudi slunk from the room. He didn't wait for Kate and she didn't want him to. The guard said nothing to her, and after five minutes she set out to make her way, alone, to her own room. She was nervous and shaken, and could sense the whiteness of her face.

23

Back in her room, Kate felt something approaching despair. She was on her own again. George had been ejected from the castle, Anni hadn't been seen since the day before yesterday, and Rudi now appeared to be a pawn of Herr Finkel. She had no obvious way of getting out of Essenheim, except by agreeing to marry Rudi. And the old Prince was still a prisoner.

Without much hope, she lifted the telephone receiver. The voice was the friendly one of Adela, but its first words were the familiar ones: 'No outgoing calls today.' Though it was what she'd expected, Kate's heart sank further. Then Adela went on, in a confidential tone, 'Is that Fräulein Kate? Yes? I have a message for you. Strictly private.'

Kate waited eagerly.

'It's from Princess Anni. Pack your bag, she says, and be ready to go. And stay in your room till she comes!'

'Is that all?'

'That's all I know. I don't want to know any more. Forget I told you. But if Anni says she's on the way, she's on the way.'

Kate put her things together. It didn't take long. Getting her bag packed gave her a sense of progress. She sat on the bed to wait for Anni. Time went by. She walked over to the window and looked out. It was raining steadily. The trees on the avenue were bedraggled; the Essenheim flag hung limp; a couple of men in capes – presumably from Herr Finkel's security squad – guarded the bridge that led towards the town. Kate went back to the bed, put her feet up, and after her previous uneasy night found herself nodding off to sleep. She didn't resist.

Scrabbling sounds from the wardrobe awoke her. She sat up with a jolt, to see Anni emerging. Her face, hands, T-shirt and jeans were smeared with black ink and her expression was joyful. She ran to embrace Kate, transferring some of the ink to Kate's own person and clothing.

'Dearest Kate!' she cried. 'We've done such tremendous things. And we're all set to get you out of here!'

'Who's "we"?' Kate asked.

'Me and George and the Mayor and Herr Beyer and Hansi. You know Hansi? He's Herr Beyer's apprentice at the printing shop. I always liked him and he always liked me and we didn't even know we liked each other because I was in the castle and he was in the town and castle and town don't mix but we did like each other all the same and now we've been doing this marvellous job together and we're going to stay together and George is great and the Mayor's great and Herr Beyer's great and everybody's great and I've never had such fun in my life and never mind heaven helping Essenheim *we're* helping Essenheim and George will come as soon as they've finished and Hansi'll have to leave the country on account of this but I don't mind because he'll be with me and oh Kate I'm so excited . . .'

Kate gripped Anni's shoulders. 'Anni,' she said. 'Tell me. One step at a time. Just *what* have you been up to?'

'It's the *Essenheim Free Press*,' Anni said. 'We've really made it a *free* press. A special number. Unofficial. A terrific editorial. George wrote it and I translated it and Hansi set it in type and Herr Beyer printed it and the Mayor stacked the copies. And now they're distributing it all round the town. Calling all Essenheimers to meet in the marketplace this evening. And *they'll* decide what happens, not the people in the castle. And one of Herr Finkel's men heard the machines running and came to see what was going on, and you know what happened? The Mayor laid him out. Wham! Pow! And we locked him in the lavatory and went on printing. And the Mayor'll lead the townspeople on a march to the castle, but we won't be there because Hansi's best friend is Riverman Flusswasser and he'll be waiting for us in the royal launch, the *Lorelei*. And you and I and George and Hansi will all be getting out of Essenheim together. George said he wouldn't go without you, and I said neither would I, and there wasn't any argument about *that*.'

'But, Anni,' said Kate, 'what about your uncle?'

'Oh, that's all right,' said Anni. 'We'll rescue him, too, as soon as George arrives. I know just how we're going to do it. It can't go wrong.'

Then she came suddenly to earth after her ecstatic verbal flight. 'At least, I hope it can't,' she said.

More time passed. Rain still poured down steadily. Anni went to her own room, washed, changed her clothes and came back with a packed bag to set beside Kate's. Then there was nothing they could do until George arrived. They sat on the bed together and talked a good deal about London. Anni sighed dreamily at the thought of cinemas, theatres, concerts and innumerable shops. She breathed with awe the names of Harrods and Libertys. Then they discussed their current prospects. Kate declared that she would on no account marry Rudi. Anni said that, much as she loved her brother, she thought Kate was dead right. They told each other they would probably never marry at all. Neither of them believed it. They played some tapes, talked some more on various subjects, tried the radio, which was the usual diet of elderly pop, and fell into occasional friendly silences. By the time the expected sounds were heard from the wardrobe, they felt they had been sisters for years.

Anni hurried to help George into the room. He came straight across to Kate and kissed her. Kate kissed him warmly back. He kissed her again. Anni said, 'Hey, what about me?' George kissed Anni. Anni kissed Kate.

George said, 'All right, the love-in's over. Let's get going. What are we waiting for?'

Kate said, 'We have to rescue Prince Ferdinand.'

George said, 'Kate, we are not in the rescuing business.'

Kate said, 'No Prince, no me.'

George sighed deeply and said, 'I thought as much. All right. Just tell me how.'

Anni said, 'There aren't many guards, you know. Finkel's men are spread rather thinly. If we could lay out the one on Uncle Ferdy's door we could probably rustle him away without any more trouble.'

George said, 'Who's "we"?'

Kate said, 'Well, for this purpose I think *you* are.'

George said, 'Why?'

Kate said, 'Well, hitting people on the head is a man's job, isn't it?'

George said, 'Who says it is? I thought you were liberated.'

Anni said, 'Don't argue, George. Pick up that vase from the window-ledge. Walk over to Uncle's room with us. Then, while we chat up the guard, you get round behind him and . . .'

Kate said, 'Bring it down, hard.'

George said, '*How* hard?'

Kate said, 'Don't ask silly questions. Hard enough.'

George said, 'I bet it's not as easy as it sounds.' But he didn't resist any more. The three of them walked through the Great Hall and over to the old Prince's room. George carried the heavy glass vase in front of him without any concealment. Outside the Prince's door, a guard challenged them. Anni said coolly, 'I want to see my uncle.'

The guard said, 'Have you a permit?'

Anni said, 'Do I need a permit to see my own uncle?'

The guard said, 'My orders are that nobody goes in without a permit from the Prime Minister's office.'

Anni became indignant and claimed that as a relative of an imprisoned person she had a right of access as a matter of natural justice. George, becoming interested in the point at issue, forgot what he had to do and listened attentively to the argument. Kate made frantic signs to him. Fortunately Anni was occupying the guard's full attention. Reluctantly recalling his duty, George slipped around behind him.

Kate couldn't keep her eyes from George, but the guard wasn't watching either of them; he was trying to cope with Anni in full flow of royal indignation. George raised the vase. With an agonized expression, either at the physical exertion or the moral questionability of his assault, he brought it down with a nasty crash on the guard's head. The guard fell instantly. George looked at him with surprise and horror, as if he hadn't expected any such result, then put what remained of the vase carefully down on the floor. Anni, with more presence of mind, pushed the Prince's door open, and they bundled the unconscious guard inside.

The Prince was in his usual chair, sitting glassy-eyed before the television set. George, recovering, took one of his arms, and Kate the other. Anni darted to the door, looked out, and signalled them to come on.

The Prince tottered between them. A servant, passing them in the corridor, gave a little bob in their direction and went on, apparently seeing nothing amiss. They entered the Great Hall, which they had to cross. Anni went ahead, looked round, and again signalled them on; there were no guards in sight. As quickly as they could, half carrying the old man, Kate and George followed.

Then there was a burst of shouting and a thudding of many feet along the passageway that led into the Great Hall from the direction of the dungeons. And into the hall poured a mixture of soldiers and students, waving guns and schlagfuss sticks. They milled around aimlessly as if, newly released, they didn't know what was expected of them. But following them up, like sheep-dogs with their flock, came a formidable group. They were the brawny cleaning-women of the castle, and directing them was Bertha, the jailer's wife.

Kate, George and Anni pressed their backs against the wall and watched. The Prince stared blankly, as if no sight could now make any impression on him. Rallying the vanguard of troops and students, Bertha pressed forward. Now her shock troops, the cleaning-women, moved ahead to lead the charge. Some with mops and brooms at the ready, some swinging iron buckets around them to clear the way, they forced a path through the Great Hall. Two or three markswomen among them picked off guards with well-aimed blocks of soap. At the spearhead, Bertha herself, protected by two stout lieutenants bearing dustbin lids, cut and thrust her way towards the Prime Minister's office.

Bodies swayed and jostled everywhere. Students and soldiers hurled themselves into the fray; grey-uniformed Finkel guards, unable to draw their guns in the crush, struggled with clusters of assailants. Bertha was out of sight now, but the battle went on. A guard freed himself enough to fire a couple of shots, but was borne to the ground by an angry mob. There were more shots from the far end of the hall, a reek of powder, and total confusion prevailed for a while. Then Bertha came into view again. She was dragging a limp, unconscious Herr Finkel by the collar towards the stairway that went down to the dungeons. A couple of guards tried to rescue him but went down in a scrum of thrashing limbs.

'Where's rotten Rudi?' Bertha yelled as she went past. 'I'll get that young man if it's the last thing I do!'

But Rudi seemed to have removed himself from the scene.

'Come on!' urged George. 'Let's get out of here, fast! Can we use the main door?'

'No!' Anni hissed. 'Always locked and bolted. And look at all that crowd. We can't get Uncle Ferdy through there! The passage! It's the only way!'

The shouting and struggling went on unabated. Schlagfuss sticks were wielded; there were more shots. A scrubbing-brush, flung by a muscular cleaner, flew past Kate's ear and felled a Finkel guard just behind her. Dragging the old Prince along, the three of them made their way from the Great Hall into the corridor that led towards Kate's and Anni's rooms. A stray guard, dishevelled and breathing hard, stood in their way; a soldier leaped on him from behind and bore him to the ground. They shoved their way past. Then they were in Kate's room. Anni slammed the door behind them.

Kate was suddenly weak with shock and could have collapsed

on the bed, but Anni went straight to the wardrobe and found the entrance to the secret passage. They followed her inside. At once the silence and darkness closed in upon them. Hesitantly they moved ahead. The Prince stumbled along as best he could, without question or protest. Anni went ahead and George gave the old man what support he could from behind. Kate brought up the rear, carrying her own bag and Anni's. Lit by intermittent light from the slit windows they struggled on. It was impossible to hurry. Kate lost all sense of time; it was an endless ordeal. Twice she almost fell and once she grazed an arm on the stonework.

They went through the little chamber where they had met a few nights earlier and continued beyond it. Farther along, a passage opened out to the left, but Anni ignored it and led on. Soon afterwards there was another opening to the right. And now Anni suddenly whispered, 'Stop! Listen!'

Towards them along the side-passage came the notes of an early Beatles tune, plucked hesitantly from the strings of a guitar. It was the tune Kate had heard on her first night in the castle.

'Friedrich!' she and Anni exclaimed together.

Anni scampered away towards the sound. Kate and George stayed behind with the Prince, unwilling to urge the feeble old man away from the escape route.

'I don't believe,' said Prince Ferdinand, making his first remark since they'd collected him from his room, 'that the boy will ever master that thing.'

The sound of the guitar ceased. Anni's voice was heard, calling to them. And the old Prince himself led the way, shuffling along the side-passage towards it.

At the end of the passage a door was open and electric light streamed out. In the doorway stood Dr Stockhausen.

'My dear Prince!' he said. 'Welcome to my refuge. It's the Prime Ministerial fall-out shelter. Who's in power at the moment?'

24

'I will give you coffee and cake,' said Mrs Stockhausen. 'I always longed to be an ordinary Essenheim housewife. Thanks to Colonel Schweiner the ambition has been fulfilled. All I wish is that I could go out and do some shopping.'

'And all *I* wish,' said Dr Stockhausen, 'is that Prince Friedrich would give up practising on that wretched instrument. If he went on much longer, Karl would confiscate it.'

Karl grinned evilly and made a pretended grab at the guitar. Friedrich clutched it to himself.

'I'm d–doing much better than I was,' he said.

It turned out that the Stockhausens were installed in a modest but well-equipped apartment with running water and ample stores. During his thirty-year Premiership, Dr Stockhausen had provided for all eventualities. His fall-out shelter, which he had foreseen might serve an alternative purpose as a hiding-place, had been built in secret between the castle foundations and the cliff-side; and the men who constructed it had been given grants to settle in the New World, so it was unknown to anyone else. With Karl as combined manservant, guard and reconnaissance patrol, the Stockhausens were in a position to bide their time indefinitely.

They declined an invitation to leave Essenheim on board the *Lorelei*.

'We are perfectly comfortable here,' Dr Stockhausen explained. 'When we learn from Karl that an acceptable régime has come into being, we shall emerge. If that doesn't happen or we grow too bored, we can make our way out, by the route which you are no doubt taking now, and can get to Serenia, where we have substantial bank accounts. There is no hurry. However, if Prince Friedrich should decide to leave now, we would not stand in his way '

Kate had the impression that this last remark was an understatement.

Friedrich beamed happily. 'I'd love to c-come,' he said. 'I'll be ready in a m-minute.'

Anni was anxious not to lose time. 'Hansi and Riverman Flusswasser will be waiting for us at the quay,' she said. 'I don't want anything to go wrong now.'

With Friedrich added to the party, and the old Prince a little revived, they returned to the point at which they'd left the main passage. A little farther on, its sides ceased to be cut stone and became rock. There was less height, and they all had to bend low. Occasional trickles of water could be heard. Once again the journey seemed to drag on endlessly; the old Prince stumbled several times and had to be helped to his feet. And then ahead of them there was dim light, filtering round an obstruction.

'We're coming out on the cliff face,' Anni said.

'What's that in the way?'

'It's only a bush. Covers the entrance.' Anni pushed her way around it. Kate, George, Friedrich and the ex-Prince followed with difficulty. They were in the open air now, on a narrow path that led round the cliff, with the sheer walls of the castle above. The rain had stopped and the moon was full. From far below, loud in the silence, the roar of the River Esel could be heard.

Kate swayed, suddenly dizzy. Anni grabbed her arm.

'Are you all right, Kate?'

'Yes.'

Slowly and perilously they edged their way round the cliff. The Prince tottered along between George and Kate, holding a hand of each. He looked as if he might fall at any moment and take them with him. Even without the Prince, Kate couldn't have managed this journey in normal times and in the light of day; her head for heights was poor and her limbs would have refused to carry her. But now there was no alternative and she struggled on, too exhausted to be frightened.

It could only have been a few minutes, but once again felt like hours, before there was the sound of water much closer at hand, and they were coming off the cliff face and into the course of a fast-flowing stream which splashed its way down into the River Esel.

'This is where we get wet,' said Anni. 'It's a good job it isn't higher.'

They waded the broad, shallow stream. Kate gasped at the coldness of the water. Then they were on the far bank, and on rounding another corner were under the supports of the castle bridge, at the town end.

Cautiously they climbed to road level. There were no guards here. Anni took an arm of the Prince in place of Kate, and they made their laborious way along the high street towards the marketplace. And in the square the people were massing. It was an orderly concourse, without much noise. Out of the dark side-streets came more and more quiet folk to swell the gathering. A voice could be heard marshalling them through a loud-hailer.

'It's the Mayor!' George said. 'It worked! They responded to the *Free Press*!'

Kate caught a note of longing in his voice. 'We can manage now, George,' she said. 'Go on. Follow the story.'

'Oh, no!' declared George. 'We're getting you away first. That's the priority.' And Kate didn't argue. They made their way round the edge of the square and continued towards the quay.

It took a long time to pass the gathering host. It seemed as if every man, woman and child in Essenheim was assembling. Not one had a weapon. And in response to a call through the loud-hailer the column moved off. The people of Essenheim were on their way to the castle. In the moon-shadowed streets none of them recognized that their Prince of so many years was passing them in the other direction.

Kate wondered for a brief moment whether it was wrong to be taking the old Prince away. But looking at him as he tottered painfully along, she knew that Rudi's cruel comment had been true. His day was over. He hadn't any further contribution to make; he didn't *want* to make any further contribution. He just wanted to get to his daughter's house in Serenia and end his days in peace. It would be wicked to throw him back into the fray, even if one could.

They were in steep deserted streets now, heading downhill towards the quay. And the sound of a running diesel engine could be heard. The royal launch *Lorelei* was under power and ready to go. As they reached the water's edge a gangplank was let down. Hansi and Able Riverman Flusswasser waited on the boat with arms outstretched to help them on board. There was a last perilous moment as George pushed the stumbling Prince ahead of him; Riverman Flusswasser leaned far out to grab his hands and pull him on board. Anni, Kate and Friedrich followed George, and they were all safe on the rear deck of the *Lorelei*.

Hansi cast off. The quay fell behind and the sloping streets of Essenheim moved past as the riverman steered the launch on its way down the Esel. The lights of new and old town gleamed high and low. Above them on one side loomed the castle; on the other side, farther away, was the red light at the top of the radio mast.

'How long will it take us to get to the frontier?' Kate asked, as the boat left Essenheim town and began to throb its way gently between vineyards.

'A couple of hours, maybe,' Anni said. 'The frontier posts are at the lock.'

'Could we be stopped there?'

'We're not *going* to be!' said Anni with determination. 'Then I'll be taking Uncle Ferdy to my cousin's, where he wants to go. And *then*' – her eyes sparkled – 'London, here I come! Just think, Kate, I'll be seeing you in London. Can you believe it?'

'Only just,' Kate admitted. She could hardly believe anything that had happened in the last couple of weeks. Even this boat trip down the river had taken on an air of unreality. Surely it wasn't actually happening.

Anni and Friedrich went with the Prince into the *Lorelei*'s cabin. Only Kate and George remained on deck. They stood side by side, leaning on the rails. Kate felt again the surge of affection she'd had several times for George, and with it another sensation: not quite the melting of her insides that being with Rudi had caused, but a slight electric sense of physical nearness. Perhaps after all the presence of George could do something for her ...

'Kate,' said George softly.

'Yes, George?'

'Kate, may I tell you something? Do you know ...?' George hesitated, then took the plunge. 'Kate, you look almost beautiful in the dark!'

Laughter bubbled up in Kate. She didn't feel insulted at all. George's assessment of her charms was roughly the same as her own. Maybe she pleased Essenheimisch taste, but she was leaving Essenheim now.

Then there was a disturbance, the creak of a door. Opening on to the deck at the rear of the cabin was a wet-locker, the kind of cubby-hole where brooms and buckets were kept. The door of the locker now moved. Something inside fell over and there was a muttered curse in Essenheimisch. And then the door was thrown wide, and out of it stepped Rudi.

Kate and George stared. Rudi was as self-possessed as ever.

'Kate!' he said. 'Dearest Kate! I stowed away in order to be with you! How glad I am, how relieved and delighted, that we are here together after all! Kate, whether I am prince or commoner, rich or poor, I'm your man. I'll never let you down!'

As recently as the day before, Kate might have believed him. At least she would have *wanted* to believe him. But, looking at him now, she realized that the magic had stopped working. She didn't believe him. She didn't want to believe him. She didn't care.

212

'You don't let *anyone* down, do you, Rudi?' she asked sardonically. 'Not your uncle, not Schweiner, not the students, not Elsa, not Bettina . . .'

'That is all past,' Rudi said. 'The only thing that matters now is you.'

George had quietly opened the section of railings where the gangway would be lowered when the launch tied up.

'Rudi,' he inquired, 'can you swim?'

'Of course I can swim,' said Rudi.

'Show us,' said George, and pushed him overboard. The last they saw of him was his head breaking the surface and his arms moving as he struck out for the bank.

'George!' exclaimed Kate. She was shocked. It was totally unlike George: so drastic, so dramatic! 'How *could* you? You're a *terrible* person! And what would the *Morning Intelligence* say?'

Then she was in his arms.

25

The royal riverboat *Lorelei* moved gently into the lock at the Serenian border. Ex-Prince Ferdinand Franz Josef I I I emerged from the cabin, climbed painfully on deck and stood at the rails between Kate and Anni.

'I must look my last on Essenheim,' he said.

At the top end of the lock was a tiny wooden hut with a lamp hanging above the door. Out of the hut stepped a man in the coarse purple uniform of Essenheim officialdom. He called something to Able Riverman Flusswasser and, as the boat came to a standstill, approached the section of the railings whence Rudi had so recently been disposed of.

'Who's on board?' he asked.

'I am,' said the Prince.

'Why, Highness!' said the man. 'It's you! You're leaving all that shambles behind, eh? I hear a different tale on the radio every hour, or so it seems, and the telephone hasn't worked in a week. But I haven't any orders to stop you, and I wouldn't stop my Prince anyway.'

He moved away, grinning, and began to spin a great wheel. Slowly the top gate of the lock closed behind the *Lorelei*.

'When you come out at the bottom end,' the lock-keeper said, 'you'll be in Serenia. Good-bye, Highness, and good luck. Heaven help Essenheim!' He came to attention and saluted.

Solemnly, shakily, the old Prince returned the salute.

'Heaven help Essenheim!' he said.

As the boat began slowly to sink in the lock, somebody leaped perilously from the rear deck of the *Lorelei* to the narrow bridge on which stood the lock gear. In a moment he had vanished into the darkness and back into Essenheim. The last thing Kate saw as the boat sank down into the cavernous depths of the lock was the lock-keeper's face as he stared open-mouthed after the disappearing figure.

'What *is* George doing?' Anni asked in astonishment.

'What do you *think* he's doing?' said Kate. 'He's seen us safely to the frontier. Now he's gone back to follow the story.'

The front gate opened, and the *Lorelei* glided out into Serenia.

26

Kate flew into Heathrow on an Air Serenia flight a couple of days later. Her father was waiting for her, having taken time out from the office.

Edward said, 'Hello.'

Kate said, 'Hello.'

Edward said, 'Well, how did it go?'

Kate said, 'Oh, not so badly.'

Edward said, 'There were telephone troubles, weren't there?'

Kate said, 'Yes, and revolutions and things. Weren't you worried?'

Edward said, 'Not much. I knew you could look after yourself. And even if you couldn't, I knew George would look after you.'

Kate said, 'Have you heard from George?'

Edward said, 'Yes, he came through on the phone last night. He's got some pretty good stuff. George is a bright lad.'

Kate said, 'Yes.'

Edward said, 'Nice, too. I like him.'

Kate said, 'So do I.'

There was a brief silence. Then Edward said, emotionally, 'Oh, Kate, I did miss your cooking!'

Kate said, 'You are an unreconstructed male chauvinist pig.'

They hugged each other for a long time.

George stayed in Essenheim for another week. He came back and wrote a series of articles in the *Morning Intelligence* under the general heading REVOLUTION IN A NUTSHELL. They attracted a lot of notice, and George won a 'Reporter of the Year' award and a hefty pay increase.

George and Kate are still fond of each other, but they aren't in a hurry to tie each other down. Kate is at the University of West Yorkshire, studying modern languages and enjoying life. She hasn't made any plans yet for her future. When she does, George hopes to be included in them.

Anni arrived in London after three weeks in Serenia. She spent a month with her friend Betsy, then came to Edward and Kate on a short visit which kept on prolonging itself. She is still there, having to all intents and purposes become Edward's daughter and Kate's sister. Hansi is at the London School of Printing. He spells better in English than he ever did in Essen-heimisch. Hansi and Anni are still starry-eyed about each other.

Ex-Prince Ferdinand Franz Josef III of Essenheim is still alive, though increasingly frail. He is living with his daughter in Serenia and seems somewhat bemused but contented enough. There is some argument, among those who care about such things, over whether he was Essenheim's last Prince Laureate, or whether the brief reign of Prince Rudolf should also go into the record-books.

And Essenheim itself? Well, when the great march led by the Mayor arrived at the castle, the soldiers and students and cleaning-ladies all poured out to meet it, and they decided there and then that they'd had enough of revolutions and self-appointed régimes, and they'd find out by a ballot of the people what they really wanted to do. And the result was that Essen-heim voted to become part of happy, peaceful Serenia.

There are some, of course, who regret its disappearance as an independent country. One of them is Aleksi, who has written a poem, universally agreed to be his masterpiece, in which he says that if he should die people should think only this of him: that there's some corner of a Serenian crematorium that is for-ever Essenheim. Sonia is also dissatisfied, believing that Serenia is bourgeois, élitist and degenerate. But Sonia enjoys being dissatisfied and wouldn't know what to do with herself if she had the misfortune to become contented, so there's no need to feel sorry for her.

Rudi didn't come to any harm from his ducking in the River Esel. He is now running for election as Essenheim's representative in the Serenian senate. He'll probably win. He may well finish up as Federal President of Serenia. Whatever happens to those around him, Rudi will come out on top.

Girls still think Rudi is wonderful, until they find he doesn't care about them. Some of them find out too late, and suffer. Yet there was one girl he did care about, as much as he was able to care, and that was Kate. If he'd played his cards less cleverly he might have won her — who knows? He'll never do so now.

The Essenheim Army has been incorporated in Serenia's. It no longer includes ex-Field Marshal Schweiner, who was court-martialled and dismissed from the service in disgrace. The army now has smart new uniforms, and its duties are purely ceremonial.

The dungeons of Essenheim Castle stand empty.

CONSTELLATIONS

Stories of the Future

edited by Malcolm Edwards

Twelve classic short stories from some of science fiction's brightest stars, including Kurt Vonnegut Jr, Arthur C. Clarke, Philip K. Dick, J. G. Ballard and Robert Sheckley, all concerning strange worlds and other times.

MURPHY AND CO.

Anthony Masters

Money is still short at Dunmore United so the Junior Supporters Club – The Mob – are intent on helping out. But their efforts look puny beside the half a million which someone else comes up with. *Half a million?* The Mob smell a rat and decide to find out just what's going on.

SWEET FRANNIE

Susan Sallis

Confined to a wheel-chair, Fran doesn't seem to have much of a future when she goes into Thornton Hall Residential Home. But pretty soon there is eighteen-year-old Luke Hawkins to think about. After all, who better than fiercely independent Fran to help a young man who has just lost both his legs in a road accident? A book of sweet and sour emotions that will bring tears of admiration and amusement as well as sadness.

THE FORTUNATE FEW
Tim Kennemore

Jodie Bell is a professional gymnast – starved to the perfect weight, worked to the point of collapse and sold to the highest bidder. A thought-provoking story set in the not-too-distant future when gymnastics has replaced football as the most popular spectator sport.

FLAMBARDS DIVIDED
K. M. Peyton

The return of her cousin from the Front signals a further dilemma for the now-married Christina. The eagerly awaited sequel to the award-winning Flambards trilogy.

I CAN JUMP PUDDLES
Alan Marshall

This is Alan Marshall's story of his childhood – a happy world in which, despite his crippling poliomyelitis, he plays, climbs, fights, swims, rides and laughs. His world was the Australian countryside early this century: rough-riders, bushmen, farmers and tellers of tall stories – a world all the more precious to a small crippled boy.